The Gori's Daughter

To
Rory
Hope you enjoy
the book.
All the best.
Love
Shazia x x

Shazia Hobbs

Ringwood Publishing

Glasgow

First published in Great Britain in 2014 by
Ringwood Publishing
7 Kirklee Quadrant, Glasgow G12 0TS
www.ringwoodpublishing.com
e-mail   mail@ringwoodpublishing.com

ISBN 978-1-901514-12-4

British Library Cataloguing-in Publication Data
A catalogue record for this book is available from the British
Library

Typeset in Times New Roman 10
Printed and bound in the UK
by Lonsdale Direct Solutions

About the Author   Shazia Hobbs

Shazia Hobbs lives in Glasgow, with her children and partner, and works at being a full time mother. Having worked in retail, offices, call centres and a variety of other jobs, she decided to study to enable her to apply for a more rewarding career. After gaining her PDA Certificate in Adult Literacy, she decided to go onto her COSCA Certificate in Counselling and at the same time got a publishing deal for The Gori's Daughter. Having completed and achieved her certificate, she has put studying plans on hold for now and has started writing her next book, The Gori.

Acknowledgements

I would like to thank:

Hobbsy and my children, my close friends and my family for all the help, support, encouragement and patience they displayed during the long process of the writing of this book.

Kashif for being there throughout the process, for reading every chapter and for his honesty.

Tom Stokes for encouraging me many, many years ago to write the story.

Ian McPherson and Magi Gibson for their invaluable support and advice while attending their creative courses at Glasgow University.

Yasmin Chaudhry for her assistance in transcribing and translating the Mirpuri dialogue. Any faults remaining are mine alone.

Yusuf for his patience and hours of phone calls to help create the right image for the cover.

All those at Ringwood Publishing – especially Sandy Jamieson and my dedicated Editors, Isobel Freeman and Margaret McInnes – who have helped get my book published.

Dedication

To:

My family, without whom this story would not have been possible.

Family Map

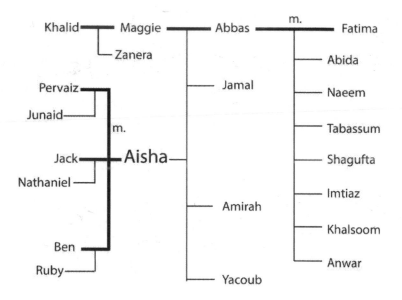

Chapter 1   Nobody knows me here.

Once again I had run away. This time from the Pakistani community I had spent the last 20 years longing to be part of again. Trying to live with that longing is why I moved home 30 odd times, why I never held down a job and was no good at relationships or friendships. I was struggling to fit into a western culture I knew nothing about, a culture I had been told was corrupted and diseased, but a culture I was forced to live in when I was disowned by my Pakistani family. The white community was a place where I felt I never belonged. I was always searching for acceptance from my Pakistani side, but after almost eighteen months immersed in the Pakistani side, running away was essential to my sanity. This story is about the struggle between my white and Pakistani sides and my attempt to find a place where I belonged.

When I first fled my abusive forced marriage I was given a flat on the 8th floor of a tower block in Thornliebank. Running again, almost twenty years later, I have now moved my two children to the 15th floor of a tower block in Dennistoun. I have moved to the other side of Glasgow. From a main door flat in the south side to the east end and an area which is predominantly white. So strong was my fear and need to extricate myself from the Pakistani community, I chose to live in a relatively rough part of Glasgow I didn't know. It felt good, so peaceful. I now have no fear from my Pakistani side for daring to write about my experiences, and no desire to be accepted by Abbas and his family.

It seems like forever I have been told to write it all down and it seems like forever I have thought about it. Now I have decided it is time to tell my story about growing up with a Pakistani father, a Pakistani stepmother, a white mother and their combined children; all living together in the big house. It hasn't been easy. Perhaps that's why so few people write their life story because it gets you thinking, analysing, digging up the past and discovering secrets. Secrets the family and the community would prefer to remain secret forever.

I was raised as a Pakistani in a Muslim household with very little contact allowed with my mum's side of the family because they were white. She had been told their Western ways would corrupt her children, and as she had grown up in care was easily persuaded not to take her children on visits to her brother. Because of this, most of my life story revolves around Pakistani people and their community and my struggle to be accepted. I think it's important to point out that although I was living in a Muslim household my upbringing was anything but Islamic. Dragged up in twisted cultures and traditions is a better way of explaining it. This story therefore is not criticising all Pakistani values and cultures, just the culture I experienced in my family and the community. Many in my family would prefer I keep quiet. I won't. Yacoub, my younger brother, always encouraged me to keep writing when there were days when I felt like giving

2

it all up and listening to the voice of Abbas, who told me I was wrong and misguided.

'Write it all down, sis. The whole truth and nothing but the truth. Our whole lives we were taught to lie, keep secrets. 'Ssshh, don't tell.' Bollocks to that,' Yacoub said.

But writing has made some already fragile family bonds shatter. Trying to get it right meant talking and asking questions, questions people would rather leave unanswered.

Growing up, my siblings and I were treated differently to the Pakistani children in the house. As the children of the white woman, 'the gori', we were despised and ridiculed at every opportunity. Mummy went out to work in Abbas's shops while Fatima, Abbas's wife, was responsible for child minding and Abbas, well he was a social butterfly and loved to be out as often as possible, escaping the mad house he had created.

At the age of three I was taken along with my older brother to Mirpur, Pakistan. Taken and left there by Abbas, at Fatima's insistence, to live with his parents and extended family. Five years later we returned to Scotland. For the longest time I resented the fact that I had been sent away. I blamed that experience for making me feel like an outsider in the family. Writing has helped me see it differently. Now I am grateful Fatima chose to send me away. Sending me away allowed me to receive the unconditional love and acceptance all children deserve and helped me see what an Islamic upbringing could be like. My grandparents idolised my brother and me. For five years I lived a happy life. I remember relatives travelling from afar to see 'the 'gori's children'. All saying the same things, 'how beautiful we were', 'how fair our skin colour was', 'Mash'Allah – 'praise be to Allah', 'weren't we the cutest things ever.'

Returning to Glasgow the praise and love ceased. Fatima had a deep hatred for us and for Mummy for destroying her 'izaat' (honour). Her way of paying Mummy back was to secretly destroy her family. Only now, having talked about it all with Mummy and my brother and sisters, can I see the devastation she caused and to an extent continues to cause. Remembering, Mummy said, 'I mind never being away from my doctor's'. Telling him, 'I am a mother to five children yet I don't feel like I am their mother.'' Unknown to the doctor, Fatima was the reason behind Mummy's bouts of madness for which the doctor prescribed more anti-depressants, leaving her for long periods of time unable to function and living in a zombified state, believing everything Fatima told her. The family doctor was aware of the family set up. Fatima was unable to speak English, so any appointments for herself or her children were made by Mummy. Mummy always came along to the appointments, sometimes taking Fatima's children on her own. The doctor was unaware however, of the way in which Fatima was undermining Mummy and slowly driving her crazy.

'Twaray bachay itnay batamese haramzady hain. Koi gul nee soonay.' (Your children are ill-mannered bastards. They never listen to me.)

When not zombified, Mummy shouted at us along with Fatima and Abbas, when he was home. Three parents and not

4

one able to show even a fraction of the love and kindness I had known for five years in Pakistan. Mummy went along with whatever Abbas and Fatima told her, especially Fatima who she was desperate to please. Maybe she felt guilty for taking her husband and this was her way of trying to make it up to her.

I couldn't speak English when I came back to Glasgow. My family in Pakistan had spoken Urdu to me instead of the more popular Mirpuri language, although I understood it and could speak it also. Urdu is more pleasant sounding compared to the harshness of Mirpuri, kind of like speaking the Queen's English compared to speaking like a Glaswegian ned. In Glasgow the children spoke English, with Mummy's children speaking Mirpuri instead of being taught Urdu. Fatima spoke Urdu only to her own children and so over time I forgot the Urdu language and spoke Mirpuri.

Desperate to fit in, I tried extra hard at school. I was always reading and writing at home, thinking if I can speak English like my siblings then maybe they will let me join in their games. A year after I had returned from Mirpur and we had moved to the big house, I had my own library card. Mummy, sick of me borrowing books on her card, had taken me to the library to get my own. Reading books allowed me to escape from the dramas that were unfolding on a daily basis in the big house.

To 'show face', which was very important to the Asian community, Fatima acted like the perfect step mother, caring for her husband's mistress's children and treating us all equally,

5

letting the Pakistani community believe she was a wonderful person. Around people she thought could be trusted and would possibly understand, she was honest in her feelings towards the gori's children. A distant cousin of Abbas's visited us in the big house, not long after we had moved, travelling from Birmingham and staying with us for a week. Maybe she felt bad for Mummy and her children and before she left told Mummy in her broken English:

'Everything good, children small. Wait they big, troubles will start.'

Mummy dismissed her warning, caught up in a fantasy that her children's home life was on par with 'The Walton's', but the troubles had already started. Mummy was made to feel guilty if she spent any time with us or showed affection. Her children were made to feel guilty if they dared to spend time in each other's company. Fatima would be quick to mock.

'Apoo khaydoh. Meray bachay noo nah balao. Eh twaray matrai pra penn hain' (Play together. Ignore my children. After all they are your step brothers and sisters.)

We were actually half brothers and sisters as we shared the same father, but Fatima insisted on calling us step and so we learned to always refer to them as the step family and they thought of us as their step family too.

We never spent time together as a family without the step side. We never went out for the day with Mummy and my brothers and sisters. We never even had a picture taken together as a family. No pictures exist of Mummy with her children or

6

her children all together and smiling, because we were not allowed to be a family. Fatima, on the other hand, made it her priority to spend time with her children, away from the big house.

When we moved to the big house, a move I'll talk about later, Fatima and Abbas's daughter, Tabassum, had stayed behind in the flat on Albert Drive with her husband. Tabassum had arrived from Pakistan a few months after I had returned to Glasgow from Mirpur, to join her husband, a nephew of Fatima's, and they had been living in the flat with us. Married girls generally leave their parents' home and live with their in-laws, but her in-laws were in Pakistan and so she lived alone with her husband in the flat that had been our home. The flat in Albert Drive is where Fatima would spend a lot of her time with all her children, leaving us behind in the big house, alone.

Mummy wasn't there, she would always be working and Pakistani families have no issues about leaving children home alone. Zanera was 15 when we moved to the big house and babysitting duties when Fatima was off out were left down to her. Even with Fatima gone, we were still too scared to bond with each other so strong was our fear of upsetting her. In a sick way all of us, Mummy, my siblings and I wanted to please Fatima and keep her happy. I have had an on and off relationship with Mummy from the day I was disowned and since I began writing, it has been more off than on. I would say our relationship is a work in progress, but for now there is no work and there is no progress.

There were twelve children in total and seven of the children were of similar ages. Three of them and four of us. The oldest of the seven is my big brother Jamal, then there is me. Seven months after my birth Imtiaz was born to Fatima. Eighteen months later and both women were pregnant again and that time gave birth days apart. Two little girls to add to the growing madness, then Fatima fell pregnant again and Mummy this time was a few months behind. This time the desired boys were produced and this brought an end to pregnancies.

I have no relationship with anybody from the Pakistani side of my family, and from my family I am in contact with Yacoub only. Yacoub was always different and when we were growing up he never ordered his sisters around, demanding his clothes were ironed or to make a snack for him. Living in London he gets to escape from it all and unlike me he has never felt something was missing because of the lack of Pakistani culture. My happiest years were spent in Pakistan. The culture was important to me, was part of me - I was Pakistani. Yacoub had no such issues and happily left his Pakistani side behind in Glasgow when he moved to London

For nearly 20 years I lived a life to please others, Pakistani and white people. Being disowned and ostracised by my family and the Pakistani community gave me no other option but to live with white people. Getting rid of my shalwar kameez (traditional Asian clothes), not talking the language and forgetting anything I ever knew about Islam. My world was totally white with no contact with Pakistani people. I had had no other choice but to change who I was, so I forgot my early years in Pakistan so I could fit in, but for the last eighteen months I had been trying again to live as a Pakistani.

It was the birth of my daughter, Ruby, that made me return to the Pakistani community. Secretly hoping Abbas would be delighted to meet his grand-daughter when he had never shown any delight in me, stupidly believing my daughter would melt his heart in ways I never could. Thinking if I could get back into the Pakistani community; Abbas would get to hear that I am raising my daughter in his cultures and traditions then he will forgive me and accept me. With the birth of my daughter my own Pakistani prejudice started to show. I did not want to raise my daughter in the corrupt Western culture. Even though I had raised Nathaniel, my son, in the white culture and managed to raise a good boy, it didn't matter. Girls, I believed, were different and needed protecting.

I wanted to win the approval of Abbas so badly that I turned my world Pakistani, keeping only a handful of white friends. They had been true friends who had always accepted me. There has been friction however with my Pakistani acquaintances since I started writing. Writing helped me see what the Pakistani community really thought of 'the gori's children'. Ghazala, one of my acquaintances whose approval I sought, always called me a 'half-caste' and regularly said she would always think the worst of white people regardless of how corrupt her own people were proved to be. The friction began with people worrying that I am going to write about the real side

9

of Scottish Pakistanis. At the same time I became fed up with being constantly told how I should be living my life, not buying supermarket chicken in case anyone popped over for a visit, not sharing the fact that sometimes I eat out at non halal restaurants, for fear of being judged. Feeling guilty for not praying, even though many others rarely do. It's the hypocrisy that makes me not want to be around the Pakistani community anymore; the double standards, the backstabbing and gossiping amongst many other things and I suppose coming to understand that I would never be accepted but would always be 'the gori's daughter'.

When I was growing up I had been brainwashed into believing white people were trash; it's why I never fully settled in the white community. From the age of eight until I was forced into a marriage at the age of 18, I had to listen to comments about how white people were beneath those who were responsible for raising me, and my marriage exposed me to people with similar views.

These past eighteen months I have spent back in the Pakistani community have shown me that it is far more complicated than that. The white people I call friends are good people while some of the Pakistanis I met could truly be described as trashy.

The Pakistani population in Glasgow is small and everyone really does know everyone. The closeness is reinforced through the practice of first cousin marriages. The big difference I noticed between the two cultures is white people generally live just one life, the majority of Pakistani people I met

10

live two, one at home and in the community where the aim is to show what an outstanding Muslim you are; the other living the life you choose always undercover and secret, known only to a trusted few. But everyone knows everyone and the community loves a good gossip, so most secrets are open secrets. A huge number of males and females drink, smoke, take drugs, go to pubs and clubs, have sex, have affairs and hide their sexual preferences. Some don't care who knows and openly do what pleases them. For this they are tagged with the label 'coco nuts', brown on the outside white on the inside, this title is meant to insult them. Nearly all of the Pakistanis I knew always at one point or another in conversation said, 'I fuckin' hate Pakis.' I could never understand why. Even though the Pakistani family treated us like dirt, even though Abbas and Fatima forced me into a marriage with a man much older than me, even though the man I was forced to marry and have a son with treated me like dirt; I still loved Pakistani people. I was half Pakistani and had been raised as a Pakistani. I had spent the best years of my childhood with good, decent, kind people who treated me as more than just 'the gori's daughter' and it's the reason I tried to hold onto the Pakistani community even when it was clear I wasn't truly welcome. Being away for so long I had forgotten the Pakistani flaws and hypocrisy, but the past eighteen months brought it all back. Writing it down made me think. Now I understand and now my story begins.

Chapter 2   The beginning

Mummy met Abbas one summer afternoon, in Glasgow, 1967. He had arrived from Kashmir like many others before him to make their fortune in a land where they believed the pavements were lined with gold. Many left their wives and young children behind, with the intention of bringing them over once settled and established. They met in a flat on Albert Drive, Pollokshields, and Mummy was sporting a black eye and split lip. Her daughter's father, Khalid, another Pakistani man, was responsible for the beating. The man was not interested in his child nor in Mummy, using her only for sex whenever he failed to charm some other white woman. Mummy was there with Mary, a back street abortionist used by the Pakistani men to terminate many a child they had created with the white women they were freely sleeping with. She was not there for an abortion, just to visit the men for the afternoon. Mary was friendly with many of the Pakistani men and had invited Mummy along on one of her visits.

Abbas was very handsome, well-spoken and a charming older man, old enough to be Mummy's father. She was under his spell after the first meeting. They agreed to meet at a party the following night and Mummy arrived giddy with excitement, her red wavy hair open and hanging loosely down to her waist, her signature black shift dress and knee length grey boots with thick black tights to complete her Beatnik look. Most clothes she

12

owned were black. Usually she wore her black polo neck and black drainpipe trousers but that night she was out to impress. A tiny size six with a childlike figure even though she had given birth to a child almost a year ago, the black emphasised her slimness. The men were all Pakistani and the women all Scottish, Catholic Scottish. No Protestant women were ever present at the parties Mummy went to. The vast majority of women at these parties were from care or broken homes. Damaged by their own families and the Catholic Church that was meant to protect them, and unwanted by their own men, the women lapped up the attention these exotic creatures were supplying. Ignoring the fact that most had a wife back home, back home was so far away, it was easy to live in the here and now with their new boyfriends. The Pakistani men all had the same dress sense. Polyester suits in the standard beige or charcoal grey, with a contrasting polo neck. Some wore a garish print shirt with a ghastly tie in shades of mustard and brown, with a V-neck jumper or cardigan in a contrasting colour to complete the look. Abbas and Mummy danced and talked. I think he liked her because she was intelligent and he was intelligent too. I was born to clever parents, they were just not very responsible. Abbas told her about his wife back home, his first cousin, he also told her about his children. Three of them were only a few years younger than Mummy and the youngest, a daughter, was almost a year old. Mummy told Abbas all about Zanera and how she was in care, how she was unable to cope without the help and support of her family. She told him all about her sad and sordid life. Her

13

foster mother didn't even know she had had a baby. Such was the shame of illegitimate children, in the eyes of her Catholic foster mother, even more so when the father was Pakistani. By the end of the party Mummy had bared her soul to Abbas, who instantly felt a need to look after this poor woman. She went back to his flat that night, never really left and he soon encouraged her to get Zanera out of care.

'It's no good, Maggie, ju no leave her. She jor daughter, ju her mother. Go bring her home.'

They spent a year living together in the flat Abbas was sharing with two other men from Pakistan. Mummy and Zanera shared a room with Abbas, the two men shared a room and the kitchen was shared by all, as was the bathroom. Mummy spent a lot of her time working hard, helping care for the elderly in nursing homes; that's where her career was headed, a nurse, before Pakistani men and pregnancy ended those college dreams. Instead she was forced to do menial tasks when she had aspired to be so much more.

Her relationship with Abbas at first was everything she had dreamt of, getting Zanera out of care and settling into a family life. Abbas was good to Zanera and kind, maybe she reminded him of his baby daughter in Mirpur, Mummy thought to herself. Zanera loved her new daddy, the only daddy she had known. The only thing bothering Mummy was that Abbas refused to discuss marriage with her. Dropping hints made no difference to him and more often than not he changed the subject completely. In the eyes of her Catholic god she wanted to do the

14

right thing and have a wedding band on her finger. And in the eyes of Abba's god he was not too worried about living in sin with an infidel. This was just one of many sins he was committing now he was living in the UK and free from family restraints. Some of the other white Scottish women were getting married. One of her closest friends, Wilma, had married and her Pakistani husband had promised to never bring wife number one over, instead choosing to send money over to Pakistan and support the family left behind. This was a promise he kept till his dying day.

Abbas had no plans to marry Mummy, ever. She brought in extra income and for that he was grateful. Yes he liked her and got on with her, but he liked partying and getting on with lots of other women too. The initial surge of sympathy he felt towards her when she shared her story had cooled down and now he was more interested in the extra income. It allowed him to save, send the required money back home and continue partying and chasing women, paying for them if he had to. Without Mummy's earnings he would not have been out as much and still Mummy happily handed over her wage packet at the end of the week. Abbas often left Mummy and Zanera at home with little food in the cupboards, a stale loaf, scraping of butter and mouthful of milk. The lodgers would cook a meal and sometimes ask Mummy and Zanera to share it with them while Abbas was out spending her money like he was a rich man. His family in Pakistan were provided for and he drank to that,

Mummy and Zanera far from his mind. The kindness of others ensuring they did not starve.

The state of Mummy's mental health had her almost sectioned on several occasions. Having only known neglect her entire life and now at the age of 20 with a two year old daughter and a boyfriend who was rarely at home, every now and again the reality of her life caused a mini break down. She would wail and scream uncontrollably, lashing out at anyone who came too close, like a frightened little child. Abbas soon learned that Mummy needed to be soothed with praise and kindness, soft voices to bring her out of it, gentleness and kindness. Every now and again Mummy faked it for the tenderness he showed her. Gossip has spread back to Pakistan that Abbas was living with a 'gori' and her child to another man. With his usual charm and self-confidence, he reassured everyone back home it was nothing but gossip.

'You know how we love a gossip, this one is with that one and that one is with this one. That's all it is, the gori she is a worker and shares a room with the boy from Lahore. Nothing to do with me.'

With his refusing to admit he was living in sin with a white woman, they had no other option but to believe him and for a while his secret life was safe and he thought to himself the best way to escape the gossip was to leave Scotland and head to England. Glasgow was where all the Kashmiris seemed to be settling. The foundations for the ghetto that Pollokshields would

16

become were being laid, with every man, woman and child that was arriving and setting up home there. Down in England it was not as bad because they were settling all over, in places like Bradford, Birmingham, Manchester and London. In Scotland, Glasgow was the place they came and Pollokshields was the district to live. No escape from the prying eyes and backstabbing that the people of Kashmir thrived on. An opportunity arose when a friend of a friend was returning to Pakistan and leaving behind a business for someone to take over. Fed up with an unwelcoming community, the cold weather and missing his life back home, he had saved for his one way ticket back to Pakistan. Abbas decided he was the man for the job and told Mummy that they were moving to Huddersfield, England, to take over the running of a halal butcher shop, which had a pokey wee one room and kitchen above it. Becoming part of a business with accommodation, Mummy doesn't need asking twice. Her life in Glasgow so far had hardly been a happy one. She had been put into care at the age of six along with her eight brothers and sisters. With such a large family it was unlikely that they would be placed together, and so her brothers and sisters were separated and Mummy along with Uncle Ciaran, the youngest brother, were fostered by a couple with a ten year old son. Her foster father died when she was eight and life was miserable with a foster mother and foster brother who didn't really have time for her. Escaping and meeting Zanera's father, who got her pregnant and abandoned her, and then Abbas, it seemed her life was destined to be miserable. Months after the move to Huddersfield,

17

Mummy discovered she was pregnant again. Abbas was hardly overjoyed at the news, thinking only of how she will keep on working whilst pregnant?

The running of the butcher shop was left mostly to Mummy, with Zanera hanging round her feet, until Mummy began to make friends with the English women on the street and then sometimes they would take Zanera for a few hours, allowing Mummy peace to work. Cutting meat, serving customers, keeping an eye on who had credit and who was behind on repayments. One afternoon a Pakistani woman entered the shop and started a conversation with Mummy in her best attempt at English, so keen was she to get some gossip to send back to Mirpur. She knew Abbas's wife and didn't like her very much, this was her way of stirring it so to speak.

'Who tha baby father? Around? Help ju?'

'What do you mean?' Mummy asked bewildered.

'Abbas, he tell my husband, jor baby father black man?' she continued oblivious to Mummy's anger.

'I live here with Abbas and I am having his baby. He is the father,' she told the woman.

When Abbas arrived at the shop later that evening, Mummy questioned him about what the woman has said, asking him if he was denying the child was his. Telling her that she probably misunderstood the woman, knowing it was true.

'No tell anyone no my baby. Ju be silly for.'

Mummy refused to be placated and sulked for the rest of the night, refusing to talk to Abbas. She was eight months

18

pregnant, her hormones were all over the place and she was exhausted. She didn't know what to think. She preferred not to think. Days after the argument Abbas arrived at the shop with a Pakistani man she has never seen before, turned the 'open' sign round to 'closed' and locked the door. Turning to Mummy, Abbas told her, 'Come, Maggie, I marry ju, here is molvi (holy man) who do it. Come we go upstairs to sitting room.'

Following behind them, Mummy made her way upstairs, Zanera running ahead. The molvi was wearing the traditional clothes, worn by all the men on Fridays, the day of Jumma prayers. Mummy had no reason to believe she was being duped. Abbas was in his best grey suit and beige polo neck, eager to get the proceedings started. Laughing nervously, due to the religious man in the room, Mummy told Abbas, 'I've no' even washed my face or brushed my hair. Look at the state of me, I cannae get married like this?'

'Ju vorry all the time for? Look at ju like a phool (flower), ju fine.'

They sat down on the sofa and the molvi sat on a chair at the dining table. Zanera was excited although too young to understand why, chattering away when one look from Mummy silenced her and she hung back, watching. The molvi started speaking to Abbas in a language Mummy didn't understand, Arabic she found out later. He informed her that they are now, in the eyes of Islam, married. Mummy chose to believe this. Even though she had not understood a single word being spoken, when Abbas had prompted her to nod her head and say 'kabul', telling her it meant 'Yes, I agree to take this man as my husband.' She was happy that in the eyes of her Catholic God she was no longer living in sin. She bought herself a gold band to wear on her wedding finger and for a long time she believed she was no longer living in sin. In the spring of her 22nd birthday, she welcomed her first son, Jamal, into the world. Jamal was coffee coloured with a head full of soft black curls. He had his father's features but was more delicate. Mummy, Abbas and Zanera were besotted by Jamal and for a while he brought his family together. Abbas spent more time at the flat and took over the running of the shop. With a new-born baby and a toddler it was just not possible for Mummy to work. For a while Mummy dreamt her life could be truly happy. Every day was a delight and it was something she had never experienced before. Abbas was doing the cooking, making sure she ate and rested, and taking Zanera away for the day, to Bradford or Birmingham even London to give her a day with just Jamal to care for. Hiring someone to cover the shop, off he went, Zanera skipping happily alongside him. Abbas would use these trips away to fulfil his need for other women, leaving Zanera with relatives in whatever town in England he visited. Those were the happiest days of Mummy's life.

By the time Jamal was a year old, Abbas had slowly gone back to his socialising ways and was hardly at home. Dropping by to get a wash or change of clothes or take money out of the till. He would spend a little time with the children and depending on the welcome he got from Mummy, he would either avoid her or try and charm his way back in. Sometimes he would stay home for a week, working in the shop, helping out with the children and spending his time with Mummy, only to disappear for a week or two in a row, no appearances even fleetingly. On one such occasion when he finally returned Mummy happily told him she was pregnant again. Three months almost. This time when he returned he didn't have to charm her much, Mummy was just glad to have him back and keen to share her good news. Abbas lashed out, slapping her hard across the face. With contained fury and anger, he hissed at her, 'Ju stupid bitch, ju vill abort.'

The unexpected reaction and the stinging blow shocked Mummy into silence. Abbas left the flat and stormed out of the shop door, leaving Mummy alone with her demons, her children and unborn child. In tears she decided no matter what, she will not abort; he will love this child as much as the other children. The next few weeks were full of tension, arguments and lots of violence.

'Ju bloody bitch. Bloody harami (bastard.) Kootee kamini zaleel aurat, (disgusting bastard bitch of a woman.) Vy ju no listen for,' Abbas screamed and taunted at every opportunity, hoping to wear Mummy down and convince her to travel to Glasgow and visit their mutual friend, Mary, the one who does abortions for the Pakistani men. Mummy refused. Abbas may have lost sight of his religion but Mummy had a stronger fear of God than she did of this man in front of her. When her belly reached the stage where it would be too late for her to abort, he calmed down on the taunting and criticism and resigned himself to the fact he was having another child to the gori. By then there were more pressing issues to be dealing with, organising his flight back to Mirpur for one, and finding somewhere else for Mummy and the children to live.

Abbas was going back home for six weeks and would be returning with his wife, brother and youngest daughter. Five years is long time to be away, more so for those he had left behind. For Abbas they were the best years of his life and home rarely crossed his mind. The swinging sixties and the Western lifestyle had appealed to Abbas on every level. His wife, Fatima, was less than thrilled on hearing that the rumours were in fact true. There was no great love between Abbas and Fatima, first cousins married through family choice and not for love or compatibilities. Fatima's pride and sense of honour was hurt more than her heart broken, and so she listened to Abbas as he outlined what he had in mind for Mummy, how they could exploit her weakness to their own advantage. Fatima was not impressed by her husband's escapades or future plans, but was keen to come to the UK so agreed, telling him 'I will never give you permission to make her your second wife, I am your only wife.'

Arriving in the UK from rural Mirpur was a huge culture shock to Fatima. The sounds, the smells, the weather, the buildings, the people, alien to what she had left behind. So many things to adjust to, and of course meeting Mummy. Mummy was standing outside the shop waiting for Abbas to return from the airport. A taxi pulled into the street and came to a halt outside the shop. Standing next to Mummy was Joyce, a neighbour from the street who Mummy had become good friends with. Zanera was playing with some of the other children and Jamal was on Mummy's hip. Abbas got out of the taxi followed by Fatima and their youngest daughter Shagufta, then his brother Haroon got out of the front seat of the taxi. Fatima was wearing a plain white shalwar kameez (tradition Asian suit of trousers and long dress) and matching scarf on top of her head, covering her hair, which was plaited loosely and hung down to her waist. She was dark skinned, almost as tall as Abbas and fat. Fatima watched as her husband marched over and started shouting in a language she didn't understand. Getting out of the taxi, she took in her rival and smirked to herself. Mummy's long wavy hair was untied and hanging loosely to her waist, she was wearing a purple paisley print maternity smock which covered her knees. Bare legs and skin so white it was almost translucent, brown and black freckles dotted all over the flesh on show. Kanjari (prostitute), she thought to herself. Half naked out in the street for all to see, what kind of a woman had her husband got himself? Sneaking a glance at Mummy's children too, she was struck, for a second, by how adorable they were. The boy was smiling and wriggling to get off his mother's hip. Fatima could see he was excited to see his father. Father, she thought, my husband. Harami (bastards), her children are nothing but harami bachay (bastard children), she repeated in her head. Her curiosity satisfied, she looked around her and at what she was guessing was her new home.

23

Showing face, head held high, she refused to let her disappointment, hurt and bewilderment show. Covering her true feelings, she looked back at the woman that had stolen her husband and she promised herself she would destroy her. Mummy sensed she was being watched and half listened to Abbas ranting at her.

'Vy ju out here for, eh? Go back in jor house, standing like a charelle (witch), go.'

'The children haven't seen you for weeks, they missed you,' she told him, looking over at her rival and begging for the affections of the man in front of her.

Turning his back on her and walking over to his wife, he told Mummy one more time to go home.

'Come on, Maggie, let's go back over to yours, and let them out the back to play. I'll make us a cup of tea,' Joyce told her, watching as Abbas led his family into Mummy's old home.

'Did you see the state of her?' said Joyce. 'Bloody hell, no wonder he cheated on her, she is like a man beast. Even from across the road I could see the hair on her face. That's what you get for in-breeding.'

'He's with her though isn't he? No matter what she looks like, he still went and got her and brought her over to live in my house,' replied Mummy.

The children had been given a snack and were out in the back garden. Zanera was five years old and was an expert at child care duties. Changing Jamal's nappies, making his bottles and feeding him, getting him ready for bed, all the things his

24

mum should have been doing. Some days Mummy really struggled to give him the attention a toddler needed, and his big sister had to take on the parent role. Mummy and Joyce sat in the front room on the sofa. Mummy's new home came furnished, a bit tatty from the previous tenants but usable. The sofa was a large drop end style in a floral print of mustards, browns, greens, purples. The favoured hues of the 60's and 70's. Lighting up another cigarette, Mummy inhaled as she wondered out loud when Abbas would come to see her and the children.

'Do you know, Maggie, you are really better off without him, I have said it to you before and I will keep on telling you. You deserve better than him, hardly ever at home and now his wife is here. What kind of life is he going to give you?'

Mummy argued that nobody would want her, two children and another on the way. She believed that Abbas was the only chance of a family life she had. She argued that she would be unable to cope on her own, even when Joyce insisted she would help and provide child care when the time came for her to go back to work. It was an argument they often had, Joyce begging Mummy to leave Abbas, Mummy refusing.

Joyce left after she had helped Mummy feed the kids and settle them into bed. Sitting down with another cup of tea and cigarette Mummy sighed. She hadn't eaten all day, her appetite gone when Fatima arrived. She was running on nervous energy. She was anxiously waiting and praying Abbas would come over. He was only across the road and Jamal was his child too, she thought to herself. She wouldn't see him until the next

25

night when the children were in bed, and what he had to say sent her into shock.

'You want me to live with her? Are you crazy?' she asked, when he told her of his grand plans for her future and that of her children. Ignoring her protests like he did with his wife, he continued telling her how much support she would have, give it time and Fatima would become a good friend to her and a mother to her children.

'Ju vill have the family life ju always vanted, ju vill see how happy we all be. One big happy family.'

Abbas needed this to work out. He was not earning enough to support two homes, at this moment in his life he was barely earning enough to support one home. Mummy got up and went into the kitchen to make some more tea, leaving Abbas smoking his cigarette. Standing at the sink, Mummy imagined a family life of happiness the way Abbas seemed to think it would all be. What was Fatima saying to it all, she wondered? Mummy came back in and asked Abbas.

'Oh, she will be delighted to watch the children while ju work in the shop,' he lied. 'It will be awkward at first,' he agreed with her. 'Neither of ju speak each other's language. Jor cultures, lifestyles are completely different but it can work out. When jor baby is born, ju come back work in shop and Fatima she watch Jamal and Zanera and jor baby. She upstairs in flat, ju downstairs in shop. If children vant their mother, ju go upstairs.'

'This is your baby too, I wish you would stop saying 'your' baby,' Mummy told him. This pregnancy had been different, he had not shown the slightest interest. She would go on to have another three children with him and, unknown to her at the time, I would be the only one he wouldn't visit in hospital or acknowledge when brought home from the hospital. Maybe when the baby arrives he will change, she told herself. I arrived less than two months later and by then Mummy had agreed to come back to work when I was a month old. Abbas didn't change his attitude towards me when I was born.

The next time Mummy saw Fatima was when she returned to the pokey wee flat above the shop, her old home. Fatima had been living with her brother in Bradford and visiting other relatives that had settled in other parts of England. Walking through the living room door, she saw Fatima sitting on the couch with Shagufta sitting next to her. On the other side was Haroon, Abbas's brother, who was very close to Fatima. They were first cousins as well as being brother/sister in law and had grown up together like brother and sister. Conversation stopped and three heads turned to stare at her. Mummy with her milky white freckly skin, blue eyes and red wavy hair hanging loosely down to her waist. Black polo neck tucked into her favourite drainpipe jeans and her kitten heels on. She was holding me in her arms and Zanera was by her side with Abbas carrying my Moses basket into the room and Jamal running in behind, a big smile on his face.

Fatima broke the silence.

'Kanjari kol koi sharam nee' (Slut has no shame.), she spat at Mummy.

27

'What's she saying, Abbas?' Mummy asked, unable to take her gaze away from this woman in front of her. The woman she had agreed to share a home and man with. The two women couldn't be more different. Fatima with her head covered and her trademark white shalwar kameez, and Mummy with her long hair flowing down her back and already back in her size 6 clothes. It was hard to believe that she had given birth only a few weeks ago.

'Oh no vorry, Maggie, she say ju very beautiful, likes ju,' he soothed with lies.

Turning towards his wife he told her warningly, 'Tu renday budhee, eh chunghee aurat hain, bhot kum karsee. (Behave woman, she is a good hard worker).'

Haroon pleaded with his brother that this was not right, this situation cannot work, asking him why he was doing this, surely there had to be another way. Turning to Mummy, he took his frustrations out.

'Ju belong gutter. Bad lady. My bhabi (sister-in-law) much better ju!' he yelled.

'And what?' Mummy screamed back. 'Is she moving out because I've moved back in, is she getting on the first plane back to Mirpur? Staying? I thought as much. Makes her just as bad and in the gutter same as me.'

Haroon started shouting when Fatima spoke and instantly he stopped.

'Meh isski pagal banai shorsa,' she told Haroon while staring at her husband's mistress in disgust. 'Saree duniya karab karee shorsa. (I will drive her crazy and ruin her entire life.)'

'Buss karo koi samaj. (Stop this at once, do you not understand),' Abbas shouted.

'Doesn't sound like nice things...' said Mummy.

Abbas and Mummy both began speaking at once.

Haroon smirked at Mummy, glaring at him she continued, 'She sounds and looks angry, look at her face. Kunjari is no a nice word, Abbas, I know that word. You said she was happy with this arrangement.'

He began soothing Mummy with the lies he so often fed her, knowing how to control her with his charm. Exploiting and manipulating her neediness and weaknesses.

'Maggie, no be silly, she trying best. No easy for all of us,' he told her.

Turning to his wife with contained fury.

'Samaj nee avnee? Kitnee varee aksa? Bootha sidda kur! (Do you not understand? How many times do I need to tell you? And straighten your face.)'

'Everyone vill be happy, one big happy family,' he said looking to Mummy and back to his wife, smiling.

Abbas saw no other way to solve his financial dilemma, he couldn't support two households and fund his love of partying and pay for his other women. Dumping Mummy and the children would look bad, his parents wouldn't have approved. They were simple, decent and kind people who tried their best to

29

live a peaceful life and would never have forgiven him for abandoning his children, regardless of who their mother was. Their religion would not have allowed it. Abbas needed the family he was creating to live together for it to work financially and allow him to fund his Western lifestyle. Fatima continued to curse at Mummy until Abbas bellowed:

'Kitnee varee aksa? (How many times will I need to tell you?)'

And she abruptly stopped, seeing the anger and rage on his face, knowing she was pushing him too far, she had after all agreed to this arrangement.

'Challo (come on), Maggie, back to work. And I go see Humza, owe money. He no pay for weeks.'

'Budhee tu choop kur aur bakwaas na tusee doi shoroo karo (Woman be quiet and both of you don't start your nonsense)' Abbas said, turning towards the door.

'You're going out? What about the children?' Mummy asked nervously already unsure about leaving us in the care of Fatima and Haroon. Thinking this arrangement was wrong yet having no strength to walk away from it, seeing no other option available to her, Joyce's offer of child minding doesn't enter her head, she wants to please Abbas and Abbas has said over his dead body will a white woman raise his children. I guess nobody saw the irony of his argument.

'Vy vorry all time for? Smile, go work. I tell ju already budhee (old lady) look after. Your children, her children.' Abbas often referred to Fatima as budhee, this was his pet name

30

for her rather than an insult because she wasn't that old and Abbas would often be called bhudda (old man) by the two women, again his pet name and not an insult.

Reluctantly and with no other choice available to her she placed me in my Moses basket and made her way down the stairs, leaving us at the mercy of Fatima. Eight weeks maternity leave without pay and then back to work, cutting meat without pay and Fatima chosen as the child minder for her children.

Several times Mummy had to leave the shop and come upstairs to stop me crying or change a nappy or make a bottle. Fatima and Haroon left me to scream, choosing to ignore the gori's children completely. Forgetting that we are Abbas's children too. Regardless of our parents, what Fatima ignored completely was the fact that we were children, children who didn't deserve the mean and nasty way she treated us.

Every time Mummy came up, Fatima watched her. Mummy struggled to show love and kindness to her children, struggling with her own demons took all her time. No kisses, no cuddles for us children. She ended up taking all her anger and frustrations out on us instead. Aware she was being scrutinised by her when changing my nappy she glanced over.

'Hai eh thay bachay naa kaam bansee (This will be child's play.)' Fatima said to Haroon.

To Mummy's surprise, for the first time that day Fatima smiled at her and Mummy thought, as she made her way back down the stairs to the shop, maybe Abbas was right, maybe we can all be a happy family.

The happy family lasted a few days before Mummy moved back out and returned to her home across the road. Living together in a wee pokey flat was impossible, living together at all and sharing their man was not possible, Mummy and Fatima had decided. Mummy though, for the time being, continued to work in the shop to earn a wage to look after herself and her children. Abbas had relented and let Joyce babysit his children. Fatima had moved to Bradford to her brother's home, moving in with his wife and young family, she had refused to return to Huddersfield and seven months after I was born, she gave birth to another son, Imtiaz.

Since moving to Huddersfield Mummy had spent a lot of time running back to Glasgow, having had enough of the unfair and cruel treatment dished out by Abbas. The rail staff were so used to seeing her they knew her by name. Usually when she left she had the standard busted lip, black eyes and bruised and battered body. Fighting with Abbas was the cause of her bruises, Abbas thought nothing of giving her a slap to keep her under his control. With her young children she must have looked a pitiful sight. Returning to Glasgow and to her foster mother.

Describing it Mummy said, 'I mind the first time I left him and came to Glasgow. I went straight to her door crying. She was the only mother I knew even though she was an auld bastard. Jamal was just a baby and Zanera was standing holding my hand. You wurnae born yet. 'You can come in Maggie but leave your black bastards in the garden.' When I told her I

32

wouldn't be coming in without my children, she slammed the door in my face.'

After that welcome at her foster mother's home, she went to stay at a friend's. With two young children it wasn't the easiest of situations and the only other family she had was Uncle Ciaran, her brother. He was fighting his own demons and insecurities, having grown up in care with Mummy and was unable to offer her a place to stay. After a few days she would return to the hell in Huddersfield she saw no way of escaping from.

When I was 18 months old, both women were pregnant at the same time and Abbas had returned to Glasgow, alone. For the next six months or so he travelled between Huddersfield and Glasgow but mostly to Bradford to visit Fatima who he provided for financially. Abbas started working as a conductor on the buses, then driving the buses and he had saved enough money to rent a large three bedroom flat on Albert Drive, Pollokshields. The butcher shop in Huddersfield had been taken over by some distant relative of Abbas's, Mummy was not able to run it with three children and another on the way. Instead she relied on her child benefit to survive and the kindness of her neighbours, and when Abbas visited she begged him for money, which he rarely gave her. Fatima and her children arrived in Glasgow a few weeks before Mummy, who was left behind in Huddersfield unaware of the plans being made between husband and wife. Mummy remembered, 'He just turned up one day and said we were moving back to Glasgow, he'd found a flat and we were all going to live together. I was to go out and work and she would look after the weans. And that was it. I remember coming back and finding she had chosen the biggest bedroom.'

People like to gossip and Pakistani people are no exception. If anything they are the biggest gossipers, making it their business to know everything. I wondered what the community thought of our family set up and asked Mummy over the phone one day.

'Nobody really said anything to our face. Of course people knew. One time Fatima and I were out getting a few messages on Maxwell Road, both of us heavily pregnant. And this one comes up sniggering and says 'Do you all sleep together in the one bed?' I told her. 'Aye, when he is fucking me she knits, and when he is fucking her, I read my book.' The look on her face was worth it. Fatima gave me into trouble for saying it but I didn't care.'

Soon after moving to Glasgow Fatima gave birth to a daughter, Khalsoom, and five days later Mummy had a daughter too. Mummy and Abbas named her Amirah, meaning princess, and this time round Abbas was delighted with his baby daughter to the gori. A year later Fatima was pregnant again and this time had a boy. Mummy was four months pregnant with the baby of the family. By this point the two women had bonded over their dislike of Abbas's womanising ways. Two women at home and still he was out 'whoring it' as it was known in our house. Soon the time came for the last baby to be born and Mummy went to the hospital unaware of the passports being applied for, tickets purchased and suitcases packed. The day my baby brother was born, Abbas visited Mummy and told her Jamal and I were being taken to Kashmir the following day. Fatima was struggling to cope with looking after all the children and now there was another baby. He brought us in the next day and we were allowed in a private room away from the ward to say goodbye. Mummy said, 'I was numb. I'd just had a baby and was having to say goodbye to the two of you. I didn't cry, just held you both and told you to be good. Jamal understood what was happening, you were too young.'

Mummy, understandably, finds it difficult to talk about this time in her life. I can only imagine how difficult it must have been for her. Guilt plays a huge part I guess. Her family was destroyed and broken by the choices she made. She accepted living with Abbas and Fatima in a fucked up version of happy families, never for a minute thinking of the impact this would have on her children's happiness and ultimately her own.

Chapter 3   From Glasgow to Mirpur and back again

My earliest memory is when I am three years old. I am crying. My nose all snotty. I am sitting next to Abbas in a strange, hot place surrounded by family members I have never met before. Nothing is familiar. My brother is sat on Abbas's knee happily playing with a toy helicopter, purchased to pacify him and obviously working. I show no interest in the doll purchased for me. Mummy is not there with us, neither is Fatima or my other brothers and sisters.

Even though I was just three years old, I understood he was leaving us here with his parents and extended family, strangers, to Jamal and I anyway. He was returning to the only family I knew, back to Glasgow, alone. Jamal was undisturbed by the fact we were being left behind and shed no tears. I continued to cry, refusing to allow Abbas to comfort me. Screaming louder when he tried to pick me up. A lady took me from him and soothed me with words I did not understand. Abbas said his farewells and left. It was lucky for us his parents were kind, decent people who adored us. In Pakistan we were never made to feel worthless, never made to feel shame for being mixed race, never being labelled as 'the gori's children'. Being so young and being very blessed to have grandparents and especially for me an aunty who adored me, it didn't take long for the tears to stop. Love and kindness had replaced hatred and contempt.

The five years we spent there we never went to school. Both of us decided we didn't want to go and our grandparents never forced it, knowing one day we would return to a completely different schooling system. They were happy to have us around. Never for a minute did I imagine a life anywhere but where I was. One of my favourite times was the monsoon season. The heat would be unbearable during the day, the sky bright with the sun when all of a sudden a chill and the clouds would slowly darken and the skies would open up and the downpour would have you drenched in seconds. I would be running barefoot in the puddles squealing with delight as any happy carefree child does. My aunty would shout at me to get inside and laughing she would gather me up in her arms and take me away from the rain. A gentle breeze would build up and loosen fruit off trees, causing it to fall on the ground. I remember being allowed to collect and eat it. Apricots, dates and pomegranate were my favourites and still are to this day. Within minutes of the rain, the sun would re-emerge from the skies, drying our wet clothes instantly and back out we would all go. I was always dirty, roaming in the barren rural countryside, out exploring on adventures with the numerous cousins that lived there. Bhai jii (grandmother) always shaved my head, maybe the curls bothered her, although I have been told it was because of the nits.

I grew up hearing stories about Jinns and black magic. Jinns are made from smokeless fire and exist in their own dimension, where they marry and have children and many Muslim people believe in them and blame the Jinns for all sorts of misfortunes. The same happens with black magic, if someone has an unexplained illness then their family will be convinced black magic has been done on them. Some of the stories I overheard Bhai jii and the other adults discussing, but most of them I heard from my older cousins, who loved scaring the younger ones with their horror tales of people being possessed because of something they had done that had angered or attracted the Jinn. Wearing strong perfume and going out late at night is one way of being possessed because the Jinn are attracted by strong perfumes and they are most active at night. Shamila, one of my cousins, was 12 years old. She told me if someone pees in their place of existence, trees and old empty houses then the Jinn gets angry and possesses that person. Lots of the women also covered their long hair if going out in the evening as this is something else that attracts the Jinn, as does beautiful men and women. I had my hair shaved off so wasn't worried about them possessing me. Bhai jii reassured me whenever I went to her, scared by some of the stories, and told me to recite Ayatul Kursi to protect myself. Even though we never went to school to learn our ABC's, we were taught to read the Quran and a little about Islam from Bhaba jii (Grandfather), so I was able to recite this verse whenever I was scared or spooked. I often asked Bhai jii to tell me the story about the lady and her vanity. The story was about a woman who had died and was buried. When this woman was alive she wore a lot of make-up and her nails were always painted in colours to match her shalwar kameez. She was very vain about her looks and took a lot of time over her appearance,

38

making sure her hair was styled in the latest fashion. Too much time, said my Bhai-jii. One day two men were walking through the graveyard when they heard wailing and cries of help. The noise was coming from her grave and so they began digging it up and helped the woman out of the shroud she had been buried in. Bhai-jii said the woman had no eyelids, no eyelashes, lips or cheeks. Her fingernails were also missing as were her toenails. Her hair was patchy and shorn. The men were horrified by what they were seeing but the woman did not notice their horror. Bhai jii said that God had done this to the woman and sent her back so the women of the village would see how God punishes those who are vain.

My Bhai jii was a plain and simple woman. She was taller than most of the Pakistani woman in the village and slim. She had bright orange hair from dying it with henna and would sit in the sun with the henna smothered in her hair. Her finger nails and toe nails were also covered in henna so they too were an orangey colour. Her face was lined and brown and her ear lobes hung down to almost her neck from the weight of the pure gold ear rings she wore. Whenever I heard Jinn stories from my Bhai jii I felt safe, no matter how scary.

In my experience child abuse is rife in the Pakistani community and here in Pakistan it was The Paedophile who abused me. Pakistani people live in large extended families and it is easy for an abuser to get a child alone. I have memories of him doing things he shouldn't have being doing. He was 24 years old and a nephew of Abbas's. Married to his second oldest daughter, my step sister. I avoided her at all costs as she was mean and nasty. She had huge bulging eyes and wore thick glasses, her teeth were fighting for space inside her mouth and she always looked angry. Years later I would see the advert for shadii.com (an online dating agency for Muslims) and it would remind me of her.

Mummy visited twice in the time we were there. The first visit was a year after we had been taken away, of which I have no memory, but her second visit, three years later I do remember and happily hugged her and accepted when told that she was my mother. I knew I had a mother somewhere even though my childhood was so fulfilling and carefree and the love and care I received from my aunty left no time to daydream of a mother. I just knew I had one like all the other children did. Jamal refused to be hugged, obnoxiously announcing, 'Eh meri maa nai, eh thay gori hain. (She is not my mother, she is a white woman.)' Not going near her to be hugged and kissed. Not having anything to do with her the entire time she stayed. I was too young to notice Mummy's hurt over this and laughed along with everyone else, Mummy included, when he continued to call her the white woman. Jamal was very possessive over Bhai jii and demanded she love him and him only. When he was six years old he told her to send Bhabha jii away so he could be her king and her only king, so strong and fierce was his love for his Bhai jii, telling her there was no need for Bhabba jii to be there as he would protect her. If I went to her for comfort he would sulk until he got his own way and got her to himself. Usually I

40

pampered to his demands and allowed him his beloved Bhai jii to himself, I had my aunty and preferred to go to her for my comfort. My aunty was beautiful, inside and out. She had little time for gossiping and backstabbing and preferred to spend her days cooking and cleaning and also teaching the Quran to the young ones in the family. Her children were in their late teens and had little need for her. Whenever I needed her she was there, showing me right from wrong, good from bad. She told me to always tell the truth, liars were not nice people, she said. If I lied about something she was not happy, and so I learned to always tell the truth.

We had no indoor toilet and no shower or bath. The toilet was a hole in the ground and a jug 'lotah' full of water was used for cleaning or if you were out roaming, then a stone or leaf. We washed outside in the hot sun, a deep bucket filled with cold water. Bhai jii decided to pierce my ears one day, with a needle. I was six years old when I was held down, by female relatives, screaming loud enough for the whole village to hear me while she pierced each ear. The needle had black thread, wound very thick, which went through the ears and was tied in a knot. Two little black hoops of black thread to keep the piercing open. Cuddles, soothing kind words, 'Oh aren't you so pretty, a proper big girl.' Along with my favourite treat gulab jammins (sweet spongy desert) and the pain was forgotten. Within weeks the threads, after much bribing and coaxing, were snipped off and replaced with small, pure gold hoop ear rings. Pakistani gold is usually 24 carat and yellow in colour. Bhai jii and Bhabha had purchased them especially for me. I did feel like a proper big girl with them on. Pakistani families are always visiting, especially when someone comes over from 'Valet' - Glasgow. Excitement in the air at the gifts they will bring, the stories they will share about the 'goray people' and their lifestyle. They described a world where the pavements were paved with gold because the government housed you and gave you money. Here in Kashmir nothing was given for free. Everybody worked for what they had and if they didn't work they didn't have. There were no government hand outs here. We were two little toddlers born to one of these 'goray people' they had heard about and visitors travelled from afar to see us. See with their own eyes the beautiful children that Abbas had fathered with a white woman. I can recall numerous occasions when relatives would appear and Jamal and I would be paraded, scrubbed and dressed in our finest Pakistani clothes. People were always cooing over us, wanting to squeeze our cheeks, touch our hair. My head was more often than not shaved and usually just a bristle of hair and still they ruffled. In awe at our uniqueness. The entire time spent there we heard 'Masha 'Allah kitnay sonay hai. (God has willed it, aren't they adorable.)' 'Insha'Allah, nazaar na lug jai (God willing, don't put the evil eye on them.)' They probably had never seen mixed race children before and for them we were a novelty. Soon more relatives arrived and the lady told Jamal and I she was our 'Umee jee' – (mother) and the six children with her were our brothers and sisters. I had no memory of her and she had never been to visit the five years I had spent there. As far as I was concerned they were not my family. Even though I was told they were, I refused to believe it. I never called the lady Umee jee, she was cold and distant towards me and I refused to acknowledge her. I was almost eight years old now, I was a strong confident happy and carefree child. Raised in a loving and mostly safe environment, it was easy for me to be that child. Fatima couldn't harm me in Pakistan or really scare me. Here I was protected and safe from her nastiness. Fatima and the gang of children stayed for almost six weeks and although I have vague memories of them arriving, I blanked them out and thought if I ignore them then it won't be real and I won't have to go with them like everybody keeps saying. I ignored my aunty when she began packing my belongings and would unpack them when she wasn't looking. Anytime Fatima or one of the children from her gang spoke, I acted like I heard nothing and no amount of cajoling or scolding would make me listen. The children were all loud and brash and spoke in a language, English, I didn't understand. They laughed and sniggered behind their hands a lot. Fatima would say nice things and try and get me to come sit beside her but I stayed away. I knew she didn't mean it, she was doing it to pretend she cared. I remember being on the roof tops with my favourite cousin Shahid watching the 'Valeti - Glasgow' children playing. They were strangers to me, from a place that held no interest. Unlike many other people living in Kashmir and as young as I was I had no desire to visit or live in 'Valet.' Here was where I belonged. This was my home.

'Tere khandaan hain, tu vapaas chalee ina dey nal. Subha tu Valet jassay, (They are your family and you are going back to Glasgow with them tomorrow,)' Shahid told me, stopping my questioning of what they talked about in their funny language.

'Nai! Fir nah koho. (No! Stop saying that.)' I cried, and went looking for my beloved aunty, this time she was unable to stop my tears. For weeks I had been ignoring the discussions and plans for our return to Glasgow. And then suddenly it was time to leave. There was no more ignoring it.

My beloved aunty told me again about how this was never meant to be our home forever and how one day we would be returned to our family.

Hugging me tightly she soothed me as I continued to cry, snot and tears all over her kameez (dress). Snot and tears when I arrived and snot and tears when I left.

'Maihairbani,' I beg in between sobs. 'Mujay nai vapaas payjo. (Please. Don't send me back.)'

Rocking me back and forth in her arms, like a baby. The tears and sadness would continue for a very long time. Years later I would learn she died in a car crash and I would cry for my beloved aunty, her life taken far too soon. There would be no contact between us when I returned to Glasgow and I wouldn't see her again until my forced marriage at 18 years old and then I was too caught up in my self-loathing and misery to thank her for anything. It was always my dream to see her again one day and thank her for the love and kindness she had shown me. She made the most important years of my life happy, without those happy times who knows where I would have ended up.

Uprooted from all I knew and loved. Jamal and I were always going to be returned to the madness that Abbas had been creating for the last five years. No matter how much I cried and begged that night, it didn't change the situation. Returning to Glasgow was a shock. I left behind the only family I have known and a world full of hustle and bustle, smells of spices in the air mingling with the smells of horse and cow dung, voices of children playing and the sun shining brightly above it all. Arriving in Pollokshields the coldness and drabness of the place was so different to the home I had left behind. Here the buildings were tall and so close to one another with no open space. There were no animals, goats, cows and horses, roaming the streets, only dogs and cats. The cold was something I would never get used to and even wrapped up in a scarf, gloves and hat when going out, I was still frozen. The flat was just as strange as the people who lived in it. Inside they had carpets on the floors, windows with glass in it and curtains to close over at night.

There was a bed I was to sleep in with Zanera and Amirah when all I had ever slept in was a munji, a bed made out of woven rope. In Mirpur when I woke up in the mornings and after breakfast, I was free to go on my adventures with my other cousins and sometimes Jamal too. Here, there was no venturing out of the flat on my own, only television to watch. Adjusting to the strangeness with nobody to stop the tears. I asked constantly to be sent back. I was told to shut up or I would be given

45

something to cry about. A few slaps later, I stopped asking to go back and kept my tears for bed time when I had privacy to cry without someone threatening to slap me. The flat on Albert Drive had three bedrooms and a dining kitchen. The biggest bedroom was Fatima's, who shared it with Shagufta, Jamal, Imtiaz, Khalsoom and Anwar. Mummy slept in the other bedroom with Zanera, Amirah, Yacoub and me, and the back bedroom was kept for whatever relative was visiting or staying with us. The living room doubled as Abbas's bedroom with his bed in the recess.

The only nice person I found in my family in Glasgow was my little brother, Yacoub. Last time I saw him was on the day he was born and now he would be five in a few months' time. Mummy idolised him as did the rest of them and she had refused to let him go to Kashmir, so really I was meeting him for the first time. Mummy had left him behind on both occasions when she had visited Jamal and I in Pakistan, leaving him in the care of Fatima and Abbas. He was easily the cutest child in the house and he was sweet natured which made it difficult not to adore him. When the other children picked on me for my lisp or my lack of English, he never joined in. Living in a home where fights were a daily occurrence was frightening. Listening to Fatima tell us that we were 'haramzaday bachay' (bastard children), white trash good for nothing was disturbing. I was shocked. All I had ever been was Pakistani, thought beautiful and loved and the way Fatima treated me traumatised me. Even though I had been sexually abused in Pakistan by Waquas I was too young to know what he had been doing was wrong and he was always kind and sweet towards me, never swearing or calling me names. My mind was unable to comprehend what was happening in my life. From kind, loving grandparents and an aunty, to terror. The family I was now living with were all used to it and knew how to survive. I would never learn. A few weeks after I had arrived Mummy took me to school one day and left me there. School was a welcome relief from the flat in Albert Drive where there was so much fighting and shouting. There were fights between Abbas and Mummy and fights between Fatima and Mummy. Cursing and swearing in English and Mirpuri, I learned the swear words pretty quickly. There were never fights between Abbas and Fatima, never did I see them shout or swear at each other the way they did to Mummy and rarely did they shout at their children. Within weeks I had learned not to answer back, not to draw attention to myself. I went from being a confident outgoing child to a quiet and nervous child. We were all living in a large three bedroom tenement flat crammed with 12 family members, all strangers to me. I had never witnessed such violence and hatred. This lifestyle was alien to me. The people were strange and their behaviours cruel. Everybody wanted to please Fatima. The worst fight I ever witnessed was a few months after I had returned and I was the reason for it. Not being able to speak English and wanting to be able to talk with Mummy and the children, although Mummy's Mirpuri was pretty good by now, I became a bookworm and devoured my school books every minute I could. The other children all got on so well, they had all grown up together after all.

Jamal being the oldest of us seven children was automatically accepted into their gang, no need to try for him. Being a boy also obviously helped. I began thinking if I can speak English better I can fit in. Maybe they won't tease me so much because of my lisp and my strange accent when I attempt to speak English. I speak a little like Abbas. English is not my first language after all. Even though Jamal did it too, he was never picked on. The evening of the fight and the adults were in the living room and the children, all nine of us, are in the kitchen. Yacoub was the youngest of the children and was very noisy as were the other children, nine children in a room was going to be mayhem. I sat quietly on the sofa reading my school book while the other eight children screamed and shouted like children do. Ignoring me as always.

Suddenly the kitchen door slammed open and Abbas stormed in yelling,

'Vat is this bludee noise!'

I looked up from my book and stared. He was a giant of a man, over 6ft tall. His face was twisted in anger and his nostrils flaring. I was unable to look away, even though my heart was racing from fear. I was terrified of him. Catching me staring, he singled me out, marched over and slapped me with all his strength, hard across the face.

'Ju bludee keep noise down, I no bludee tell ju again,' he screamed at me. And with that he left the kitchen.

I instantly put my hand to my cheek which was stinging with the pain as hot fat tears poured down my face. I realised Abbas didn't really like me.

Within a few minutes Mummy was in the kitchen. The children were quiet now and seeing my tears she came over and asked me why I was crying. I lift my head to tell her and she was shocked to see the imprint left on my cheek.

'What on God's earth has happened to you? Who did this? What is going on in here?' she asked, while tilting my head to the side gently.

The children all started talking at once.

'She didn't do anything'

'Uboo jee (daddy) slapped her and...'

'Quiet!' Mummy shouted. 'Shagufta tell me what happened.'

'Uboo jee slapped her for making a noise and she was just reading her book, we were all shouting and he thought it was her,' Shagufta told her smugly.

'Is that true?' Mummy asked me. 'Did your father slap you?'

I nodded my head.

'Ya bloody bastard, ya fucking swine, wait till I get my hands on you. Hit ma lassie would you, you wait,' Mummy screamed at the top of her voice. Storming out of the kitchen and into the hall where she continued shouting.

Abbas came out of the living room smiling.

'Maggie vat is this bakawass (rubbish) Ju is bludee crazy, woman.'

Mummy screamed at him that he had gone too far and threw herself at him. The children watched from the kitchen door as she pulled his hair and attempted to scratch him. Abbas easily held her back and gave her a few slaps across the face, usually enough to finish the fight. Mummy was a force to be reckoned with and was not backing down this time. There were crates in the hall for storing ginger bottles and she picked one up and sent it flying at Abbas, screaming, 'Mayaddah bhenchod harami! (motherfucking sisterfucking bastard!)'

Angered by her insolence, insulting him in his mother tongue, he grabbed and punched her hard this time, bursting her lip. All the while Mummy was screaming that she would kill him and cursing the worst words I have ever heard, some of which I didn't understand. Yet. Abbas continued to slap and punch while Mummy fought back, refusing to back down. Both of them screaming at each other while the children watched. Eventually Fatima came out from the living room, her trademark white shalwar kameez on with matching headscarf wrapped loosely over her hair, and broke up the fight with her loud but firm voice. The one she used to take control, because she is in control.

'Buss,' she demanded looking straight at Abbas and turning to Mummy she told her firmly, 'Gamaandi kee sochsun, iss vakat buss karo eh larai. (Think of what the neighbours will say, stop this right now. No more fighting.)'

50

We watched as they stop fighting, still cursing and swearing, until Abbas turned his back after a last slap across Mummy's face and walked into the living room followed by Fatima. Looking at Mummy, standing crying in the hall, with her torn denim shirt, one shoe on, the other fallen off in the fight, broken nails, scratched face, busted lip and black eyes, I realised she really loved me. Defending her children against Abbas was easy for her, protecting them and herself from Fatima was a battle she was unaware she was fighting.

Months passed by and I kept trying to fit in. My efforts were rewarded and I began to speak more English and was reading books from the library borrowed on Mummy or Zanera's card. I had not yet lost the accent that caused the children to roll about the floor laughing, and still was crying every night before I fell asleep, praying I would return to Kashmir. I was missing my aunty and grandparents, missing the sunshine and freedom, missing the happy days. Here in Glasgow, apart from going to school and mosque, we stayed indoors mostly. During the warm weather we would be allowed out in the shared back gardens or be taken to the Square Park, just round the corner, but not during the winter months. For as long as I could remember I only ever came indoors to sleep, spending my every waking hour outdoors. Sometimes even sleeping on the roof tops on a 'munjee' bed woven with rope, with my grandparents and Jamal.

Abbas arrived one day driving a van and everyone rushed downstairs excitedly. Mummy was at work, earning the money that helped to buy it. It was a dark red colour. At the front sat Abbas, proudly, and Fatima opened the door and climbed in, her older daughter, Tabassum, following and closing the door behind them, big smiles on their faces. Owning a car meant status in the community, it proved to others that you were doing well. The door at the side was opened by Jamal and in the back it was all metal, no seats. It'd been bought for the cash and carry run to stock up the newsagent Abbas was in the process of purchasing. Nine children all climbed in and someone closed the door. Sitting on the floor of the van, the boys standing to show off, we went for a short drive and then returned to Albert Drive. Fatima began to make lots of big fat cushions, stuffed with old clothing and spare material, for those who would be sitting in the back of the van for long journeys. Trips to England to visit numerous relatives were being planned and I could hear the excitement in their voices. Weeks later we broke for the summer holidays and I was disappointed when we finished early on the last day, knowing it would be weeks and weeks before I could return. School, along with reading, was my only escape. Coming home, Fatima was all flustered, hurrying the younger children out of their uniforms and into their shalwar kameez for the girls, and trousers and jumpers for the boys. We were going somewhere, that's why there was an urgency. Usually there was no hurry to change out of uniforms. Even though she was ignoring me, I still hurried with the others and got changed. Going to the window in her bedroom she looked out and told the children to all go down. Abbas was downstairs in the van.

'Aisha tu ithay reh. Koi jaga nee twaray vastay. Tu jassay judoo au vapaas ajasan. (Aisha, you stay here, there is no room for you to go. You can go when they come back.)' said Fatima, seeing me hurry to join the other children.

I stopped and stayed back while the other children hurried out. Watching them from Fatima's bedroom window as they all piled into the back, laughing and joking, all together. Standing behind me she told me reassuringly.

'Eh tay khair karan gain, vapaas ajasan tay tu jasay. (They are just away for a drive, when they get back you can go.)'

I spent the afternoon glued to the window. Patiently waiting. Only moving to go to the bathroom or to ask for something to eat when I got hungry. Hours passed by and I still believed my turn would come. I saw Mummy walking up the street, coming home from work and waited out in the hall for her to come through the front door.

'When are they coming back? I've been waiting for ages and she said when they come back I can go,' I blurted out to her.

'Let me get in, hen, and what are you going on about? Going where?' she asked while taking off her jacket to hang up.

'They all went away in the van after we finished school and she...' I began to tell her what happened when she interrupted me.

'They've all gone to Bradford, ya eejit, they'll no be back for weeks. It's the summer holidays.'

Leaving me in the hall she continued into the kitchen where Fatima and Tabassum were sitting. Tired and hungry after a long day working, Mummy didn't notice my tears. Going to my bed, I hid under the covers and cried. I cried for my aunty, my Bhai jii and Bhabha and mostly I cried for a mum and a dad who loved me. I knew Fatima treated us unkindly and cruelly favouring certain children over others. I was not allowed to question why she did this. I felt so sad that she lied to me, left me standing waiting and hoping, knowing all along they were never coming back. Even though I knew there was more than enough room for me to go with them, I believed her because I still wanted her to be nice to me. At first when I got back to Glasgow I would call her 'Umee jee' and tried my hardest to please her. In Pakistan nobody forced me to call her by that name and it was easy for me to ignore her. Here in Glasgow Mummy insisted and demanded that I call Fatima 'Umee jee', 'she's your mother too and that's what you call her,' so I did but it wasn't long till I avoided using the word mother for her and when I needed to speak to her would make eye contact. I didn't like the other children not being there. Mummy was out at work all day and Fatima never tired of telling me I was a good for nothing, trashy, ugly, dirty, little bastard girl. When visitors came to the house she would put her fake smile on and for the sake of her izaat (honour) play the perfect step mother role. It was a confusing time. Fatima was saying all these nasty things with pure hatred and visitors would come and tell us 'Mash'Allah aren't you all beautiful' in awe of our mixed race beauty. Aunty

54

Wilma was a regular visitor. She wasn't blood related. She was a friend of Mummy's, she was married to a Pakistani man, Uncle Omar, and they had adopted a mixed race baby and named him Joseph.

Aunty Wilma was one of the few kind people in my life. Every week she would visit and bring sweets, little pokes with cola cubes or bars of chocolate, sometimes a magazine. Once she came with three dolls for us younger girls and they had different smells. Soft bodied tiny dolls almost like a beanie baby. I picked the strawberry smelling doll. If you held the face next to your nose you could smell strawberries. She was wearing a red dress with a strawberry print. I cherished that doll and took it to bed every night. It was the first toy I had in Glasgow, in Pakistan toys didn't really interest me as I preferred to be roaming and running about with my cousins. Although I looked forward to guessing what treats she might have when she came to visit, it was the hugs and kisses I looked forward to the most. It was those few moments when she would hug me and tell me what a good girl I was, that I lived for. Who to believe?

***

Two big events took place the year I returned to Glasgow. Abbas and Fatima's oldest son, Naeem, got married and we moved to the big house ten days later. The marriage was a love marriage. It was unheard of in 1979 and is still discouraged in many families today. Many families still prefer the practice of first cousin marriages, usually arranged at birth and sometimes forced when the time comes. Naeem had the courage to say no to his parents, telling them he regarded their choice of wife as his sister. His arranged wife was Fatima's niece, they had grown up in Mirpur playing together with the other cousins and his sisters. Naturally his cousin he treated like a sister, so it was wrong in his eyes to make her his wife. Maybe seeing the choice his father had made with Mummy gave him the courage and strength to stand up to them and pick his own wife. His wife to be was a cousin of my aunt in Mirpur. My aunt's marriage to Abbas's youngest brother had also been a love marriage. Neither of the women had been related to Abbas or anybody in his family or extended family including Fatima.

Weddings are a huge celebration and the build up to the big day can last for several weeks. Families travel from all over the UK and even from Pakistan to witness the joyous occasion. Fatima's brother and family, from Bradford (known as the Bradford lot) came the week before the wedding and stayed with us in Albert Drive. He had five daughters and two sons. I believed Mummy and Fatima were both my mothers. All the younger children believed this to be true. We called them both mother. Mummy for the white one and Umee jee for the Pakistani one. Therefore they both were. We never questioned the fact that we had two mums, to us it was normal.

'Which ones of you are brothers and sisters?' asked one of the Bradford lot.

'We are all brothers and sisters,' replied Imtiaz. 'Why are you being stupid?'

'Who is your mum then?' she asked.

'Mummy and Umee jee,' he replied.

'You are the one who is stupid. You can only have one mum,' her sister laughed at him.

The seven of us all started shouting at the Bradford lot that they didn't know anything. Of course they did. Even when I insisted, 'My head and arms came from Mummy, and my bottom half came from Umee jee.'

The other six agreed and gave their own versions of how we had two mums. It had to be true, our parents had told us.

That winter afternoon, all of us in Mummy's bedroom, we learned the truth.

'Imtiaz, Anwar and Khalsoom, you are Umee jee's children and real brothers and sisters. And Jamal, Aisha, Amirah and Yacoub, you are Mummy's children and real brothers and sisters,' they told us seven younger children, smugly and all knowing. Days later the wedding took place and the other children carried on seemingly unaffected by what we had been told. I couldn't stop thinking about it. Even though I have asked Mummy many times about the wedding in the hope that it will jog something in my memory, not one detail ever comes back apart from sitting and listening to the truth for the first time. Fatima wasn't my real mum. I was thinking all day long about the way she treated us. Was it because she was our stepmother?

All around me there were celebrations and I remember only Fatima and her fake smile, for when visitors were around. I was pretty good at reading by now and had read stories like 'Cinderella', 'Sleeping Beauty' and the rest of these tales all with the classic evil stepmother. It went over and over in my head, never giving me any peace until one day I would get why she hated us so passionately. Fatima had been forced to share Abbas with Mummy and that was the reason why Fatima hated us. The fairy stories made me think about step mothers, but I didn't really understand until after we moved to the big house. There the differences in the treatment of Mummy and her children would really start to manifest, or maybe I just noticed more because now I knew the truth.

Chapter 4   Moving to the big house

Moving to the big house was exciting. It was a 15 minute journey in the back of the red van, but to us children it seemed to take forever. It was the Christmas holidays, not that we celebrated Christmas. Santa Claus was forbidden from coming down our chimneys. Although we did have a celebration of sorts on the day with a family get together and a huge feast prepared because it was Quaid E Azam's birthday. He was the founder of Pakistan and like Jesus he was born on the 25th December, so it's a special day for Muslims too.

We were all happy and united for a change, no bitching, no backstabbing, and no picking on the gori's children. Compared to the cramped conditions in Albert Drive the big house was like a mansion. Entering the big house I was in awe. There was a cloakroom and a hallway big enough for a snooker table, two sitting rooms, a dining room, a family room, a kitchen and a shower room. Up the huge staircase, 18 stairs to the landing and then another six to bring you to the top of the house, there were four bedrooms and a family bathroom. Outside there was a garage and out shed. It was surrounded by gardens to the front, back and sides. These gardens would become Mummy's pride and joy, nurturing her plants and flowers with the love she was unable to show her children. The best thing about the big house for me was that I could hide upstairs in my room reading, undisturbed by the dramas going on in the family. The sleeping arrangements stayed pretty much the same, only now Abbas had a bedroom and not the recess in the living room. Fatima continued to share with her two daughters, and Mummy with her daughters. Jamal, Imtiaz, Anwar and Yacoub got to have their own bedroom and no longer shared with their mothers. Downstairs one of the sitting rooms was used as a bedroom for the newly married Naeem and Amina.

The big house unfortunately was in an area which was predominantly white. Glasgow in the 70's and 80's was not so welcoming to Pakistanis, the white women that lived with them or the mixed race children that were born to them, especially the mixed race children. We went from Pollokshields which was the hub of the Kashmiri community to an area where we were the only Asian/mixed race family. At school we were picked on and called names. We were the only brown children, so it was inevitable. I had been used to racism resulting from my being half white. Fatima reminded us on a daily basis that we were white trash and somehow inferior to her children, the pure ones. I had never been picked on or bullied for being brown.

Mirpuris were rapidly becoming the majority in Pollokshields. Many of them were choosing to settle there, tempted by the cheap accommodation in comparison to the other areas in the south side, and also by relatives and friends who had arrived from Kashmir before them and had set up home. Many are still living there today. They arrived en masse from Mirpur, families saving every rupee they earned to send their oldest son or sons if they could afford it to come to the UK to make their fortune. These men came and set up home in the tenement flats of Pollokshields, three or four men from the same village sharing rooms, to cut down on costs to save money, which for some was almost thirty times what they could earn back home. Also the Mangla Dam was being built in the Mirpur District and to allow this to happen, hundreds of villages had to be emptied, entire families evicted and displaced. There was a reported 100,000 families moving to Britain. For those moving to Glasgow, the West End was too expensive and even today there are fewer Asians living in the West compared to the South.

Where we used to live in Pollokshields, at school and out in the shared back gardens, there were lots of other brown kids and a few other mixed race children too. In some places there were more brown than white kids. We belonged and never thought of ourselves as being 'different.' Life outside the family home was carefree and out in the back garden we would play alongside the other children, whatever their colour. In our new family home we were only ever allowed in the gardens to play and never out in the streets, and at our new school we stood out. We looked different, we spoke with a slight accent and the girls dressed differently, having to wear trousers underneath our pinafores, no way do you show your legs. We smelled differently too; smelling of spices, thanks to daily curries cooked at home, and mustard oil, which was massaged into all the children's hair. The hair massaging was always done on a Saturday afternoon and left in overnight and then on the Sunday it would be washed out when we were bathed for school the next day. The oil softened the hair, made it shiny and sleek and many Pakistani families carried out this ritual, it just didn't smell very nice. We were easy targets.

Out of the seven of us that were in Primary school, I was the one who stood up to the bullies. I loved school, it was my escape from the big house. At my old school there was kindness, praise and, most importantly, fun. I wanted the time I spent at school to be happy. There was enough fighting, name calling and insulting to be dealing with at home. I had no choice but to fight to keep school a happy place. At home I was powerless to change the way in which we were treated. Who would listen to me and who could I hit back in defence? At school it was different. At school I had the power and the courage to change the way we were being treated, I could stand up to the bullies. They called us 'smelly pakis', spat on us, laughed and ridiculed, tripped us up and even threw stones on one occasion. The teachers didn't know how to deal with it. They had never had to deal with racist behaviour from their pupils.

Amirah had told Mummy when we got home from school that day, and the next day Mummy marched up to the school screaming at the head teacher that she was sick and tired of her children being picked on, and if the school didn't punish those responsible then she would be taking further action. Mummy's screaming and shouting didn't resolve the problem. The insults continued day after day after day until one day, Michael, who was in my class, shouted one too many times, 'You're a wee smelly paki.'

I ran up to him and slapped him hard across the head, just like I've seen done at home a thousand times, to me, to Mummy and her other children. Looking down at his scared face, taller than him and all the other boys in my class, I screamed, 'I am not wee and I am not smelly and if you call me a paki again, I will hit you again!' All my anger and frustrations were being taken out on Michael, not the biggest bully in the class; that was Gavin who had no problems pulling my pigtail hard or slapping me on the arm or back, even punching me in the head. Poor Michael, who had never hit me, wasn't to know that Abbas had slapped me hard across the face the night before. I had refused to help wash the dishes after dinner, choosing to go to my room to read my latest Enid Blyton book. I had borrowed it from the library after school and decided 'The Magic Faraway Tree' was a better choice than washing the dishes and because no fuss was made I stayed in my room. Fatima told Abbas when he came home and I was called down from my room and slapped for my disobedience. It was Michael's bad luck that he chose to call me names that day. I slapped him across his head and punched him, shoving him away when he tried to hit back. When word spread that I had fought with him, I was challenged to fight boys on a daily basis.

Most play times I could be found surrounded by a ring of boys and girls all cheering 'fight, fight, fight.' Jacket off and sleeves rolled up, fists in the air ready to strike whatever boy faced me. I wasn't scared or angry, I just wanted the bullying to stop and for them to accept us. The girls were far friendlier or maybe they were just too scared to fight me. I was in Primary 4 and would happily fight against boys in Primary 7. Anything to stop the bullying and make school fun like it was in our old school.

Once, I remember being caught fighting with Gavin, we would fight many times before we called it a truce, surrounded by a group of boys and girls we were pulling and shoving at one another with slaps and punches being thrown around. Mr Costello broke it up and we were sent to the head teacher. We were both given lines to write, 'I must not fight.' 100 times it was to be written as though that would in some way change our behaviour.

The teachers, worried about Mummy's reaction I think after her previous visit to the school, didn't inform the big house. If the big house had found I was fighting I would have been in big trouble. It would not be seen as acceptable for me to stick up for myself. One of the many fucked up views of the big house. Fucked up because it seemed Abbas, Fatima and Mummy were allowed to hit us for whatever trivial reason they chose but I wasn't allowed to hit someone for picking on us. The fighting ended when the boys just gave up, realising I would never stop fighting them. Slowly we were accepted by most of the children at school.

Out of school was a different story and the racism from neighbours would continue for many years before the area began to accept that Abbas and his family were not going to be forced out. No matter how many times they smashed our windows, scrawled in paint 'BNP' and 'Pakis go home,' on our garden walls, or spat at Mummy and called her a 'paki lover' when out at the local shops, we were staying put. We would never be accepted though, tolerated maybe.

No matter what happened on the outside, inside the house the racism would never end. The locals actually called the big house, the white house, because it was painted white. For obvious reasons it was never referred to as the white house by those who lived in it. The big house even had its own flag pole. Not that we ever hung the Kashmiri flag from it, or even the Scottish one. There was a Mercedes in the drive, red, to go with the red van and a burgundy Datsun. 1980 Glasgow was not yet the flash and bling society it has become. Abbas was ahead of his time and enjoyed flaunting his wealth.

For the first year we were there, we were dropped off and collected at school by Fatima even though the school was literally round the corner from the big house. When children asked us who she was, we came up with the idea of saying she was the maid. I have no idea why or how, it just seemed like the most believable story.

'She looks after us and the house while our mum and dad work,' all of us replied to our new friends when describing Fatima.

We were starting to realise we were not your normal family set up, ashamed to admit we had two mums and a dad. We knew it was wrong that our mums and dad lived together. Fatima's own children told that lie for a long while too, all the way up until I left primary 7 to go to secondary school we were still pretending Fatima was the maid, when in reality Fatima was the queen of the big house and it was Mummy who was the maid.

Within six months of moving to the big house, a 'for sale' sign appeared in our next door neighbour's, the Wilsons, garden. At first they had been friendly allowing their two daughters to play with Zanera and Shagufta, the girls were similar in age and sometimes they let us younger girls join in their games. The Wilsons would sometimes be invited into the big house and loved tasting the curries we had for dinner most days, although some were too spicy for their taste buds. It didn't take long for the friendship to sour.

The Wilsons were disturbed by the way in which we, Mummy's children, were treated and shocked that Shagufta was allowed to talk to us the way in which she did. We were playing out in the front garden, the girls from the big house and the Wilson girls. The neighbours had no sons and the boys in the big house were discouraged from playing with girls they were not related to. Pakistani families don't like their boys and girls mixing freely. Shagufta liked to pick on me the most, commenting on my looks or my hair or the way I spoke, confident that she would never be punished for being mean. Suddenly she blurted out, pointing to Zanera, Amirah and me, 'They are all bastards you know.' Her words didn't bother me because we were always called 'bastard children' so I had heard it numerous times before. Shagufta often said it in front of her Pakistani friends when they were visiting, and they laughed and sniggered along with her. The Wilson girls were not laughing and Mary, the oldest, told her to stop. Shagufta ignored her and continued, 'I mean look at the size of her forehead. She is so ugly and my mum says I am more beautiful than her.' This was directed at me. Shagufta was always insisting I was ugly and she was beautiful. The Wilson girls got up and left the garden ignoring Zanera when she told them, 'Oh come on, Shagufta is only trying to be funny and get a reaction, she always does it. Just ignore her.'

Quietly and quickly they made their way into their own home and that was the last time we played together. By attempting to stick up for us, they showed me that I wasn't crazy, that we really were treated and spoken to cruelly. In my head when we were spoken to like that I always thought 'this isn't fair' and sometimes I found the courage to voice those thoughts, yet none of the adults agreed with me, telling me 'be quiet' or asking me 'what do you know?'

A day or so after the incident, some of us children were in the back garden playing, making the most of the summer weather. Mrs Wilson was in her back garden, alone, digging up some soil for planting flowers and wasn't her usual chatty self. When some of the children asked if her girls were coming out to play, she replied with a 'no' and continued with her digging. Usually she would be asking us how we were doing or what game we were playing and giving us biscuits or crisps as a way of making up for all the curries we fed them. Usually her girls would be out playing in the garden too. That day she was not doing any of her usual things. Amirah went in and told Fatima and Mummy that Mrs Wilson was behaving strangely. Mummy came out and went over to the low wooden fence that separated the two gardens.

'Hello, Janette, is everything okay?'

Mrs Wilson was silent for what seems like ages and then looked up at Mummy and said,

'It's not right, the way some of the children are allowed to treat the other children. I am reluctant to let my girls come over and play after hearing the language from Shagufta the other day.'

'Oh away you and don't talk rubbish, I don't believe you. They all play nice together, they're brothers and sisters after all and I'm sure they have their arguments like all others do.'

'No, it's more than that, it's the way they speak to your children, my girls heard Shagufta calling them bastards,' said Mrs Wilson in a whisper.

'How dare you, the goddam cheek of it. Let me tell you this, none of the children swear in this house, they know better not too. As for your girls, they are no longer welcome in this garden or in the house.'

Mummy went back into the house leaving Mrs Wilson stunned by the way she had reacted, refusing to even listen to her. In the living room Mummy relayed the conversation to Fatima and they called for Shagufta to question her over the incident. Shagufta denied any wrongdoing, with her eyes and mouth wide open she protested her innocence. That was enough for the two mothers and she was allowed to go back to whatever it was she was doing. Life was easier for Mummy if she believed whatever Abbas, Fatima and their children told her, rather than listening to her own children or other people. Even when we did try and tell, we were all learning quickly that it was pointless, we would be accused of lying. The truth didn't come out fully until years later, when all of Mummy's children had left the big house and even then Mummy had a hard time believing us.

It was a few week after this incident that the 'for sale' sign went up.

'Ju all sell jor bludee houses and I vill bludee tell all my family to buy,' Abbas would rant. Telling everyone how racist our neighbours were. The reality was that our neighbours were good decent people and couldn't bear to live next door to our pathetic excuse of a family. There was screaming matches in the big house on a daily basis, just like in Albert Drive, Mummy screaming at her children, Fatima and Abbas screaming at her children too and screaming at Mummy. Mummy was strong enough to scream back sometimes and that ensured her a slap or two, maybe a punch from Abbas. The walls weren't thick enough to drown out the screams of the adults or the screams of the children.

Abbas ended up buying the house next door. Six months after we moved into the big house, Naeem and Amina were given the keys for the newly purchased house. It would be known as 'the house next door' and would be their home for the next fifteen years. Their old bedroom became the boy's new bedroom, and the boy's old bedroom became the girl's bedroom. Not having to share a room with Mummy was a joy. I was going to be ten soon. What child wants to share a room with a parent? Especially one who is as sad as Mummy. Sometimes she would lie in her bed and cry, and because she had never been shown affection she wouldn't allow us children to comfort her and so we ignored her tears.

I shared with Amirah and Khalsoom. I put up posters of Michael Jackson, hidden inside the door of my wardrobe. I wasn't allowed to hang pictures of pop stars on my bedroom wall although I was allowed to listen to them singing and watch them on TV. I drew pictures and hung them up on the walls instead, pictures of rainbows, clouds and houses, happy pictures. Having the privacy of my own bedroom to escape to was heaven. Amirah and Khalsoom were always playing games together. With only a few days between them, they were closer in age than to me and had bonded while I was in Kashmir, and with Fatima forever scolding Amirah and I for daring to play together we rarely did. If she caught me and Amirah together, and if Zanera was with us, she would wail as though it hurt terribly.

'Khalsoom aur Shagufta twaree sukee penn nee, tah ina dey nal ni khednay. (Khalsoom and Shagufta are not your real sisters, that is why you don't play with them.)'

Fatima was happiest when Mummy's children ignored each other and spent our time in her children's company. If Zanera was hanging out with Shagufta then Fatima was happy and if Amirah was hanging out with Khalsoom she was happy.

70

The boys in the family she allowed to play together, but Jamal and Yacoub never really hung out together, there was too much of an age gap between them for a start.

I soon realised I was better off hiding away from it all and at the same time I still wanted desperately to fit into this mad family, not realising yet that I would never find my place in it because there was no place for me. My time in Kashmir had helped seal my fate. I was too different. I was honest even if it meant a slap or a beating. No matter the punishment I was honest. The others had learnt to be sneaky and lie and connive to survive. That was all they had known. I had lived with good, kind and decent people. I had only known happiness.

When we moved to the big house I really became aware of the clothes we had to wear. At school we were the only Pakistani/mixed children and we, the three girls, stood out. I used to beg Mummy sometimes and ask her if I could wear tights because I wanted to be like the other girls at school. Thick tights will cover my legs just as good as the trousers and some Pakistani families weren't as strict so I hoped she would fight my battle. Mummy never did and would tell me, 'Shut your face, are you stupid? Showing your legs is not what good Pakistani girls do.'

Mummy had only recently started wearing shalwar kameez because of Haroon, who had told her that one day her daughters would want to dress like her and what would she say to them? How could she tell them no if she was dressed like a Western woman? I guess that's maybe why I thought she would

71

allow me to wear tights because for as long as I could remember she never wore Asian clothes or covered her legs.

Everywhere we went in Mosspark, to the shops, the supermarket or the library, we were the only Asian family. In our shalwar kameez we stood out instead of blending in like we did in Pollokshields. Everyday shalwar kameez was never as bling as suits worn for Eid or weddings or parties. Fatima always picked plain browns, mustards or a sick green colour material with a horrible print on it, to sew mine and Amirah's suits. Zanera never really got anything beautiful sewn for her either. Fatima or Tabassum would sew the outfits together. Most of my shalwar kameezs were plain and dowdy. The kameez – the dress - would be sewn in the printed material and the shalwar – trousers- plain with a scarf sewn in the plain material too. Even though we rarely had to cover our head with the scarf, it still had to be worn, flung over shoulders and hanging down your back. Sometimes the hem of the trousers had the material from the dress stitched along it which to me seemed wrong, but I had never had a say in the way my clothes were sewn.

Chapter 5 Mummy's breakdown

During the first year in the big house Mummy had a breakdown, serious enough to have her admitted to hospital. At the time I didn't know what was happening or where she had gone to. I was too young to understand the monsters she was fighting in her head, too busy trying to survive my own monsters. Mummy had spent the entire first year working all the hours she could possibly do, working to fund the big house, the cars in the drive and the money which was sent to Kashmir to build a family home. She was also working for Abbas's socialising money. Leaving for work when her children were asleep and returning from work when they were asleep took its toll on her. Her pay was taken from her and given to Fatima for child care fees. She had hardly any time off before she was back at work. Working in Abbas's newsagent and take away.   The newsagents meant leaving at 5am to get the newspaper and bread deliveries and the take away meant not getting home till after midnight. At the weekends she would come home even later with the take away staying open till 3am to cater for the drunks coming out the pubs and clubs and all wanting a kebab or pakoras, but she got the weekend off from working in the newsagent so was home for a few hours during both days.

When Mummy was ill we were completely ignored and left to fend for ourselves. Fatima chose not to feed us if she could avoid it. On the occasions that Abbas was home and she had to give us something, she would feed us scraps, never any meat from the curry just bones, one chapatti or the smallest portion of rice. If you were still hungry after this you stayed hungry, while their plates were piled high and second helpings always offered. All her children were overweight. Housework was delegated to Zanera, Amirah and me while her daughters did very little. Their time was spent learning how to sew, learning prayers and about Islam and when they were older, gossiping and backstabbing.

The boys in Pakistani homes are regarded as kings and so never have to lift a finger, their every whim and need taken care of. Mummy's boys were lucky that this rule applied to them too. When Mummy was ill there was no goodnight at bedtime, we were sent to our rooms after dinner. There was nobody to tell us to brush our teeth and make sure we were clean. Nobody cared and when Mummy came home she too did not care either. She was worn down and weary and under Fatima's spell again. It didn't take long for her to treat her own children in the way Fatima had been treating us. Telling us we were good for nothing, ungrateful bastards, and that we should try and please Fatima, make her happy, she looked after us after all.

At weekends we usually had English dinners, taking a break from curries and rice and eating homemade fish and chips with beans or fresh veg, macaroni cheese, pastas. One Sunday, while Mummy was still in hospital, we helped Zanera wash and peel a huge sack of potatoes, wash the fish, dip it into whisked eggs then breadcrumbs and pile them onto a large plate ready for frying. Too young to help with the frying and cutting of potatoes, I escaped to our bedroom before some other work would be found for me, and Amirah went into the family room to join the others. All of us eagerly waiting until dinner was ready, looking forward to the English dinner after a week of spicy food. I was debating in my head whether to have bread sauce or tartar sauce with my fish. The hustle and bustle of dinner being dished out stopped my thoughts and I waited for my name to be called signalling my turn to get a plate. I heard nothing. I went downstairs to the living room and Fatima was sitting with her children. All of them had plates. Mountains of thick cut greasy chips with crispy golden fish, beans on the younger children's plates, carrots, cauliflower and peas on the others. Everybody ate oblivious to the gori's children, except Jamal. Jamal was eating along with her children. Fatima never excluded Jamal and rarely mocked or belittled him. He was included in her family as one of her own, she never ridiculed him for being white. By doing this Fatima alienated Jamal from his real family. When in Kashmir he had refused to go near Mummy, insisting she was a white woman therefore not his mother. Fatima had taken him under her wings keeping him safe from the 'white woman' when we returned from Kashmir. Jamal went along with her plans, too young to understand and happy to be away from the white woman. This ensured he treated his real siblings with contempt for being 'the gori's children'.

Yacoub was watching TV, glancing sideways at them eating. Amirah was next to Fatima smiling eagerly, hoping her smile would win her a plate of dinner. No such luck this time. I watched Fatima as she stabbed a chip with her fork. Pointing it in my direction she asked, 'Kassay? (Do you want a bit?)'

Shaking my head, I told her 'no thank you' and walked out the room and go into the kitchen. I found Zanera there making tuna sandwiches.

'Are you hungry?' she asked when she saw me coming in. Amirah and Yacoub followed behind.

'Why can we not have fish and chips?' we all asked her at once, our voices trembling, close to tears. The oldest of Mummy's children, she tried to look after us whenever Mummy was away.

'You just can't. She said so and what she says goes, alright.'

We sat at the kitchen table and ate the sandwiches, while all round us the aroma of fish and chips lingered.

By now the other children were starting to behave differently towards us. Mummy's first hospital visit had kept her away for almost a month. Enough time to destroy the confidence and spirit of her children.

'Your mum is pagal (crazy, cuckoo),' mocked Imtiaz while turning his finger round and round at the side of his head.

Mummy's children sat quietly, not defending her. We were all sitting in the cupboard under the stairs. The hangout for the seven children, a place where we could escape from the adults. We had blankets and cushions provided for comfort. For a while it was where we were always to be found until the boys kicked us out and declared it a girl free zone. There was no point in saying anything to defend our mother. Fatima would accuse us of loving Mummy more than we loved her. This was her war cry and what she said to Mummy anytime we tried to tell Mummy what was happening. For weeks we have had to listen to her constant wailing of 'Meh tusanee matrai maa, tha tussa istra karnayo mere nal. (I'm your step mother, this is why you behave this way towards me.)'

Mummy always believed her complaints, easier to be on Fatima's side, the winning team, than to defend her children. If Mummy didn't believe her, she would have to deal with the way we were being treated and she was having a hard enough time dealing with her own issues.

Hearing the front door open and the voice of Abbas booming stopped the bullying.

'Ver are ju children. Look who come home it's jor Mummy.'

We all scrambled out from the cupboard and saw Mummy in the hall. I didn't recognise her at first. It seemed like ages since I had seen her. She smiled when she saw us. Yacoub and Amirah were the only ones that had visited Mummy while she had been away. Nothing was ever explained and all I was told was that she would be back soon.

'My weans, my weans,' gathering us in her arms and leading us into the living room where Fatima was sitting with her two older daughters. The three of us sit down with Mummy on the couch, Yacoub perched on her knee. Hugging him tightly to her she looked over and saw Zanera and Jamal hanging back.

Smiling and laughing Mummy asked us how we've all been, 'How's school? Have you been good?' So many questions for so much time spent away from her children. Before any of us could answer, Fatima bemoaned her bad luck in having to care for such ungrateful children.

'Twaray bachay itnay batamese hain, koi gal nee soonay. (Your children are so bad, they won't listen to a word I say)'.

Disappointment in her face, Mummy listened as Fatima continued to berate us. Disappointment in her voice, Mummy asked why we let her down time and time again. We, her children, were too scared to tell her the truth and all the while Fatima was smirking, knowing full well she was winning in her fight to destroy Mummy and her family.

Later that week the seven children were in the kitchen. It was the girls' job after dinner to tidy the kitchen. The boys usually hung out with the girls although they took no part in the washing of the dishes or the drying and putting them away. We were all still young and to an extent innocent and rather than sit with the adults in the TV room, the boys preferred to be in the kitchen being silly like boys are. For some reason I started talking about the way Fatima treated us. We were all in agreement that she was unfair and picked on Mummy's children. Feeling confident that everyone would agree I blurted out, 'She really is a nasty bitch!'

Imtiaz slapped me. Stunned I ran out of the kitchen and straight up into my bedroom. Out of them all, I was closest to

Imtiaz, we were in the same class at school and it hurt me to think that he would slap me. He had never hit me before. Jamal came up a few minutes later. Smiling he said, 'I can't say anything to him or hit him for slapping you, she's his mum. You can't swear about her to him.'

In my naivety I had honestly expected everyone to agree with me.

It was round about this time I started hearing stories from Mummy about her childhood. When she was suffering from severe depression and bed bound for several days or weeks, her children were sometimes sent to sit with her, even though she was not lucid and was reliving her own nightmares. It had been decided by Abbas and Fatima that we were old enough to cope with her grief. Children should never have to hear their mother revert to being a little girl begging her abuser to stop, but in the big house that was seen as acceptable. They knew what Mummy had suffered and they knew what Mummy said in her fragile state, but they never thought to protect us from it. I remember the first time I was sent to sit with her, I was absolutely terrified. Having never seen her in this state, I went straight back down to the living room and demanded, 'You have to come.' Maybe the fear in my voice or my determination made Abbas follow me back upstairs. I had never demanded anything from Abbas, never told him he had to do something, never had a relationship with him and never spoke to him unless he spoke to me first. There was no way I was moving from the door way until he got up. The fear of his tongue lashing or slap across the face for my insolence at not listening to him was nothing compared to the fear at seeing Mummy in the state that she was.

'Mammy daddy, oh mammy daddy,' Mummy moaned, grief stricken, oblivious to us coming into the room, lying half under the covers her head twisting from side to side as though trying to escape her demons. I stared at her. Her signature cry of 'mammy daddy' would become legendary in the big house and the cause of much hilarity. Easier to joke about it than deal with the issues haunting Mummy, and for Mummy it became easy to laugh it off too and keep taking the anti -depressants she was prescribed by her doctor. Fatima could often be heard saying 'oh mammy daddy' in her strong Pakistani accent when getting up off the couch as though it was a struggle or Abbas would say it if he was tired, and we children would say it whenever we wanted to make the adults laugh.

'There, there, Maggie. Ju here, look everything is ok,' he told her. Turning to walk out the room he told me, 'Just tell her everything ok.' Left alone with her I tried to soothe her and failed. I was terrified by what I was hearing.

'No, stop, please stop,' she cried 'I don't want to, I'm a good girl. No, please don't hurt me.'

'Oh Mammy Daddy,' she said over and over again. No matter how much I told Mummy 'It's okay,' it never ever would be okay. This is how her children learned from a young age, about Mummy's childhood, her life in foster care, being sexually abused, and life in Huddersfield, pregnant and being told by Abbas to have an abortion.

During the first year in the big house I also turned ten. I cried and everybody laughed. A doll was the cause of my tears and everybody's laughter. A black doll given to me by Mummy. Fatima had told her to buy it and Mummy did whatever Fatima said. The year before Khalsoom and Amirah had given me a birthday card with a black girl on the front. Not a real picture, just a cartoon of a girl with a huge afro. I looked different to them all. With my wild curly hair, freckles and African features, I was the complete opposite of your typical Kashmiris and their poker straight hair and freckle free features. They were forever taunting me that my real dad was a black man. Huddersfield in the 70's was a popular place for the West Indian and Caribbean men to settle and many took the jobs of milkmen and postmen. The postman that delivered our mail in Huddersfield, Shagufta often told me, was black and therefore, she suggested, he was my real father. All of them would laugh, Fatima and Mummy joined in with the laughter too. I wondered if it was true. Anything, I was starting to realise, was possible in this mad family. However I knew I looked like Abbas though less scary and foreboding, but we had similar features. I have a smaller version of his nose, much smaller than the version he passed onto his children with Fatima. Still I wondered if that was the reason why Abbas hated me so much because he was not my real father. Was that why he wanted me not to be born? The doll was chosen to ridicule me, make me feel shameful for the way I looked and remind everyone that I was different to all the other children so they could have another excuse to laugh and snigger at me with my black doll. I refused to play with the doll, no matter how much they shouted at me. They can't make me, I told myself. They tried but I stubbornly refused to give in and they eventually moved onto some other drama. I spent my birthday in my room listening to music.

By the time I was ten my love of Bollywood songs had been established and I counted my blessings that the big house allowed music. Endless music. In many Pakistani homes it is forbidden or listened to secretly. In the big house it was part of everyday life and we could listen to either English or Asian. Mummy loved Bob Marley, Fleetwood Mac and many Motown artists and Abbas listened to Mohammed Rafi, Lata Mangesker and Asha Bosle. Fatima didn't listen to music, preferring to sit and gossip or watch her Indian dramas on the video. Music made me happy and some songs even today can send me straight back to the crazy world in which I grew up and make me smile, I refuse to feel sad.

Chapter 6   The extended family

Fatima's hatred for people didn't stop with Mummy and her children. When her son married Amina she was heartbroken and for a while she made her daughter in law's life even more miserable than ours and like us the aftermath of that still affects Amina's family. Amina's children grew up without the love from their grandmother and today Amina's only daughter struggles with her self- worth and has an eating disorder.

Amina had come from Islamabad from a loving and educated family. Marrying into the big house she was unaware of the nightmares that would unfold. It was a love marriage, which was unheard of in the 70's although Abbas's older brother in Pakistan had chosen his own wife, the aunty that had raised me along with my grandparents. Amina was one of my aunt's nieces and was one of the many visitors to my grandparent's home to see the 'gori's children and it was then she had met Naeem for the first time and both of them fell in love. Even today many Pakistani families are against the notion of a love marriage, choosing to force their children into an arranged marriage with a first cousin.   Fatima had chosen her daughter-in-law but when her son refused to marry her she had no choice but to give in. Naeem was adamant he was marrying Amina and using his father's love affair with Mummy as a precedent, he won his fight. For weeks he argued that his Uncle had also chosen his own wife and even though Mummy wasn't his wife Abbas had also chosen her. Naeem refused to marry the first cousin chosen for him, telling Fatima that his cousin was like a sister to him and that he would marry Amina whether they agreed or not. Amina's family were happy for her to marry Naeem; educated and much more open minded than our family, they agreed with her choice of husband because it was what she wanted. With a smile on her face and through gritted teeth all for the sake of 'izaat', Fatima got through the wedding and then in the privacy of the big house the real Fatima appeared.

For the first six months of her marriage, Amina was sworn at, hit, punched, scratched and kicked. She was told on a regular basis that she was ugly. The children were all encouraged to be nasty to her. Anything to please Fatima and because picking on Amina meant we were left alone for a while, we all joined in, Mummy included. Poor Amina. There was nobody to defend her or make it stop, even Naeem was helpless to stop it. At work all day he had no choice but to leave her alone with her abusers. When he returned in the evening the abuse would stop and we would all play nice, showering Amina in fake kindness. Nothing was ever done in front of him and everyone denied there had been any ill treatment. Naeem wasn't blind and could see the bruises, scratches and sadness in his new wife's eyes. He would ask Fatima why his wife was being treated like this and she would reply, 'Choot marnee eh charelle. Meh kuj vee ni kitah. Envay rolay sholay bananee eh. (She is lying, the witch. I have done nothing to her, causing trouble for no reason.)

Fatima denied all wrong doing, denied it while staring into her son's eyes.

'Meh akhai see iss kootee nal shadii na kur? (I told you not to marry the bitch, did I not?)'

Naeem knew his mother was lying, yet was powerless to stand up to her. He had fought against his mother's wishes to marry Amina and now she was his wife, he had no strength left to protect her, from his mother and her rage.

Amina was traumatised and one day wrote to her parents begging for help. She had just discovered she was pregnant and the abuse showed no sign of stopping. Sometimes Fatima attacked her like a woman possessed. I would watch as she launched herself on her, slapping and punching, scratching her face and pulling her hair screaming that she had destroyed her life by marrying her son and she would destroy hers in turn. She told her she would never allow her happiness. Anything could set Fatima off in her attacks, verbal and physical against Amina; the way she replied to something she was asked, a slap for being rude, the way she cooked dinner, sworn at for ruining it or just if Fatima was bored. Fatima was becoming an expert in destroying lives and Amina was secretly becoming an expert at escaping and one day walked out of the front door and across the road to where her older brother was waiting in a car, they drove to Birmingham where they had relatives. Letters had been exchanged and arrangements for her escape planned. The big house was stunned, never for a moment believing she would be capable of pulling something like this off. There was a huge family meeting. Naeem was distraught and threatened to leave the big house forever if they continued behaving the way they were. Amina had not told him of her plans either. I was out in the hall with some of the other children listening as the loud voices cried out. I heard him screaming at his mother that he loved Amina and could not imagine a life without her.   Amina stayed in Birmingham for several months with weekend visits from Naeem. After one visit he returned with his wife, her pregnant belly clear to see. The violence stopped, although the emotional abuse continued; Fatima was unable to be nice.

When their daughter, Mirrium, was born, Naeem gave out 'mithai' a sweet traditionally given out for the birth of boys, never girls. Naeem had already broken tradition by having a love marriage so it made sense for him to continue with further breaches. A girl's birth is not celebrated as she is seen to be a burden and an expense. She incurs the cost of a dowry for her marriage and then she leaves when she is married to go and live with her in-laws, making no contribution to her own family. A boy's birth is celebrated because he will grow up and work, continue to live with his parents and when he marries, his wife will come live with her in-laws and the parents' hope they will be looked after in their old age. Naeem didn't view his daughter as a curse or burden and was besotted by his beautiful new-born baby daughter and wanted the community to know he was just as happy as if she had been a boy.

Mirrium was adored by Abbas and Mummy and tolerated by Fatima. Mummy became her grandmother and Fatima took nothing to do with her. Mummy ended up pouring all her love and devotion into the granddaughter Fatima rejected, the granddaughter cast aside to punish the parents. Fatima allowed Mummy to love Mirrium in ways she never allowed her to do with her own children for a number of reasons. Partly because it was her son's daughter, not the gori's, so Fatima tolerated it, but mostly to hurt us, watching the ways in which Mummy loved Mirrium and knowing she would never love us the same way. I apologised to Amina for the way I treated her and for calling her names. There was a really ugly Bollywood actress and she was really fat, that's who we had said she was. 'Toon toon.'

'You have nothing to be sorry for, you are just a child. It's the adults in this house who should be ashamed,' she said, smiling at me as she spoke. Amina was more beautiful than some of the Bollywood pin ups and I couldn't understand why we were told to call her ugly. I couldn't understand a lot of things that were being allowed to happen in the big house.

One day I discovered the family allowance book. I am not too sure what age I was maybe twelve, maybe older. Sometimes ages and events and life in the big house get all muddled up. Bored and taking a break from reading I went snooping in the kitchen. The other children were all busy in their activities and sometimes it was easier to be alone than try and join in, sensing I wasn't wanted anyway. On top of the fridge it sat, tempting me to look at it. 'Mrs Margaret Ali '' printed in black and underneath 'Mr Haroon Ali.'' My mind went into overdrive coming to the wrong conclusion as to what it meant, as I stared at it.

It said Abbas's older brother, Haroon, was married to Mummy. Did that mean he was our real dad the way Mummy was our real mum? I went to find Mummy. Finding her upstairs, lying in bed, reading, I tried to discuss the thoughts whirring round my mind, wanting her to make sense of the nonsense that was fighting for space in my head, amongst all the other nonsense. The big house was built on lies and secrets and anything was possible.

'Is he my real dad?' I asked her, silently saying a prayer that he was. 'Please God.'

She laughed. And then she laughed some more. Shaking her head, 'No. No,' all the while laughing even harder. Tears of laughter rolling down her face as her book lay upturned on the bedcovers, forgotten. I never understood why she laughed so much. We had two mums so why not two dads? Finally the laughter eased a little and she told me.

'It wasn't a real wedding, I didn't really marry him, hen. It's just so he can stay here. And he's not your father.'

I was confused. Why would she marry him if she didn't love him? I was too young to understand the fake marriage concept. I was disappointed that Haroon was not my real dad, any dad would have been better than Abbas. As I got older I understood that Mummy had been used. Used for her British passport. She had been married to Haroon so he could obtain the desired red passport, married only on paper then divorced allowing Haroon to go home to Kashmir. With his British Citizenship stamped on his passport he was free to go back to

Mirpur. A year later he returned to Glasgow with his wife and ten year old daughter, who had been waiting for almost seven years to come and make their new life in the UK.

Bhai jii (grandmother) came to visit the big house the following summer. I was really excited at seeing her again after so long and I was delighted that she had bought with her the freckle removing cream, a little silver tin which I believed held magic cream to remove my dreaded freckles. Children believe anything you tell them and Bhai jii told me they would disappear. Even though they never did, I still believed.

For Bhai jii's visit I was allowed to wear my gold hoop ear rings, Fatima took them out of the locked wardrobe in Abbas's bedroom with a key. The key was wrapped in a little pouch with rolled up notes and tucked into her bra for safe keeping, like so many other Pakistani women, their bras are their purses. I had worn the earrings for Naeem's wedding to Amina and hadn't seen them since.

Bhai jii spent a lot of her days out visiting, she was taken away most days by Abbas. If she was at home then Abbas would be next to her along with lots of different relatives who were visiting us, or alone with just the big house family. Seeing Bhai jii reminded me of the carefree times in Kashmir and I secretly hoped she would demand to take me back, where I felt I belonged. Scared of Abbas's constant put downs, I had learned to avoid him whenever possible, spending as little time in his company as I could. I would be engrossed in my latest Enid Blyton adventure, upstairs in my bedroom, alone, even though I loved her and wanted to spend time with her and get to know her again. Abbas always being around his mother meant I stayed away. The times I did sit with her I was quiet, scared to say the wrong thing, scared Abbas would yell, and only spoke if she asked me something. Six weeks later and Bhai jii returned to her home, without me. I never did get to know her again, never did have any real quality time with her. The earrings were taken off me and returned to the wardrobe.

During the summer holidays the following year, Mummy called me in from playing in the back garden and told me Bhai jii had died. She stood looking at me waiting for me to cry I guess. Instead I went upstairs to my room. Sitting on my bed I waited for the tears. Jamal came into the room and sat on Amirah's bed.

'You ok?' I asked him.

'I feel like I should be crying,' he said in a sad voice.

'I've been trying to make myself cry but I can't.' We sat in silence for a while. Jamal and I rarely spent time together and the only times he talked was to tell me to do something, whatever it is he couldn't be bothered to do himself. I felt sadness, sadness for Abbas who had lost his mother, no matter how cruel he was to me. I loved my Bhai jii very much and had spent five years with her, she was Abbas's mother and he had a life time of memories with her. I felt sadness for all the other relatives who had adored her also, sadness for Jamal and I, that we would never see her again, even though I knew Jamal was her favourite.

At breakfast the next morning I remembered my earrings. It's the only thing I had which were given to me by Bhai jii. When I asked Mummy if I could have them to wear she told me go ask Fatima. Mummy was never allowed to say yes or no in most matters, we always had to ask Fatima or Abbas. This was another way in which Fatima undermined Mummy.

'Meh apnae kantay lessa, Bhai jii mikee ditay sun. Mummy akhai tussah nal pucho. (Can I have my earrings please, Bhai jii gave them to me. Mummy said to ask you.)' I said to her politely.

I had been warned on numerous occasions to speak nicely to her and always did; unfortunately my facial expressions were unable to lie and I was always being told, 'Straighten your face', any time I showed dismay and disappointment in Fatima's treatment of us.

'Ley! Eh thay Eid aur shadii vastay, hur din vastay nee, (They are for special occasions, Eid, weddings not for everyday wear.)' she laughed at me.

'Judoo Bhai jii ithay sunn meh hur din latee sah (But I wore them every day when Bhai jii was here),' I reminded her.

'Buss! Jah daffah oh koi kumshum ja kaar. Ramnee. (Enough! Away you go, get in the kitchen and tidy up. Bastard.)'

She dismissed me with the wave of her hand and a look of sheer hate. Lip trembling I left the room and went upstairs to my bedroom and cried. At last I was crying for Bhai jii, triggered by Fatima's unkindness and greed and crying at the unfairness in the big house. I never saw the ear rings again. They were melted down and made into a ring for one of Fatima's granddaughter's fifth birthday presents.

The summer before I started secondary school, another family event took place. The Bradford lot were visiting. A tradition that would continue for years. One night I was lying on the top bunk awake, the younger children all asleep. Our bedroom was the only place without an adult and the three girls had sneaked away to gossip. 'Check and see if they are sleeping.' said the Bradford sister. I heard Zanera get up and I pretended to be in a deep sleep and fool her. They chatted for a while about boys they liked and then the bombshell.

'So what do you think your real dad is like?' Shagufta asked.

'Sometimes I do wonder but Abbas has been my dad for as long as I can remember,' Zanera answered. Lying on the top bunk I froze, my blood running cold, goose pumps and tears. I was almost thirteen years old and never knew we had different dads. Not once did I suspect or even guess. My world was turned upside down and my crying got so bad that I started sniffing, nose blocked. Zanera was my half-sister like the others.

'Hey, are you crying?' Zanera asked. I ignored her and continued crying, unable to stop. Feeling her standing at the bunk bed, I turned my face away.

'Oh, don't cry, it's alright. I'm still your sister,' she said kindly.

Shagufta laughed, finding the situation hilarious. 'What you crying for, you idiot?' she mocked. I ignored them all, unable to find words to describe how I'm feeling. I cried myself to sleep and the next day asked Mummy if it was true.

'It doesn't change anything, she is still your sister,' was her response. It was such a big thing for me yet it had never really been a secret. It seemed everyone knew apart from me. Having my nose in books allowed me to escape from the harsh realities of the big house, oblivious to the gossip and secrets, listening and sometimes not understanding. I was different. I always knew it.

Chapter 7 Secondary school

The night before I started secondary school was frightening, even though Imtiaz was also starting with me and Jamal was already there in second year. Shagufta too was in her final year, Zanera had been taken out of school to prepare her for marriage and hadn't been to school for two years. I was upstairs in my room checking over my schoolbag and uniform, making sure everything was perfect, when I heard Abbas shouting.

'Aisha, come down stair, I talk ju, hurry up.'

I had that gut retching feeling I always got when he called my name then realised Abbas wanted to talk to me, instead of the usual screaming and swearing, accusing me of some wrong doing or another. Nervously I entered the sitting room and sit down across from him.

'Ju go big school tomorrow, yes?' he asked.

'Yes,' I replied, head down, scared to look at him, scared to see the blatant loathing in his eyes.

'Ju no talk to boys. If tha teacher make ju sit next to boy, ju tell her no. Against my religion. Ju understand. No talking with tha boys,' he repeated.

'Yes,' I mumbled.

'Ok go,' and with that he dismissed me. I remembered going upstairs and being very quiet, brushing my teeth and going straight to bed. I was sad that the father daughter moment I had been secretly hoping for never materialised. Abbas was never going to be a father to me, no matter how hard I tried, no matter how good I was. For him nothing I ever did would be good enough. He would never like me the way he liked the other children. With them he was kind and affectionate, full of praise. All he was able to show me was contempt and hatred. Still I held out hope he would accept me, one day he would change and see that I deserved his love too.

Secondary school was full of Asian children and was a pleasant surprise after being the only brown faces for so long. Jamal and I, along with Aunty Wilma's son, Joseph, were the only mixed race children at Shawlands Academy. The Pakistani and Indian girls didn't want to talk, choosing to look down on me instead. Having had only white friends in primary school it was easy for me to make friends with the white girls and Anita Tollan, the toughest girl in first year, would become my best friend along with several of her cousins and childhood friends. She was heavy back up. There were a handful of Asian girls who made my life a misery for the first few weeks. There were lots of name calling at lunchtimes when I was parted from Anita and had to walk the fifteen minutes to Albert Drive, where we went every day for lunch throughout secondary school, with Shagufta and her friends. They shouted, calling me an 'ugly half caste bitch.' Children born to first cousins are generally not blessed with good looks. Science has proven that marrying so close causes problems in the children that result from the marriage. A lot of the girls picking on me, at school, were from the practice of first cousin marriages. Shagufta would laugh along with the girls and half-heartedly tell them, 'Oi, leave her alone.'

It had been a long time since I had been in a fight. The last time I fought I was defending my brown side and here at secondary school I was having to fight the brown side. 'Half caste' 'Mongrel' 'Gori bitch' they would taunt as I passed them, always when I was alone. Eventually I returned the abuse, fed up with not being able to enjoy my time at school, although part of me wanted the Asian girls to accept me. So what if I have a white mother? It seemed that it was ok for them to call me names but when I dared call them 'Pakis' or 'Smelly Indians' they went and told Abbas. We were collected every day from school by Abbas or another adult. One day when I got in his car, he glared at me through the mirror.

'Ju vait I bludee get ju home. See vat I do? Swear at those girls and call them 'pakis', ju think that vat I bludee teach ju. Bludee bashtard.'

'They call me half caste all the time.' I pleaded in my defence, hoping he would understand why I insulted them.

'Ok ok ju no swear, no say paki to them.' he told me as Imtiaz climbed into the car and the incident was forgotten, the threat of a beating lifted, from me anyway. Abbas dropped us at the gate of the big house and drove off without coming in, telling us children to tell our mothers he would be back the next afternoon. Wherever Abbas was off to was the reason he let me off on this occasion.

'One love, one heart, let's get a Paki and beat her up,' I sang in time to Bob Marley's 'One Love' along with Anita and the other white girls. I sang it at break time, and when lunchtime came and I had to walk to Albert Drive their name calling didn't bother me. I would get my revenge on them. When the afternoon break time came I fought them along with Anita and my other white friends. Using slaps, punches, pulling of hair and scratching, we won. Violence doesn't solve anything, I know, but in this situation it made the bullying stop. After that fight we mostly ignored each other and they never called me half caste bitch again, not to my face anyway. Friendship between myself and the Asian girls at school didn't develop until the following year.

Before we broke for the Christmas holidays I had started bunking off school with Anita. Her aunt and grandmother lived in a flat close to the school and we would go there. Anita had a key and was allowed to go to eat her lunch there and check on her gran while her aunt was at work. During school hours I would bunk off and go there with her, at lunchtime I had to walk to the flat on Albert Drive. Even though her gran terrified me I loved going there. It was nice and quiet and there were cupboards full of chocolates and biscuits. We would sit in the kitchen gossiping and eating. I don't think her gran even noticed we were there. She sat in her wheelchair with a blanket over her knees, her face all droopy and drooling. Anita would shout loudly when we went in.

'Hi Gran, it's me.' Going over to kiss her cheek. She was the sickest person I had ever seen and every time we went there I worried she would be dead. Her gran never replied. She was unable to communicate.

Anita's aunt soon realised we were going there. Her supply of chocolates and biscuits disappearing gave her the clue. Anita's key was taken from her and someone else was given the job of checking on gran. Still we continued bunking off school, hanging around the tenement flats and the grounds of a church nearby.

Anita asked me time and time again to meet at the weekends or after school. I asked Mummy the first time who told me to ask Abbas.

'No, she is white girl. No good. Vy no friends with Pakistani girls for?' was his answer.

'Pakistani girls don't want to be friends with me,' I told him, disappointed I was not allowed to visit my best friend. He began the lecture of how white people would never accept us, how Anita wasn't really a true friend, how white people thought we were dirt and that I should not be fooled by their falseness. Only Pakistani people will accept us. I agreed with him, scared to question the flaws in his rant, wanting to ask why he called us 'goray harami bachay,' (white bastard children), along with Fatima, and ask why we were never allowed to forget we were dirt for having a white mother.

Being in the same class as Imtiaz was tough. Competition was always fierce. Who was the smartest? Mixed or Kashmiri? I like to think I was smarter. Towards the end of 1st year 60 or so top pupils were chosen to go into 2A or 2B. 2A pupils were the elite of the two classes. How you had performed throughout the year and the exam marks achieved determined who got in. Imtiaz got into 2B and Fatima organised a huge family dinner to celebrate. A few days later I came home with my results. I had got into 2A and was delighted. There was no special dinner for me and nobody apart from Mummy even congratulated me. Abbas never acknowledged my achievement either, which although disappointing, was not surprising. Considering I had bunked off school on a weekly basis for the last six months of 1st year, it proved to me I was smarter. I was never in lessons while Imtiaz swotted away and still I beat him. Throughout secondary school I bunked off. I was an expert at forging Mummy and Abbas's signature.

Abbas told me not to talk to boys. I talked to boys.

At the end of first year and by the start of the dreaded summer holidays I had a boyfriend, a Sikh boy. We hadn't really spoken although I had noticed him glancing at me and once his friend shouted, 'Hoy, ma pal fancies you.' I ignored him. The last day of school he approached me smiling and alone. I was going in the opposite direction to where my classmates were going, heading to the lane at the back of the school where I was meeting Anita. 'Will you go out with me?' I blushed and told him, 'No, I am not allowed. My brothers will kill you if they find out.'

'So, I like you, I don't care,' he continued smiling, making me blush even more. He started following me, smiling and paying me compliments. Anita arrived and the three of us sat on the wall that ran through the back of the lane. The Sikh boy knew Anita so no introductions were needed and we sat chatting

99

about what we were planning on doing for our holidays. The Sikh boy was having a similar sort of upbringing to mine and his holidays would be spent working in the family shop and not much else. Mine would be spent at home, cooking and cleaning. Only Anita was looking forward to the bell going and the start of the holidays. An hour before lunchtime Anita left us alone and wandered off heading towards her home. School was finishing for six weeks. Walking back to school with him I agreed to be his girlfriend. I was blind to the turban he was wearing, refusing to even think of the beating I would get, being a Muslim girl and having a boyfriend. The beating would be so much worse because he was a Sikh boy. Similar to the views which existed, and in some places still do, about Catholics and Protestants dating. We held hands walking back only letting go when the lane ended and the school was in sight. Kissing me on the lips, softly, he whispered, 'I'm going to miss you.' Those summer holidays were probably one of the longest periods of my life. Amirah and Khalsoom knew I had a boyfriend and thought it was hilarious that I would date a 'turban head', and now had something else to tease me about. He was nice to me, I liked him because he paid me attention. Nobody else was nice to me. Nobody else said kind things.

At last the holidays ended, the night before school arrived. Shagufta has been learning to sew and had been given the task of sewing the girl's pinafores. Khalsoom's had turned out perfectly, surprisingly enough, navy blue material, buttons at the shoulders and pleats at the sides. Mine was a mess and

Amirah's pretty much the same. The pleats were uneven and out of shape, sticking out at the sides, looking like a disaster. I was excited to be going back to school yet miserable at what I was being forced to wear, knowing we would be laughed at. It was bad enough having to wear trousers under our school pinafores. Thankfully Mummy saw the mess Shagufta has made of our uniforms and promised she would buy us new ones the next day. She borrowed the money from Abbas telling him the pinafores were a mess and we never had to wear Shagufta's creations again. The next morning I had to hide my cheesy grin, excited to be seeing my boyfriend, scared Mummy would know something is up. It was rare to see me so happy.

I met him at break time, behind the music department where there were no other pupils. I wanted to talk and ask what he did during the holidays. He wanted to kiss me. For a few minutes I let him. Hugging into him I told him I wanted to talk not just kiss. I told him I wanted lots of hugs. Nobody in the big house gave me hugs. Craving affection I would allow him to kiss more often than talk. At the afternoon break we met again. By the end of the first week I had managed to bunk off for an afternoon with him. We went for a walk strolling through the park, holding hands and promising each other we would be together forever. We were no different to any other love struck teenagers. The big house, for me, was all but forgotten about. That weekend I spent a lot of my time trying to hide my happiness. Knowing I had my Sikh boy made the weekends bearable and when the other holidays came they were more bearable too. My bunking off school increased now that I had a boyfriend. Sometimes I would pretend to be sick at school so I could be sent home for the rest of the day. The school would phone the big house and I would be collected by an adult. The next day I would pretend to return to school and bunk off, usually two days, sometimes the rest of the week. I was always with the Sikh boy. When I returned to school my absence was never questioned; I had been sent home sick after all and my forged note was happily accepted and filed along with the others. Spending hours getting Abbas and Mummy's signatures just right had paid off. My closeness with Anita had gone. We were still friends but it was difficult to be best friends when we were never allowed to do anything outside of school hours. I became close to an Indian girl and a Kashmiri girl both in 2A with me and spent some of my break times hanging around with them or sometimes if they bunked off school too then they would hang out with me and the Sikh boy. I decided one day to ask Abbas if I could visit my new Kashmiri friend's house one Saturday. Again the answer was 'no' with a little extra 'she come from no good family, I know she's good girl but her family it is no good. They bad people. Ju no go.' I didn't dare ask about my Indian friend, or ask why Shagufta was allowed to visit her Kashmiri friends, some of whom had boyfriends and smoked. Stating the obvious only got you a slap and I had long stopped questioning the differences in the treatment of 'the gori's children.' I remember once Fatima telling Mummy's girls that we were not allowed to wear our hair up high in a ponytail.

'Eh tussah kyon bhal kii kurso? Munday vastay? Istra nee karna harami. (Why do you want to style your hair like that? For the boys? You will not be wearing your hair like that, you bastards.)'

Shagufta and Khalsoom were allowed to wear high ponytails and have their fringe cut, their hair was long but nowhere near as long as the gori girls' hair. Ours was long enough for us to sit down on, no haircuts or fringes allowed for us, no visits to hairdressers either. Fatima tried her hardest to make us look as plain as possible, no latest fashion for the white woman's children. Looking back I wish I had the courage to tell her, boys looked at us anyway even with our greased down, middle parting and two plaits. The plainest hairstyle you could style, and still Mummy's girls were beautiful next to Fatima's. In Fatima's eyes we were always dirty little children and needed to be reminded on a daily basis.

Throughout second year I bunked off school and passed all my exams. Apart from the mosque for two hours every day after school, all our time was spent at home. For us the mosque changed many locations over the years until we stopped going by the time I had reached 14 years of age, Abbas having decided that Fatima would teach us at home. One location was an old church, hired by a pretend molvi (priest). He was a pretend molvi because he never taught us to read the Quran. We were picked up in a white minivan and dropped off there with a handful of other children collected along the way. Boys went into one room and the girls into another. Most of the time the molvi never turned up and we would go exploring in nearby Mount Florida. When he did show up there was no lesson either, he preferred to sit and read his newspaper, ignoring the children in his charge.   Not one of us told anyone in the big house and Abbas continued paying our fees to a molvi who was pretending to teach his children Islam and prayers. We went there for a few months until one of the other children told their parents, who in turn told Abbas, about the lack of teaching. After that we went to a tenement in Maxwell Road, Pollokshields. This time Abbas would take all seven children in the Mercedes and drop us off outside.   We would enter through the close door and wait inside the close hidden from view, and once Abbas had driven off we would sneak back out and roam through the Shields, not caring that we may be spotted playing in Square Park. Living in a white area was tough and it felt safe to be in the 'ghetto' again. It felt good to see lots of other brown faces and not be the odd ones out. Those were some of the best memories of childhood, most of my best memories involve no adults, and so more fees were paid for Islamic lessons we rarely attended.   The Pakistani children happily skived off too, it wasn't just 'the 'gori's children.' Children want adventure and to go against their parent's wishes regardless of skin colour.

A lot of my time I spent in the big house was still in my room alone, reading books, studying and daydreaming. I was able to read over notes and relevant sections in my school books and with some help from Imtiaz when something needed explaining, it was easy for me to pass exams even though I didn't go to school. I pretended to Imtiaz that I didn't understand when my teacher was explaining in class, not letting him know that I had bunked off. I let him think he was smarter than me. By the time I finished second year not one teacher had questioned my attendance. Maybe it was because I was an A+ student, maybe it was because when I did attend class I was a well behaved student or maybe it was because my parents' forged signatures were perfect. I also ended my relationship with the Sikh boy. I was happy with cuddling, talking and sometimes kissing, but the Sikh boy had no such patience and was always asking when I would sleep with him. I believed my virginity should be kept for my husband. Mummy had raised us to not sleep around. I valued my virginity.

Fatima held no such value. During one summer break, when Amirah turned 13 and I turned 15, a few months later, I overheard a conversation that filled me with a new fear.

'Payjo Mirpur, lorsa koi bhuda bachay nal thay ina nee shadii kursa. Eh thay vee inay vastay bhot chungha hai, (Send them to Kashmir, find a widower with children and they can become his wife and their mother. Even that is too good for them)' she said, smiling at me as I happened to come into the room.

Apparently Abbas agreed to this and was happy for Fatima to arrange it. She was positively glowing at the prospect of getting rid of us, forever. Mummy was having one of her episodes and once again cocooned in a fuzz of anti-depressants unable to grasp what was being planned and was happy to go along with Fatima's wishes. This was also the time when Haroon had divorced Mummy and was waiting to fly out to Kashmir to bring back his real wife. His thank you present to Mummy was to take her youngest two daughters to Kashmir, to be married off.

Living with us in the big house at the time was Uncle Yasin, Abbas's brother in law. He was the husband of his oldest sister. He too had come to the UK in the 60's and had lived in London for the last 20 years. He had never sent for his wife and children, choosing instead to send money back and support them all while living alone in the UK. When he came to stay with us in the big house, he spent the majority of his time in his bedroom upstairs. This was our old bedroom. We had been moved in with Mummy to make room for him. He was also Zanera's father in law. The only time he came out of his room was to use the bathroom or go to the shops for cigarettes and to watch his favourite programme, 'Blockbusters' or as he would shout coming down the stairs, 'Oh Blackbastards shoroo hoya (started)?' Everyone would laugh no matter how often he said 'Blackbastards instead of Blockbusters.

When he overheard the plans he hit the roof. Being older than Abbas and as his brother in law, he was respected and the plans thankfully came to nothing. I never knew this part until recently when discussing the marriage plans with Mummy, and she told me it was Uncle Yasin who put his foot down and refused point blank to listen to their plans or allow them to happen. No wonder he used to tell Amirah and me to 'run away, they will kill you.'

It was awful to be hated by the people who were meant to care for you. For seven years I had listened to constant put downs and ridicule. Even though I believed I was a good person and deserved better it was hard not to believe what I was being told on a daily basis, that I wasn't. By now we had stopped going to mosque and were supposed to be getting taught at home by Fatima. I remember performing the ablution- washing, all the children had been gathered in the dining room for our first prayer and Islamic lesson at home. Going into the room I noticed just her children were sitting.

'Leh, ja kaydh. Me tukee kujvee nah dusnee. Batames bansay, faida kia. Ja daffa oh, lor apnae penn praa. (Huh, go play in the back garden. I'm not teaching you anything. You are just going to grow up and be shameful. No point wasting my time teaching you. Go, find your brothers and sisters.)' Fatima sneered at me.

Somehow she always made me feel like scum even though I was as innocent as her children, more so than even some. Islamic lessons and prayer time was now offered only to the Kashmiri children, and so we never learned.

All the girls and all the boys in the big house were dating, both the Kashmiri's and the mixed race ones, even though it was completely against the rules. We all had boyfriends and girlfriends. As soon as we got to secondary school, Imtiaz for some reason attracted many an Asian girl, Indian and Pakistani and was never without a girlfriend. Shagufta and Zanera set the pattern for the younger girls. We were never really allowed any freedom. Trips to the library were permitted as long as we went with another sibling. Outings alone were not allowed. Shagufta and Zanera got smart quick and discovered if they took one of us younger girls they would be allowed a little extra time away from the big house. The adults did not for a minute dream they would be up to no good with boys, well men really. I was almost 13 when they started taking me on their outings to the 'library'. We would head out and be picked up by men in their car, Pakistani men that they were dating. We would get into the car and they would drive off somewhere near a park or sometimes a flat. I would always be left in the car with some random friend while they paired off and disappeared. One random friend gave me a Valentine's Day card, weeks after I was first left alone with him. With only one verse, handwritten inside

'When apples are red they are ready for plucking

When girls are 13 they are ready for fucking.'

I almost vomited. He was as old as Abbas. When the others returned and I showed them the card, they laughed. The two girls found it very funny. The next time I was left alone with him he spent the entire time trying his hardest to molest and kiss me. I kept quiet about it when they returned thinking it was pointless to tell. They would only laugh at me. My sisters would laugh the loudest. After that I refused to go on their outings no matter how much they bribed and cajoled and even threatened me.

Whenever we got caught doing something we shouldn't be doing, for Mummy's children the sin was broadcast for all to hear, but when Fatima's children were caught they were quietly taken to the flat in Pollokshields and reprimanded accordingly but away from prying eyes. There were no such privileges for Mummy's children. Everybody heard how we were caught smoking or talking to boys and bunking off school.

Running away in the 80's was unheard for a Kashmiri girl. Amirah was one of the rare girls that did, not returning from a visit to the library one afternoon. I was clueless as to where she was. She hadn't confided in me, being closer to Khalsoom and sharing her secrets with her. The police were called and the children questioned. We all claimed that we didn't know anything and those that did know weren't saying. Fatima called me into the living room the day after Amirah had gone.

'Aja mere bhaitee, meray nal behja. (Come here my daughter, sit beside me.).' Soothingly in a gentle voice.

A voice she had never used when talking to me. I did as I was told. In her sweetest, kindest voice she continued talking to me. Telling me I was a good girl, stroking my hair. I did not see her plan. Fooled by her false kindness, I wanted to make her happy. I was completely under her spell with just a few kind words.

'Duus menoo kithay gai eh, saray pershan hain. Twaree penn eh tuhkee pata hain. (Tell me where she is, everybody is worried sick. You must know, she is your sister.)'

I wanted her to keep liking me and talking kindly, and so I told her what I knew. Not caring that I was telling on

Amirah, only caring that Fatima was being kind to me. Foolishly I thought if I told, she would always be kind.

'Koi vadhay munday nal gul karnee hain. (There is an older boy she talks to at school.)'

As soon as I have said these words she brushed me aside, reaching for the phone. Dialling Abbas at the shop she told him, 'Kaar ao, Aisha noo sub kooch patha hain. (Come home, Aisha knows where she is.)'

I started pleading with her that I had no idea where she is. Laughing she told me, 'Tennu sub kooch patha hain. Ajj threyha passlah pansan. (You know everything. Today you will get your ribs broken.)'

Abbas was home in no time. The minute he stormed in and headed for me on the couch, I wet my pants. I was a teenager and long past the stage of wetting myself. It was the fear I had of the beating that was coming my way. The fear of Abbas. We had been slapped like a lot of other children were in the UK but this I knew would be the mother of all beatings. His precious Amirah had been gone a night and a day. His shoe was off as he approached me and he whacked it across my head. Kashmiri people reading this will know that the shoe is the favourite item for hitting, it delivered more pain than the hand alone.

'Ver is she!' he screamed.

'I don't know,' I cried. Still he smacked and screamed. 'Bitch. Mayaddi (motherfucker). Bastard. Ju bludee know ver

110

she go. Tell me or I pukkin kill ju.' He was slapping with his hands now, the shoe back on his foot. He was shaking with rage and he continued to scream, demanding I tell where his precious princess is. I had no idea where she had run away to. No matter how much he hit me, I couldn't tell him what he wanted to hear. I didn't know but I didn't know how to lie to make him stop hitting me. All I knew was that she spoke to a boy, I kept saying over and over again. Finally, after what seemed like ages, he stopped slapping and smacking, ordering me out of his sight, unable to even look at my pitiful state. He left me bruised and sore. The hurt inside was more painful than the marks on the outside. That was probably one of the worst beatings he gave me. After that I stopped loving him and I started wishing he would die along with Fatima. That was the day I started really hating both of them. Yet given a chance to please, shown some false kindness and I would be charmed once again.

Amirah came home later that day, returned by the police. No checks were carried out on our home life, no one asked why a barely teenage girl had run away with an older boy. The connections Abbas had in the police force and with the politicians ensured questions were not to be asked. Using the 'culturally sensitive' card he was doing like so many other Asians all over the UK and getting away with the unjust treatment of their children. Once all the drama had died down I said to Amirah, 'Next time you decide to run away take me with you. They will beat me up again so might as well be for something I have done.'

It was almost a year later that I ran away with her. Although in that time Amirah had been running away on a regular basis, staying away for a night or two. The longest she went for was a week and when she returned life became even more hellish. Nobody spoke to us, instead they gave us dirty looks. I had not run away and yet was being treated as if I had although I was never beaten as badly as the first time.

An extended family dinner had been organised on the night we ran away, celebrating something or another. Sitting in the dining room with Amirah we contemplated life and ending it. Amirah wanted to be with the older boy and said if she couldn't she would rather be dead. I said I would rather be dead than live in the big house any longer. I was 15 and Amirah was 14. We had taken some of Mummy's pills. Opening the bottle we both took one and swallowed.

'We'd be better off dead. That's the only way to escape,' Amirah said, taking another tablet and passing one to me.

Tabassum came in from the hall, barely glancing at us she continued into the kitchen to check on the huge pots of rice and curry on the cooker, simmering slowly, almost cooked to perfection. When she went back into the hall and living room to the family festivities, Amirah and I looked at each other. We didn't want to die, life really compared to other children's issues was not so bad that we had to end it. Escape, yes. Suicide, no.

'Let's run away,' Amirah said.

Returning the pills into the bottle we waited a few minutes and with my heart racing I followed her into the kitchen and out the back door, through to the garden and towards the archway that led into the house next door. The house next door was empty, all the family were in the big house. Minus two. We made our exit out of the side and onto the street. Undetected and so far unmissed. Wearing shalwar kameez and wandering down the street towards the library.

'We'll go to the police,' I told Amirah. 'Tell them everything, they aren't allowed to be cruel. We can go into care.'

We had no money and really no sense of danger. There was a family having a barbecue in one of the gardens we passed, making the most of the last of the summer days, and we both stopped. We blurted out we had run away from our two mums and dad and needed help. They helped by giving us a lift to the nearest police station which was in Govan. Dropping us off outside and wishing us luck. The policeman wasn't nearly as helpful and when hearing about our troubled upbringing he told us the station was closed for the night.

'Come back in the morning when it's opened. There's naebody here but me.'

Govan today is still classed as one of the rougher parts of Glasgow where, let's be honest, Asian people are not really welcomed. Amirah and I came out of the police station and wandered the streets looking for help. We hadn't taken any money because we didn't have any. We walked down streets and went into a block of high rise flats. Knock knock. We tried random doors hoping to find someone willing to help. So strong was our fear and misery of the big house we were prepared to knock on the doors of complete strangers to ask for help. Somebody opened a door and told us to 'fuck off.' Still we knocked at more doors. The whole world can't be horrible. And then an old lady answered her door and invited us in. Reprimanding us for knocking on doors because it wasn't safe, she gave us lemonade and put out a plate with biscuits. Child Line had been set up that year in Scotland. Huge adverts on prime time TV. Phone them, she suggested when we told her why we were running. They offered no help. In the mid 1980's Glasgow was just addressing white Scottish children's rights to a life free from abuse. Emotional, physical, sexual abuse and neglect. Addressing the rights of a child from a minority ethnic background was not part of the training given to volunteers who manned the helplines. When I got through to a counsellor she told me to go back home and speak to an aunt or uncle about how we were feeling. When I told her that this was not possible and that Amirah and I would rather die than go back home she told me to phone the Samaritans. I did and they advised me to try Child Line.

'I have already, they can't help either,' I told the man on the other end of the phone. It was quite sad that there was no official agency able to help. Amirah rang the older boy she knew and he shouted and screamed at her for sitting in a stranger's home and for wandering through Govan. He told her to get the address from the old lady and phoned a taxi for us to go to his female friend's house. She was an Indian girl who had ran away from somewhere in England and was dating his friend. We thanked the old lady and left when the taxi arrived. The taxi took us to Maryhill. By now our absence had long been discovered and the police called. The worst thing Fatima and her daughters did that night was put crayons into the pot of rice that had been cooking and ruined it so they could blame us. They wanted to show everyone how bad we really were.

'Look at what they did. They are ill-mannered. Here is the proof.'

Our only aim that night had been to escape. We had no time to go looking for some crayons to put in the pots and ruin their dinner. We hadn't even any time to look for money or pack a bag to take with us.

We had been sitting for a few blissful hours planning our future with the Indian girl. Her parents had tried to force her into a marriage in India and she had run away to Glasgow to escape a life of misery. Here in Glasgow she felt safe, as her family were down in Wolverhampton with no idea of where to look for her. The girl suggested Amirah and I run away to England where there was less chance of our family finding us, when the door was hammered upon accompanied by the shouting of, 'Open up, it's the police.'

Amirah got up and went into the bedroom and hid under the bed. Abbas had gone straight to the police and blamed the older boy, by now Amirah had been running away with him regularly and the police visited him at work, a restaurant in the city centre. The boy told the police where we were staying. The policeman continued banging on the door and shouting. I have no idea what the girl's name was but she opened the door and the police came into the living room where I was now standing, acting brave and feeling terrified.

They asked me my name and then asked where Amirah was. One of them wandered off back into the hall and soon came back in with Amirah following behind. They told us Abbas and Mummy were downstairs in the car to take us home. We were adamant we were not going home with them.

'He will beat us. He always does.'

'It's horrible having two mums and a dad, the one that isn't our real mum treats us like shit. She wants to send us to Pakistan to marry some old men.'

I tried to argue that I was nearly 16 and could leave home and get a flat and look after Amirah. The policeman told me in England I could but in Scotland I had to be 18. The policemen took our fears seriously and refused to turn us over into our parents care, instead they took us to Maryhill Police Station where we were put into a cell until they could decide what was to happen next. Unlucky for us though, was Abbas's connections within Strathclyde's Police Force. By three o'clock in the morning we were out the police station and in the back of Abbas's car being driven home. The only saving grace was that we were to return the following morning, at eleven a.m, and be interviewed by a social worker, so loudly were we demanding to be taken into care. Even as we were being taken from the cells we were begging the police for help. Abbas could not stop this chain of events. Or could he?

During the journey home Abbas tried to persuade us not to say anything about our family, telling us over and over again how dreadful children's homes were.

'Look at jor mother, ju know vat is happening to her there. Ju vant same happen ju.'

'I don't want to live here anymore,' I replied every time, confident help was on its way at long last. Somebody had finally listened. When we got in, Abbas continued with his subtle lecture. The anger and rage held at bay, no slaps, and no punches for our refusal to be controlled. Eventually we were allowed to go to bed and woke the next morning, tired but excited. I looked around my room and silently prayed that I would never return.

The social worker that interviewed us both was a Kashmiri man. He was from the 'shame on the community' brigade and a few minutes after meeting him we both realised he was not going to help us escape. Abbas had used his connections to ensure we spoke to a Kashmiri social worker, a white person would have been horrified by what we were sharing. For most Kashmiris however it's part of the norm. The social worker was only interested in returning us home for the sake of izaat.

We never ran away together again after that one time. Again and again however Amirah ran away and on one occasion ended up at Aunty Wilma's flat in Pollokshields, too scared to come home. Aunty Wilma was at work and her husband, Uncle Omar, and son Joseph had allowed Amirah to wait for her to come home. As soon Aunty Wilma arrived she rang the big house knowing how worried everyone would be. Abbas and Mummy went to collect her. Once home with her Abbas questioned Amirah over what happened in the hours before Aunty Wilma had come home from work. Amirah said she watched TV and had something to eat. Abbas refused to believe her, in his sick head Amirah had been sexually abused by Uncle Omar and Joseph. Aunty Wilma was the nicest, kindest person in our life and this accusation would ensure she would no longer be a part of our life. She was enraged when Mummy relayed what Abbas had been suggesting and told Mummy she would never be back in the big house. Amirah was eventually sent to Kashmir to 'fix her and her wild ways.' Mummy had no say in her daughter being taken out of school and sent away from her. She was gone nearly two years but like an offender experiencing prison she returned with more knowledge than she had left with.

By the time I had got to 5th year I decided I wanted to be a social worker specialising in special needs children. When I told Abbas one day of my ambitions he scoffed.

'Ju think I pay for university for ju wipe someone's bum? Ju bludee fool no, social work no good job.'

Chapter 8   Leaving school

Further education wasn't an option available for me, I just wasn't aware of it yet. Zanera had been taken out of school soon after she turned sixteen and got engaged. Jamal had also left school and was happy to work in Abbas's shops. I was clever and thought I would be allowed to continue with my studies, but like my mother I was only good for working and bringing a pay packet into the house. After I left secondary school, I enrolled on some secretarial courses at Langside College, chosen by Abbas. A few months after I started I was made to drop out. Abbas had found me a YTS job at an office in the city centre. I would be working three days in the office and two days at college for which I would receive £35 a week. My wage was given to the big house at the end of every month. It was paid directly into my bank account and seeing as I did not go anywhere nor do anything, I never spent the money, withdrawing it at the end of every other month and handing it over to Abbas for him to spend on his women, gambling or drinking.

My 18th birthday was a quiet affair with no special gifts. The people I worked with at my YTS placement made a bigger effort than my own family had. The ladies in the office brought in a cake and put up some decorations and they had also had a collection and gave me gifts of perfume, chocolate and a handbag.

Round about this time I started seeing my ex again. I had bumped into him one day on my way home from college and arranged to meet up the next day. The five days from 8am to 6pm were the best times, weekends and holidays as always were filled with unhappiness. The older I got the worse it got. Never being allowed to be part of Fatima and her family, not being allowed to be part of my own family. Days spent cooking, cleaning, shouted at, picked on put down laughed at and mocked. Escaping at every opportunity to my bedroom. Alone.

One Saturday morning I remember being told to get ready. All four girls were going out with Abbas, me included. Most Saturdays were spent around the house with maybe a trip to the library to break the monotony.

'Where is he taking us?' I ask excitedly not caring that the only reason I am allowed to go is because I would be home on my own otherwise.

'Cat Stevens is giving a talk at the mosque and we are going to listen,' Shagufta replied, ironing her favourite outfit.

'Who is he and talking about what?' I continued with my questioning. I had never listened to Cat Steven's songs, too busy listening to Michael Jackson.

'Oh just shut up and get ready. Who cares, there will be males there too.' At 24 Shagufta was still unmarried which was unheard of in Kashmiri families. Zanera had been engaged at sixteen and married off at eighteen with no say in the matter. Lucky for Shagufta it was different for her, she was allowed to say no to any marriage notions claiming to be too young, even though she was older than I was and only a few months younger than Zanera, and wanting to study.

A few hours later and we were all ready to go to the mosque, to a mixed event. Turned out Cat Stevens was a pop star, known as Yusuf Islam and was in Glasgow to give a talk about his conversion to Islam.

Once the talk was over the girls sat at the side waiting for Abbas to finish his socialising. Shagufta noticed our cousin Iftikar.

'Wonder who they are with Iftikar? Check the skinny black one staring,' she remarked.

Glancing over I recognised Iftikar, the other three men were strangers. The skinny black one was indeed staring.

'Ha,' I laughed 'He is staring at you, Zanera.'

Embarrassed, Zanera told me to shut up. Before I could continue with my teasing, Abbas came over and we left. The skinny black one forgotten about. For a while.

Three months after I started my YTS, it was Christmas and time for the office party. The office was closing early and everybody was going for lunch and drinks.

'I'm not allowed to go,' I told the three women in the office and Andy, my boss. Even though the answer was always no in the big house, I had asked Mummy who told me to ask Abbas who told me no, even though Shagufta was allowed to go to her work's outings. Unknown to me Andy had a word with Abbas and the week of the party I was told by Abbas I could go but under no circumstances was I to drink alcohol. No matter what anybody said. I was given a curfew of 9pm and Andy had agreed he would put me into a taxi.

Finally the day arrived and I left the house happier than most days. I was at last being allowed to do something the Kashmiri children in our house took for granted. I was to have three extra hours out of the big house away from their prying and controlling ways. It was the first time I had ever eaten in a restaurant and I was nervous. There were eight of us in total for lunch and after lunch partners and friends joined the festivities bringing the total to twenty. Abbas was right, I was offered alcohol with my lunch. I said no and nobody pressurised me. However after lunch I made the choice to have a Tia Maria with coke. Maybe it was seeing everyone laughing and joking and having a good time. Nobody in the group was being rowdy or aggressive with the drinking. I wanted to fit in and be part of that. At first Andy refused to allow me but as the afternoon wore on and his intake of alcohol increased, he relaxed a little. Maybe because Abbas had ranted on and on about not drinking, I decided to disobey and have a few. I got a little drunk. It was the first time I had ever tasted alcohol and it went straight to my head. At that point I was too drunk to care about the big house. I still had a few hours before I returned and time to sober up. For a while I forgot everything, enjoying the way the alcohol was making me feel, tipsy not drunk. By 9pm I was getting out of a taxi outside the big house and my cocoon cast aside. Abbas opened the front door. He was waiting to make sure I had kept to my curfew.

'Salam a lekum (hello),' I greeted him head down and made my way straight upstairs. Shutting the door he came in

122

behind me and when I had almost climbed the twelve steps to the landing, he shouted.

'How was it?'

Stumbling more out of fear than the two glasses of alcohol still in my system I began to tell him when as usual he interrupted.

'Vat is wrong with ju? Ju been drinking?' he accused.

'You scared me. Anytime you shout at me I get a fright,' I told him, standing up and looking down the stairs at him. Standing in the hall he stared at me and I stared back.

'Go to jor room,' he finally told me. Another war cry in the big house. When they were unable to face the truth about our lives we were sent away from the adults. 'Get out my sight' was another favourite if you dared question the reason for anything.

I did as I was told and went to lie in my room. Still a little tipsy I closed my eyes and daydreamt of escaping from my life.

After Christmas Abbas returned to Kashmir to visit Amirah. During the two years she spent there he would make several visits. I continued going to my YTS, paying my entire wage into the big house and bunking off college. I bunked off college because secretarial studies did not interest me and I used the time to see the Sikh boy. The women in the office were shocked by the little I told them and sometimes they allowed me to finish a little early so I could go and have a coffee with the Sikh boy. With Abbas away I became less cautious about being caught and was seen with him, bunking off college one afternoon. Returning home I was oblivious to what lies ahead.

'I saw you with turban head,' Anwar told me. 'And when Ubboo jee (Daddy) gets back I'm going to tell him.' Standing in the hall, my jacket still on, I looked at him, pointing out to him that he had a girlfriend, his sisters had boyfriends, but that made no difference. This was another difference in the treatment of the two sets of children which was not allowed to be voiced. Taking my jacket off, I went to my room, terrified. I was thinking they would most certainly marry me off now, or send me to Kashmir like Amirah. Whatever they decided would be severer than any punishment given to the Kashmiri children. Fatima was the main punisher and there was no way she was going to punish her children harsher than the white woman's children. This was Fatima's revenge on Mummy and us, her children. I made a decision that night. I was going to give my virginity to the Sikh Boy. Everything else was out of my control. This was the only thing that was mine. Zanera never got to see her 'husband' until her wedding night. She was given just a picture. She had been taken to Mirpur at the age of eighteen and married to Abbas's nephew without Mummy or her siblings attending her wedding. There would be a wedding back in Glasgow when she returned and applied for her new husband's visa, which again thanks to Abbas's connections did not take long to be approved. I knew without a doubt the same fate lay ahead for me. The Sikh Boy was overjoyed when I told him, and soon after, my virginity was gone. I cried after and he hugged

124

me. I was crying because in my heart I believed it should have been given to my husband but whatever 'husband' Fatima had in mind would never be worthy of it.

Weeks later Abbas returned from Kashmir and Anwar started his taunting. He began bossing me around and made me do all his menial tasks, knowing he had information which was going to destroy my life, if he used it. I lived on egg shells for a while. Anwar like the others in the big house was an expert in manipulation having learned from the master, Fatima. For about a week this mental torture continued then Anwar stopped me in the stairs one day, just after I got home. 'I'm telling Ubboo jee when he gets home tonight. Just so you know.' he sneered nastily.

Trembling from head to toe I stood in my bedroom. In my head I was forever day dreaming escaping in some scenario or another. This time not thinking but acting I changed into my shalwar kameez and stuffed a top and thick black tights into my satchel type bag. Thinking I have money saved for the big house in the bank, I decided I can get a train ticket to London. Somehow in my head I always ended up in London. I went downstairs on autopilot. The house was unusually quiet, Fatima was at Albert Drive at her daughter Tabassum's home, where she spent a lot of her time. I was not sure where Mummy was, she might be next door at Amina's or at a neighbour's. Without stopping to think, I went straight out the back door and out through the back garden. Going the long way round to get on the main road and into a taxi. It was dark already. Spring was almost here but not quite. Arriving in town the trembling fear of Abbas was replaced by another but lesser fear of being alone in the city. I went to Central Station with every intention of making my way to London. In the toilets I changed into my top and tights. Venturing out, I was so terrified of being caught by Abbas or the boys in the family that I continued walking straight out and into town, finding myself at the Odeon on Renfield Street. The cinema was somewhere to hide while they were no doubt out looking for me. Purchasing a ticket and some popcorn I watched 'Cocktail' for the next few hours. I was not paying much attention to the film, focused on 'what to do now?' Funnily enough, I have never liked or watched anything with Tom Cruise in it since. All too soon the movie was over and the cinema emptied onto the street. I stayed in the foyer watching, lingering. Everyone had someone to be with and somewhere to go. Someone spoke to me, asking if I was waiting for a lift or a friend and I blurted out my dilemma. Phone the police, the kind cinema worker suggested, or go to a homeless shelter. I had no idea where to find a homeless shelter. I would have called the police but we had tried before and they were no help. I still believed they would be no help. So they were never an option available to me. The cinema was closing the worker said, and I too needed to leave. I wandered into the streets aimlessly. The fear of being on the streets alone at this point was preferable to what awaited in the big house but it was getting dark. I phoned the Sikh Boy but he was unable to rescue me. His father would kill him before allowing him to marry me. The Sikh boy didn't even have to ask as he knew how his family felt about Muslims. With nothing else to do I wandered some more and ended up on Sauchiehall Street. There were some people about but I still felt no fear. I walked up Sauchiehall Street spotted some benches and sat myself down. Lost in thought I did not spot the man watching me from the shop doorway. Becoming aware of his presence I started to feel uneasy. It was half past twelve at night and the number of people around was few.

Getting up quickly I started walking away and he followed me, smiling. I walked towards the phone boxes and called the big house. Mummy answered.

'There's a man following me and I'm really scared and don't know what to do,' I started crying. Relief at hearing her voice and not Abbas's or Fatima's.

'Where are you?' she asked through gritted teeth.

'In town,' I told her.

'Get a taxi and come straight home.' There was relief in her voice.

'I am too scared to come home. You will batter me.'

'Don't be silly hen, we just want you to come home. Everyone is worried sick. Nobody is going to batter you.'

After a few minutes I agreed to get a taxi. What else could I do? Within twenty minutes I was walking up the steps to the big house. Mummy opened the door and ushered me in, she gasped when she saw me.

'What on God's earth are you wearing? Get upstairs and change before you go in and see your faither.' I hurried up the stairs and changed. She had a point. If Abbas saw what I was wearing, he would have blown a gasket. And he was already angry enough.

Returning downstairs in my shalwar kameez and scarf on my head for good measure I entered the living room and found the three parents. Sitting down I waited for the showdown to begin.

'So who this boy? Ver ju meet him, when ju see him?' began Abbas.

My heart is beating like crazy as I answered him.

'I met him at school in first year and sometimes I meet him at lunchtime and sometimes I bunk off college.'

'Thay Sikh munda hain, (And he is Sikh.)' Fatima butted in disgusted.

I remained quiet.

'Ju think he vant to marry ju? Ju think his family allow a bitch like ju in their house? Shall I phone and ask his mum and dad? Vat ju think they say yes?' Abbas mocked.

I didn't answer him, head down. I avoided making eye contact with Abbas.

'Vat is his number I bloody phone,' he shouted at me.

Giving in, I recited it as he dialled and I heard him asking to speak to the father. Like a man deranged he demanded to know if they would accept me as the bride of their house. The Sikh Boy's family weren't aware of our relationship until Abbas rang. Still the reply was 'over their dead bodies.' Hanging up he

128

continued to mock and berate me. I heard Mummy through his rant advising me:

'Just answer him hen, just tell him what he wants to know.' I waited for him to physically abuse me but that night it seemed he favoured the mental abuse. He quizzed me on every little detail of how when and where until he finally got to the question where it had all been leading to.

'Did ju sleep with him?'

Silence. My mind was working overtime. Tell the truth or tell a lie. Tell the truth or tell a lie. He asked the question again and the truth won before I could think of a lie.

'Yes,' I replied. Silence, only Fatima moved, getting off the couch she stopped in front of me. When I looked up at her she slapped me hard across the face. 'Haramzadee (bastard),' she shouted. 'Get to your room,' Mummy chimed in. Abbas was unable to speak or look at me and thankfully was too shocked to hit me. Since I was eight years old Fatima had told me I was a good for nothing trashy slut bastard child. For her then to slap me for losing my virginity was a bit hypocritical.

I went to my room angry that she dared to slap me. Yes, I deserved a slap, but certainly not from her. She had no value for my virginity so why had she acted like she was devastated it was gone.

The next morning I got up and started getting ready for work. No one stopped me until I was about to leave. Then I was told 'No more YTS. You are staying at home now. Not wanting you to run away again.' And as easy as that I was trapped in the big house.

Behind the scenes the hunt was on for a suitable or more than likely unsuitable husband and within three months I would be forced into a marriage.

Chapter 9   Forced into a marriage and life of misery

It was a warm, sunny spring afternoon when Shagufta smugly informed me of my punishment, a punishment given to me for daring to run away, for losing my virginity, for being defiant but mostly just for being the gori's daughter. A fate which I am sure would have been chosen for me regardless of what I had done.

'Remember that skinny black guy? Well guess what? You're marrying him. Ha-ha, they just said yes to your rishta (marriage proposal).'

I went looking for Mummy who is upstairs in her bedroom. Vague memories of the man chosen for me came to mind and I begged her to tell them no.

'He's horrible, old and so black,' I told her. 'I didn't even know him. Please tell them there is no way am I marrying him!' Mummy is unable to help.

'What can I do, hen, they've said yes. Just think you will be getting away from here and they seem like a nice family,' she told me, not realising that the niceness was probably fake.

For weeks I had been stuck at home never being allowed out in case I ran away again. I told everyone who would listen, I told Mummy and my siblings, too scared to voice my opinions to Abbas or Fatima, that I was not marrying him, they couldn't force me, I said confidently.

'I am 18, I live in Britain, nobody can force me to marry anyone I don't want to,' was my cry for several days after I learned of my 'marriage.' 'In our religion it's wrong too.' Even I knew that much; it seemed like no one else cared that I was being forced to marry against my will.

Naeem called me in the living room one afternoon, he was the only nice one from the step side. He is fifteen years older than I am and rarely spoke to me. When he did he was pleasant enough, we just didn't have anything in common and I had never spoken to him alone before. Waiting for me to sit down before he began talking.

'Aisha, you have to marry Pervaiz. Think of the family honour, if you don't, Uboo jee will kill himself. He has rope in the boot of the car, I saw it when I went into it for something and it wasn't there the other day.'

Listening to him I felt sorry for Abbas, I didn't want Abbas to die, I just wanted him to like me. Could I live with the guilt if he used the rope as Naeem was suggesting?

Emotional blackmail is something most Asian children are very familiar with. It is regularly used by parents to control their children. Talking about the importance of honour in the big house was a joke, my parents were living in sin and were worried about how my not marrying someone they had promised me to would affect the family honour. Abbas never had any intentions of taking his life, certainly not for my sins but listening to Naeem, I visualised Abbas hanging from the rope. How could I live with myself, I thought, if he hanged himself. Abbas was loved by his other children and by the women in the big house, he was my father too and even though he never showed me any love I loved him and I didn't want him to die for my sins. The emotional blackmail did the trick and I no longer shouted about my rights, instead I resigned myself to the fact there would be no escape for what had been planned for me.

The wedding was arranged for three months' time. The thought of marrying a stranger terrified me. There was to be no meetings and no getting to know each other, even chaperoned obviously. That apparently was only allowed for the Pakistani children. When it was their turn to be married they were allowed to have chaperoned meetings. Many Pakistani families let their children meet under the watchful eye of an aunt or sister or some other elder, getting to know their future wives or husbands before they agree to being married. I resigned myself to the fact that I was being forced into a marriage to a complete stranger, with whom I would have nothing in common. There was nothing else I could do. Shopping trips for clothes, jewellery and a wedding outfit were planned in preparation for the big day. I had no say in any of it, and most of it was arranged by Fatima and her older daughters. Mummy went along with the plans, same as when Zanera had got married. Fatima and her daughters were pure Pakistani therefore understood the Pakistani culture and traditions so knew how to prepare for a Pakistani wedding, but really I think they did it to show face. 'Look we treat the children no differently.' 'Mummy's children really are like my own.' I was swept along by everyone else's excitement, and in a sick way enjoying being centre stage for a change.

Shopping for underwear proved problematic, I remember going with Mummy to get measured, one of the few things delegated to Mummy, and was a 28A - trainer bra size, purchasing something sexy was impossible. No breasts to put into a grown up bra for the dreaded wedding night. This caused much laughter amongst the women in the big house, when really it was no laughing matter. I was known as the 'beanpole' tall and gangly, a bit of a tomboy. Dressing up, hairstyles and makeup had never interested me. Experimenting with makeup only emphasised my freckles and playing hairdressers only reminded me of my afro like hair which was not easy to style like the other girls' poker straight hair. I was also very childish and in no way emotionally ready for the responsibility of marriage, but that didn't stop the big house from forging ahead with the plans.

The three months flew by. It's what happens when something dreadful is coming up. When you are waiting for a happy occasion it takes forever; Sod's law. My wedding dress was chosen for me, a red and gold traditional lengha (skirt) and top, heavily embroidered with threads and weighing a ton, my nose was pierced in preparation for the nose ring that forms part of the jewellery worn by an Asian bride, along with bangles, earrings and necklaces, the more gold the greater the dowry. Mummy had taken me to the clothes shop down the street, from the big house, and the shop keeper pierced my nose with a gun. Having my nose pierced was a sign that the wedding day was getting closer. Pakistani girls used to get their nose pierced because they were getting married, nowadays it's a fashion statement.   A few weeks before the wedding relatives from Pakistan begin to arrive, including Waquas, the paedophile, Abbas' nephew and son-in-law.   The week before the wedding, cousins from England arrived and there was a party atmosphere in the big house which had been decorated for the occasion. Tinsel was hanging over the banisters and round the huge mirror in the hall downstairs, the main room for entertaining was like Santa's Grotto without the Santa. Reds, gold and greens were the colours of the decorations inside the house, and outside fairy lights were hung from the trees in the front garden, the big house was united in the celebrations.

All too soon it was the night before the wedding, the mendhi night, the big house was full to capacity as was the house next door. The 'groom's' family came over for the celebrations. The males stayed in the house next door until the celebrations were over. The females stayed in the big house. I was the focus of attention as I was the reluctant bride to be. Mendhi (henna) was applied to my hands, oil was massaged into my hair and sweets fed to me by most of the females as was tradition. The males from my side of the family also participated in these rituals and fed me sweets. There was more massaging of oil into my scalp and then the females, apart from me, went in to the house next door and the same activities were carried out there for the 'groom.' I was not allowed to see him, yet. It was easy to forget I was getting married in the morning, and I just enjoyed the attention and fake kindness from Abbas and his family, everyone was being nice, smiling and showering me with attention in front of all the visitors. The previous day I was ignored, and after my wedding I would be ignored too. Abbas and Fatima would be glad to get rid of me.

It was easy to get caught up in it all and play the role they had chosen for me and I ignored the frightened little child inside of me. Dhol playing – a dhol is a large barrel-shaped wooden drum, double sided, which is banged upon with hands to create a rhythm and beat for singing and dancing - and laughter continued late into the night, food eaten and much gossiping. Many a female relative had made a point of telling Mummy, 'Aww it's like a light has come on in their house now with your daughter marrying into their family.' My new family to be were all very dark skinned, almost black and with my fair skin in comparison, it was a topic for gossip. Pakistani people and other Asians prefer lighter skin to darker skin tones - gori means fair skinned - and those with fairer skin are thought more beautiful. Pervaiz's family didn't really care what colour my skin was. They were more interested in the colour of my passport and that by marrying me to their son, he would be able to apply to stay in the UK permanently.

Once the visitors had left, the girls got the makeshift beds ready in the living room, where we were sleeping. They put blankets and pillows on the floor and we chatted through the night. Many times we went upstairs to see if Shagufta was going to join us. She had chosen to stay upstairs in the bedroom with Waquas, her older sister Abida's husband, and his three year old son. Shagufta was spending the night, sleeping on the single bed while he lay on the double bed with his son. Not one of the adults in the house seemed to think this was wrong but we, the younger girls in the family, did, so we kept going up to catch them out. Eventually Waquas roared at us to stay away, the 'looking for a pillow' 'do you want a cup of tea?' excuses wearing thin, the giggling and sniggering that accompanied every visit beginning to annoy him. Left in peace they spent the night together. No one asked any questions.

At nine o'clock the next morning, the molvi (a holy man, like a priest) and Pervaiz, my husband to be, arrived at the house next door with his relatives and friends, and Pervaiz agreed to marry me. In Muslim marriage ceremonies the bride and groom do not have to be in the same room to be married. Abbas returned to the big house with the molvi and it was my turn to agree. Sitting upstairs waiting with a feeling of dread, unwashed and in an old shalwar kameez as is tradition, I heard Abbas telling Zanera to bring me downstairs. The excitement of last night had gone. The fear of what lay ahead for me was making me shake. Mummy was in the kitchen, not allowed to witness my punishment. The molvi spoke and I zoned out, not hearing anything he has said, not that I would have understood as he was speaking in Arabic. There was silence. Everyone was waiting for me to nod my head and say 'kabul(I agree.)' I didn't agree so I didn't nod my head and say 'kabul'. Fatima and Abbas with their fake kindness tried to coax me, smiling sweetly at me, calling me daughter when all I remember them usually calling me was bastard. Up until this point I was praying for a miracle, hoping

137

someone would rescue me from this forced marriage, pretending it wasn't real. Agreeing to the forced marriage makes it real and I knew that there was no going back once I had said 'kabul'. There was nervous laughter while I remained still and mute, not falling for their charm this time. How could I agree to marry a man I had never met, never spoken to, a stranger? Unable to seal my fate I remained silent, hoping the molvi would tell them the wedding is off. Forced marriages were not allowed under Islamic law. Abbas went out the room and came back in with Mummy who told me tearfully:

'Listen, hen, you need to do it, just say what they want you to. You have to marry him.' Now I knew there was no escape, the molvi was not stopping the wedding from going ahead even though it was clear I did not want to be married and then Mummy was begging me to agree to this joke of a wedding. I had no strength to defend myself and without any help from those meant to protect me I nodded my head and reluctantly mumbled 'Kabul, I agree,' and with those words I was forced to marry a stranger from Kashmir, 16 years older than me. As soon as I said those words, Mummy started crying loudly and returned to the kitchen. I was taken upstairs and a bath was run for me and soon the preparations were underway to transform me into a bride. I wore a huge gold hoop through my nose which has a chain with an elaborate hair clasp which is pinned into my hair. My hair had been styled into a bun. I had 12 gold bangles on each arm, one set from my family and the other from the groom's. There were rings on every finger, a massive gold necklace. There were whispers that the gold the groom's family had given was superior to the gold given to me by my own family. Once ready I was taken to the central mosque in the Gorbals where the guests were arriving and I was sat down at the top table. The 'groom' was there, with his family, waiting, we were not seated next to each other, friends and family were between us. A Pakistani bride is not supposed to smile on her wedding day but to show her sadness at leaving her parents' home. I didn't smile and tears came easily, only to be told 'don't cry, you will ruin your make-up.' 'Ruin my make-up,' I wanted to scream, 'What about my life?' The whole day was a blur, at times I thought about screaming 'Help me!' Who would help? The police? There was a table full of Strathclyde's finest invited by Abbas, they were his friends and not about to help, I had tried that before and got nowhere. My husband and in-laws were unaware of my attempt at running away from home, they were also unaware of the fact that I was not a virgin as was most of the Pakistani community. It wasn't something Abbas wanted broadcast as it would look bad on him that he was unable to control his daughter. Abbas had been aware of the fact that Pervaiz's family had been searching for a wife for some time for him, and when I ran away and came back home he called them and offered me as his bride. They had been unable to find a wife for Pervaiz as his family was very religious and they had been looking for a religious, five times praying a day, kind of family.

I was allowed to invite my friend from school even though I hadn't seen her for nearly a year, it would have looked bad if I didn't have a friend to sit next to me throughout the day as is the custom, in any religion. Fatima, not wanting to look bad in front of the community, had suggested it and Rukhsana helped me get through the day. She was laughing and joking to take my mind off the dreaded wedding night which was getting nearer, bless her. I asked numerous times, 'What does he look like?' 'He's alright, I've seen worse,' she replied, reassuring me with her kindness. Throughout the day, guests would come to the top table and congratulate the family and money would be pressed into my hands as a gift and blessings given. Twenty pound notes, fifty pound notes, more money than I have ever been given before, 'Mash'Allah (praise be to Allah) you both have a long and happy life', 'Insh'Allah (god willing) you will be blessed with children.' Sometimes babies were thrust into my arms while all the women laughed and joked. 'Hold a baby on your wedding day and you will be holding your own in nine months time', is a well-known Pakistani saying. Most Pakistani newlyweds have a baby in nine months' time, fulfilling another tradition to keep the families happy. All the money was being stuffed into my purse and it was getting difficult to close it over as the evening wore on. Soon the last of the guests were leaving and it was time to return to the big house, the 'groom's family would then arrive to take me to my new home. Briefly I got to speak to my 'husband' when he came over to say hello, and I handed him the money from my purse. Pervaiz was surprised and told me it was my money and to keep a hold of it. I insisted he take the money, the purse was sitting on my lap and literally bursting at the seams and I could think of no other thing to do. The minute I arrived back at the big house, Fatima took me straight upstairs to her bedroom, alone, pretending she had something important to tell me.

'Saray baar kud pessay. (Take out all money),' she commanded, pointing to the purse as soon as we are upstairs.

'Kuj nee. Pessay Pervaiz kee dittany (There is nothing, I gave it all to Pervaiz),' I showed her.

'Eh tuu kyon kita? (Why did you that?),' she asked, barely controlling her fury and rage.

'Is vaste maara janaa eh. (Because he is my husband),' I told her as Rukhsana came in.

'The groom's family are here, you have to come downstairs,' Rukhsana said, unaware of what she was interrupting, and Fatima had no choice but to leave it and not cause a scene, the money did not belong to her. Walking out the room and seeing the look on Fatima's face at the loss of all that money was almost worth the forced wedding she had masterminded. Funnily enough she never mentioned it to me again, although Mummy later asked me why I had given the money to Pervaiz and I told her that I figured it was my money so why should I give it to Fatima to spend on herself and her family, I had had a feeling she would ask for it the minute I returned from the mosque, it's the way she was.

When it was time to leave the big house I clung onto Abbas crying, the crying came easily and I clung on tightly not wanting to go to my new home. Holding on for as long as possible because it was the first time in my life Abbas had ever held me, and the prospect of having to go and live with strangers was filling me with dread. The thought of being alone with the husband he had chosen for me was making me cry uncontrollably. Family members prised me from him, males and females all crying, all fake and all for show. Arriving at my new home, I was greeted by lots of different people. Zanera had come with me along with Rukhsana and they stayed a few hours until it was time for bed. The celebrations continued there, Pervaiz's mother had flown over for the wedding and she sat me beside her while all round other women sat staring and chatting.

More food was served and more traditions were carried out. These traditions have no foundation in Islam. The Pakistani culture has adopted these from the Hindu culture. One of Pervaiz's nephews was told to sit on my lap, at ten years old he was a little shy, and told not to get off until I had given him money. He got off my lap as soon as I handed him a twenty pound note. Zanera had asked Pervaiz for some of the money I had given to him earlier as most of the rituals involved the handing over of cash to younger relatives or to the mosque. There was much laughter and the young boy was told to get back on my lap for more money and to not get off until he got at least £100. It was usually a younger brother that sits on the lap of the bride but Pervaiz was the youngest brother and that's why the nephew had been chosen.

Another ritual involved a bowl of cloudy water (I think it has been mixed with milk) and the finding of a ring in it. For this one Pervaiz was called in and together we tried to find the ring, whoever finds it was the dominant partner in the marriage. Needless to say it was Pervaiz that found it, shoving his hand into the bowl before I even had a chance, and again there was lots of high pitched laughter and screaming from the women in the room. The tradition that required me to read from the Quran was one of the last ones carried out and I heard Pervaiz's mother ask Zanera if I was able to read the Quran. I thought to myself, 'You married your son to me without asking my family if I could read the Quran and now that I am expected to read a line or two and place money inside it for the mosque, you think to ask? And still wriggling, squirming crying babies were placed in my arms for luck.

By half two in the morning I was exhausted, Rukhsana had gone home, Zanera was still with me.

'I want to go to bed,' I told her for the tenth time at least, scowling and with my lip pouting. The day had been long and tiring and I wanted to sleep, having had no sleep the night before, I was now exhausted. Eventually Zanera was allowed to take me into my new bedroom with Pervaiz's sister-in-law, Salma, following us into the room. Salma handed me a white piece of cloth and told me, 'Put this underneath you when you sleep together.'

'Why?' I asked her confused.

Salma and Zanera laughed and Salma told me to just do as I was told as she left the room. I asked Zanera what I was supposed to do with the cloth and when she told me I panicked. I told Zanera I had to use the bathroom and brushed my teeth, scrubbing my face clean of the layers of heavy make-up that is standard for an Asian bride, even the reluctant ones. Returning to the bedroom I proceeded to remove my jewellery, Zanera came back in and stopped me.

'Oh god what have you done to your make-up? You are meant to keep it on for him to see you. Put your nose ring back in and stop being silly.'

'All I want is to curl up into a ball and sleep,' I told her refusing to put the jewellery back on, trying not to cry. There was a knock on the door and Pervaiz entered the room. Zanera said goodbye and left and Pervaiz locked the door behind her. Sitting down on the bed he spoke in his funny English.

'You vant I speak English with ju, or in Urdu?'

'I would prefer to speak English because that's what I always speak,' I replied. Apparently that was the wrong answer because Pervaiz continued speaking in Urdu. When I insisted that Abbas even spoke English to me, he paid no attention. From the start he was letting me know he made the rules regardless of what I chose. All I want to say about my wedding night was that I was glad I never saved my virginity for him.

Almost a week after the wedding when the party atmosphere had eased off, Salma came into the bedroom one morning and asked me for the white cloth she had given me. I was prepared and told her Pervaiz had thrown it out in the bin the day after the wedding. Salma was fuming and asked me what I was thinking. I calmly told her it was dirty and she never asked me to keep it for her, so why should I have? There was nothing else I could do, I couldn't hand it back without any blood. Years later I would learn some brides prick their finger and smear the cloth with blood. Proof they are virgins even when they are not. I was never that smart.

Every day of the marriage was mostly miserable, apart from the days when I went back to big house, smiling on the outside, dying on the inside. The big house was the lesser of the two evils. We were totally incompatible: he liked politics (he was seeking political asylum after all) and I liked Top of the Pops. I was very immature and childish and he regarded himself as the font of all knowledge. I had been blessed with good looks and he was not so blessed. Sometimes I pretended it wasn't real and I would wake up back in my old bed in the big house. Some days I had no idea how I got through them. Trouble started in the marriage quite quickly. Pervaiz wasted no time in telling me I was not the sister he had wanted to marry, he had fallen in love with Zanera who was already married and the only reason why he had married me was because he needed a British passport.

Growing up I was never allowed to cut my hair and it came down past my waist in soft natural curls. Mummy would trim it herself every now and again to keep the split ends under control. I had never been to a hairdressers and days after the wedding he took me to the hairdressers and had them chop it off to below my shoulders. The first hairdresser he took me to refused saying I would regret it and it was too beautiful for her to chop off, the second hairdresser had no such issues and happily took the money and cut my hair to shoulder length. I had never been to a hairdressers before and was happy to go along with whatever Pervaiz suggested, I had never had it cut so short before either. Mummy cried when she saw what he had done and she cried again when weeks after the wedding, I told her I was pregnant.

I had been put on the pill months before the wedding. Mummy, insisting I was too young to have a baby, had taken me to the doctor's. Fatima was happy to go along with what Mummy wanted for a change because she didn't care what I did once I was married off. Pervaiz's sister-in law had found the pills and I was made to flush them down the toilet, all the while being shamed in front of his family for preventing Allah's will. Pakistani families believe strongly in having a baby within nine months of the marriage. Birth control, especially for newly-weds, is not acceptable no matter how young the married couple are. Also having a baby would strengthen Pervaiz's application to stay in the UK. I conceived instantly. The pregnancy test was not needed because of the severe morning sickness I was experiencing. My being pregnant with his child didn't change Pervaiz's opinions and attitudes towards me.

Three months after the wedding Pervaiz's mother was returning to Pakistan and I begged to be allowed to go with her. I was so desperate to get away from Pervaiz and the marriage and the horrible sex he was making me perform most days, I was willing to go live with strangers. Just after my 19th birthday and almost three months pregnant, I boarded a plane to return to the place I grew up. I was happy to be escaping from the misery that was my life, hoping for happier times.

Arriving in Pakistan I forgot all my troubles back home. The first week was filled with meeting all of Pervaiz's family and adjusting to living with the in-laws, a very religious praying five times a day kind of family. When the females in his family went out they wore the niqab, - similar to the hijab (scarf) which covers head and chest- but covering you from head to toe with only a slit for your eyes so you can see where you are walking. Back in Glasgow, I sometimes wore a scarf over my head. I always did this whenever Haroon was visiting as he was religious and believed females should cover their head. If your head was uncovered he would shout at you to go and get your scarf, and sometimes when other male relatives were visiting, as a sign of respect. I never did understand why the covering of hair was essential. Even at a young age I thought surely the female body was more attractive to men than her hair. Wearing the scarf was more embarrassing than anything else. Back in the 1980's the wearing of a head scarf was not as popular as it is today in Glasgow. Wearing the niqab I felt like I was suffocating, especially in the intense heat of Kashmir, so I preferred staying indoors and coping with the severe morning sickness which lasted all day.

I was desperate to see my own Pakistani family and soon the arrangements were made for me to return to my childhood home. I went with my mother-in-law and older brother-in-law early one morning and arrived a few hours later.

They were happy to be leaving me with my father's family, knowing I hadn't returned since I left at the age of 8. Seeing my Bhabba jii (grandfather) and other relatives was lovely, Bhai jii (grandmother) had passed away when I was 13. However, I had changed completely from the care free, confident child that had left many years ago, now I was quiet and shy, speaking only to answer a question, scared to say the wrong thing and at the same time eager to please everyone. They were as strange to me as I was to them but were so welcoming that it didn't matter. I felt accepted and wanted by them and yet I only ever got to stay the one night.

My in-laws had stayed for a few hours and chatted with my family and then they had left late afternoon. When it was time for bed I was told I would be staying with Abbas's and Fatima's oldest daughter, Abida. Preferring to stay with my aunt and cousins in my Bhabba jee's house, I found the courage to speak up. However Abida insisted I stay with her and the discussion was over before it really began, with Abida arguing that I should be staying in Abbas's house, the one Mummy had worked so many years to pay for. During that night, Waquas snuck into my room. I had last seen him when he came for my wedding and had slept with Shagufta. He was married to Abida and they both lived in the house with their five children. I woke to find his hands in my pyjama bottoms.

'Get your hands away from me!' I hissed in his face.

Continuing to grope, he told me, 'Ssshhh'

'I will scream the place down,' I threatened pushing him away and getting up.

Quietly and quickly he left the room and I stayed awake for the rest of the night scared in case he came back.

In the morning I phoned Pervaiz's family and told them to come and collect me. I wanted to go to their house immediately, no longer caring that I wouldn't spend time with my grandfather or beloved aunty, just needing to be as far from the sick, twisted man as possible. All that had been going through my head was, 'I am pregnant and still he abuses me.' I made such a fuss - stubbornness is a trait inherited from Abbas - and I refused to stay, constantly asking to be allowed to go back to my in-laws until my aunt, who had given up asking what was wrong, eventually called them. By evening I was back at the in-laws and made it clear I did not want to discuss with anyone what had happened. Pervaiz phoned asking what was going on and I told him I wanted to come home, back to Glasgow. I now no longer wanted to stay in Pakistan.

'No ju stay six months. Only been two weeks ju can't just come back. Vat happened in jor Bhabba's house vy no stay for?'

'Nothing, nothing happened. Why do you have to keep saying something happened? I miss my Mummy and want to come home.' I was unable to tell him the truth, part of me ashamed that Waquas had abused me.

In the end I stayed for another two months and the week I was leaving I was called back to Bhabba's house to say farewell. I had never gone back to see them since that first visit. I went with Pervaiz's mother and father this time. We spent the afternoon with all of Abbas's family, saying goodbye to my aunt when I had never really had a chance to say hello.

Waquas was in bed, supposedly ill, and I was sent into his room to say goodbye. I opened the door.

'Don't tell anyone, please,' he begged from his bed.

Standing at the door I looked at him with pity and shook my head.

'You are sick.'

Thankfully that was the last time I ever saw him.

Back in Glasgow the misery of living with someone I did not love continued with the added bonus of beatings and daily insults. I got slaps and punches usually because he was drunk and because sometimes I was defiant and refused to have sex with him. I was insulted often, with him swearing and mocking to keep me under control, angered by my defiance. I ripped up the marriage certificate and threw it at him. 'I divorce you, I divorce you, I divorce you.' Say it three times and it's granted Islamically, but witnesses are needed and I didn't have any. Still it didn't stop me from screaming it at him to let him know how much I hated being married to him.

Running away wasn't an option. Glasgow was blind to the forced marriages being carried out and ignorant as to how to deal with them. I had tried to get help when I was younger but had got none. Where would I find help now that I was married and pregnant? No-where, I thought, and so I stayed living an

150

extremely unhappy life. Pervaiz took pleasure in telling me that I was ugly. He married me only to get his red passport. He told me I was a rubbish wife, I didn't know how to cook and I didn't know how to have sex like a real woman. I would argue back with him and tell him, yes he was right, I was a rubbish wife because I didn't want to be his wife. Yes, I didn't know how to cook and I was unable to have sex like a real woman because I was still a teenager, I was only nineteen.

He was an alcoholic and lost his driving license due to drink driving a year after the marriage. He hid it from everyone, told them all he had lost it because of too many points for speeding. I saw his license when it was sent back in the post and saw the truth. When I asked him, he laughed it off. Pervaiz thought nothing of dragging me out of bed in the early hours of the morning to make his chapatti. He was drunk and staggering all over the place, shouting and swearing, slapping me if I dared answer back or refused his demands. He would verbally and physically abuse me not caring that I was pregnant. The big house knew of the beatings. There are only so many doors and cupboards you can claim to bang into, but nobody said anything. I was some other family's problem now, but they didn't care either. We were living in Pervaiz's brother's home with his wife and three young children. On occasions when the arguments got too loud, they would intervene and calm the situation down, but generally they ignored us, turning a blind eye to his drinking and the fights we would have when he returned home drunk in the early hours of the morning.

It bothered him a great deal that I refused to tell him what happened in Kashmir and one night he came in drunk and started slapping me and saying it would only get worse if I didn't tell him. Fed up with constantly being told, 'I don't want to talk about it' or 'nothing', Pervaiz meant business when he demanded menacingly that I tell him. Realising that this was going to be a really bad beating, I told him everything. I begged him not to repeat it to anyone but to keep it a secret, and I told him about the other girls in the family and about Shagufta and her 'affair' with him. He promised not to say anything but he lied. He discussed it with Abbas's brother, Haroon. Secrets never stay secret for long, especially in Asian families and one afternoon Shagufta turned up at the front door.

'Ubboo jee (Daddy) is down in the car, you've to come down now! What have you done? He is really angry for some reason.'

'Let me get ready, I'll be down in a minute,' I replied closing the door on her face, leaving her standing outside, and my heart racing. I panicked. Instantly I knew why he had come for me even though it had been a few weeks since I had told Pervaiz. I was absolutely petrified thinking about what was going to happen. I rang Pervaiz at work.

'Abbas is downstairs waiting for me and I have to go to the big house with him, he's going to kill me. Why did you tell, I asked you not to? Nobody will believe me!' I cried down the phone hysterically.

'Don't leave the house, I'm on my way,' he instructed.

152

Shagufta rang the bell again and when I opened the door she told me, 'He said 'Don't make me have to come up' Do you want him to come up and drag you down?'

Unable to stall him, I left the house, went downstairs and got in the car. I hadn't seen him this angry for a long time, not since the first time Amirah ran away. Dropping Shagufta off at Albert Drive, we continued to the big house in silence until he spoke,

'Is it true?' he asked me quietly.

'Yes,' I replied cradling my hands over my huge pregnant belly. 'I remember things he did when I was little and he tried again when I was in Kashmir but I stopped him.'

'When ju go in house ju say nothing, I vill ask Khalsoom and Amirah if they tell me ju a liar, ju watch,' he continued.

'I'm not lying, it's the truth,' I pleaded, terrified at the thought of the beating I knew he would give.

The rest of the ten minute journey continued in silence, neither of us speaking. My heart was racing like crazy. I was always more terrified by Abbas's silent anger than his screaming and shouting. I could not bear not knowing what he was thinking.

Entering the front door of the big house he called the girls down. Mummy was out at the shops and Fatima was on one of her trips to Bradford unaware of what was unfolding, Abbas choosing for just now not to tell her, maybe he knew she would tamper with his attempt to get at the truth. At first both girls denied any wrong doing by Waquas towards them. Trembling with fear I started sobbing and pleading with them.

'Tell him, I'm not lying, you both know it's true.'

The doorbell rang. Pervaiz had driven from work and turned up at the door demanding to be let in. While they were arguing I begged Amirah and Khalsoom to tell the truth.

'He's going to batter me, you know he will, he doesn't care that I'm pregnant. Please think of the baby, it's not like I made it up. He is a pervert. We call him The Paedophile for a reason, both of you know it's true,' I pleaded.

When Abbas returned he asked the girls again, and this time they told the truth, the whole truth and nothing but the truth. Abbas was visibly shocked, his face which was full of anger and rage, became drawn and sad. He said nothing, just put his head down and stared at the floor, unable to look at his daughters. Mummy returned from the shop and all hell brook loose, when she found out what had happened, crying and swearing that she will kill him. We were sent upstairs, Pervaiz was in the house now and he sat in the living room with Mummy and Abbas. The three of us wondered what was going to happen now. Voices carried upstairs to the landing where we were standing listening. The phone call had been made to Pakistan and Abbas was speaking with his brother.

'Meh afsa kaal thay kootay noo maree shorsa, pistol maaray vastay khareed, haramzada zaleel. (I'm coming in the morning get me a gun and I will kill the dog, the dirty bastard.)'

154

Even though Abbas was discussing a murder, I was smiling inside, positively glowing because he believed me, he was on my side. Phone calls were made to Albert Drive to tell Shagufta to come to the big house at once and also to Bradford to let Fatima know. I was called downstairs and I left with Pervaiz. There was no goodbye from Abbas, just Mummy who saw us out.

Later on I heard, from Amirah, that once Shagufta arrived she was beaten to within an inch of her life for the 'affair'. To my knowledge Abbas had never raised a finger to her before and part of me felt sorry for her. Waquas was years older than us and now as an adult I could see he 'groomed' her for his own sick pleasures. I doubt she willingly had an affair with her older sister's husband. Their affair had been going since my wedding, with them both sneaking off at every opportunity.

Later on that night while on the phone to Kashmir again and with Waquas declaring his innocence and swearing on the Quran that it was all lies and with Fatima cutting short her stay at her brother's to return straight back home, Abbas's initial rage simmered to anger. Other female relatives in Kashmir told their parents about their experiences once they heard what was happening. He was always trying to touch and grope and kiss and slobber, they said, but still he said it was all lies. I like to think Abbas believed me, I didn't get a beating so he must have.

That night when Fatima had returned she begged Amirah to change her story. She touched her feet, something which is usually done to someone older and is seen as a sign of respect and subservience, and begged her to reconsider what she was saying. Waquas was married to her daughter so her family honour was at stake here. She was willing to forget that he had abused a whole lot of kids and probably still was, as they tend not to retire. Amirah refused to deny what had happened but Khalsoom happily agreed to her mother's demands. The next morning she told Abbas, 'He only tried to kiss me like a brother'. This was all Abbas needed to hear. It supported Fatima and Waquas's claims that it was lies. He didn't book his ticket or purchase a gun to shoot the bastard like a dog. His hands were tied, he would claim. Waquas was the husband of his daughter and the father of his grandchildren and also his nephew. The father of Waquas was Uncle Yasin, his brother-in-law. Fatima said Amirah and I were just lying, jealous, out to cause trouble. Jealous of what, and why we would want to cause trouble, I could never understand.

And that is how most Pakistani families deal with abuse, get angry and then forget the anger choosing to focus on the 'izzat.' What will people say? Not giving a damn that their child has been violated, protecting the abuser and shaming the abused and so the abusers continue undeterred with no fear of being punished, instead they punish their children.

Being pregnant was something I mostly tried to ignore which wasn't easy. The morning sickness never eased and I suffered right up until the end. My entire pregnancy I suffered from depression which went undiagnosed. Depression is such a taboo subject in Pakistani families that I would not have been able to discuss with anyone how I was feeling. Some days I did not want to get out of my bed, washing myself was an effort and reading was something I did very little of in my marriage. I read a few pregnancy books although they held no interest for me either. Suicide was something I thought of often. Even though I had resisted the marriage, part of me had hoped that married life would be better than living in the big house like Mummy had suggested, but it was worse. The insults didn't stop, Pervaiz ridiculed and put me down in the same way Fatima and Abbas had. It was worse in many ways because I had to share a bed with him. In the big house I could escape to my bedroom with a book. Being married, the books were replaced by a man. Regarding me as trash didn't stop him from sleeping with me.

Towards the end of my pregnancy the mortgage for a flat I was buying was finalised, with a moving in date of a few weeks away. I had purchased the flat fraudulently, wage slips had been created for my supposed job at a relative's shop, proving I had been working since I was 15. These lies were told because Pervaiz was unable to apply for a mortgage, he was still waiting for his desired red passport.

Everybody in the family and community were involved in some type of fraud and nobody thought what I was being made to do was wrong, nor were they surprised by the fact I had no say in the matter. This was the norm amongst some families. Some Pakistani families have made their wealth from defrauding the benefit system. They live in big houses, mortgages paid for, having rented it to a close relative who would claim housing benefit for them or they may be working in their own business and claiming benefits and driving big cars, everything they own having been cheated from the western society they despised.

I visited the Bank of Scotland with my heavily pregnant belly hidden under a loose hijab style outfit worn to disguise my unborn baby. The bank manager was not made aware of my pregnancy and I was told not to act pregnant. Now I had a fake mortgage to go with my fake marriage.

Living with his brother and sister in law, Salma, caused many problems, Salma especially never liked me much. The incident with the white cloth had ruined any chance of friendship we could have had. Salma was from Bradford and a distant cousin of Abbas, she was a very religious woman and prayed 5 times a day and her home was spotless. She would scrub her pots and pans until they were gleaming and like new and nothing was ever out of place, even the youngest child's toys were put up high on top of the wardrobe so there would be no mess. If I'm honest, it was the shame of not being a virgin that made me behave the way I did towards her. Sometimes I would catch her looking at me and think, she knows why I binned the white cloth. When Mummy came to visit, I would tell her Salma was being mean and making me do lots of housework and so Mummy would shout at her, threatening to tell Abbas that I was being forced to wash clothes by hand when there was a perfectly good washing machine sitting in the kitchen. Salma was not scared of Mummy and her threats, and would shout back at her that I had to learn how to wash clothes properly, by hand then in the machine. If

158

Zanera was visiting then I would sit and laugh and snigger at Salma, mocking her hairstyle or the clothes she was wearing. Anything mean I could think of, I said it to her. Although Salma never asked me if I was a virgin or not, I had a feeling she knew. Why else would I have thrown the cloth away?

During the day, with Pervaiz at work, she refused to feed me or allow me to go into her kitchen without her permission. She never let me be part of the family, only talking to me to tell me what to clean or to tell me to watch her children while she went out. There was little to eat in her fridge and cupboards. Like most Pakistani families most of the meals were prepared from scratch. Her cupboards held mostly spices and pulses, and the fridge fresh uncooked meat. Any goodies she had, she kept in her bedroom under lock and key. At feeding times I was ignored and a plate was never put out for my lunch or dinner unless Pervaiz was home. When he was home, then she fed me. Zanera was living round the corner and I would go round to her house for food and when my pregnancy neared the end she would come round with plates of food for me. By marrying and moving from the big house to here, I had gone from one hell into another sort of hell.

The birth of my son lifted some of the depression, for a while. He was perfect and thankfully looked like my side of the family. He was born with a head of thick shiny black hair and much fairer skin than his father. I know all mums say it but I had never seen such a beautiful baby. I stayed in the hospital for six days with him and Pervaiz visited daily. After one of his visits a nurse said to me

'Your dad is great, he comes to see you both every day.'

'He's my husband I tell her, my dad has never visited.'

The shock on her face was something I was used to. It was the same wherever we went and someone found out he was my 'husband.' I could easily pass for his daughter so I understood people's reactions.

Coming home with Junaid was a happy peaceful time. The fighting stopped for a while. Pervaiz pleased with me for giving him a much sought after son and his status guaranteed. A wife and now a son, it would be only a matter of time before his red passport arrived. I had known early on in the marriage that this was the only reason for him marrying me. Pervaiz I found out was a much better dad than a husband and adored his son. I tried to be a mum and failed miserably, depression taking over any joy I may have felt at the birth of my son. Mummy visited three days a week, sometimes more, and cared for her grandson. Making up his bottles, taking over his feeds and nappy changes. She was able to lavish him with gifts and love away from the critical eye of the big house. It was as if she was making up for the love she had been unable to show her children. Bathing him and cooing over him in ways I was unable to because to be honest I had no idea how to love him, it hadn't come naturally like all the baby books said. There had been no antenatal classes attended and there were no play groups available for Pakistani women. It was the early 90's and I doubt I would have been welcome at the play groups run for white women.

A couple of weeks after the birth and Pervaiz was pestering me for sex again, refusing to listen when I told him the hospital said to wait at least six weeks. I was miserable, tired and sore and the more I struggled to love my son, the more depressed I became. When Junaid was a few months old we moved to Coatbridge and to the flat I was now the owner of, and there life became even worse. I naively thought life would have been better living away from his family. When we were no longer living with his family, his drinking escalated. He was free to drink in the privacy of his home, safe in the knowledge that no one would turn up unannounced, Coatbridge being a 30 minutes' drive away from Glasgow. Relatives would ring to make sure we were at home before arriving en masse. Not that we ever went anywhere, I was stuck at home night after night. During the day I only had Mummy and Zanera's visits to keep me sane. Fatima and Abbas had done all they could to stop us having friends, and living out in Coatbridge there were few Asian families so any chance of making new friends was nil. The thought of joining a local play group scared me, I didn't think I would have anything in common with the other mums and Pervaiz would have forbade me from going. He would be scared I would be led astray by the goris.

No one else from the big house visited, not once. If it wasn't for the visits I made to the big house, sometimes I preferred to go and stay there for a few nights to escape sex with my husband, then I would never have seen them again. I wanted to visit them because they were my family, good or bad it was all I had known. I never asked why they did not visit me. That's the way it was, we lived by their rules.

The first night in the flat, once I had unpacked a few things and Junaid was asleep, Pervaiz brought out a bottle of vodka. Putting it on the table with a bottle of coke and two glasses he instructed me, 'Pour two drinks and we celebrate.'

I had no idea as to how much vodka to pour out and opened the vodka bottle and poured the vodka into the glass. Pervaiz shouted, 'Stop! Fool what are ju doing, here give it me.'

He took the bottle from me, putting it down, lifting the glass he poured half the vodka into the other glass. Topping them both up with coke, he passed me one.

'Cheers,' he said 'Drink up.' I took a sip and gagged.

'I don't want it,' I told him putting the glass down. 'It tastes disgusting.'

Laughing at me, he lifted the glass and drank from it.

'It's nice. Try little sips not a big gulp,' he said passing the glass back.

'You shouldn't be drinking, that's haram (forbidden),' I told him, refusing the glass. Forgetting the few Tia Maria's I had drunk at the office party, which now seemed like a life time away.

'Oh be quiet, ju know nothing. Go do work, empty boxes in kitchen,' he snarled at me, dismissing me with his hand. I went to the kitchen and did as I was told, just like the big house the truth was not to be faced. Unpacking the boxes I was glad to be out of his sight and tried not to think of the demands he would make once he was drunk.

Mummy and Zanera visited often and on one of their many visits they discovered the stash of alcohol, hidden in the back of a cupboard behind some pots and pans. Mummy had brought chicken and meat and was planning on spending the afternoon cooking. Rummaging for the things she needed she was surprised to find the bottles and cans of alcohol. Refusing to believe I had been married off to an alcoholic, Mummy decided it had been left behind by the previous owners. Easier to believe the unbelievable than face the truth and the life that had been chosen for me.

The months passed by in a blur, spending my days alone at home with Junaid while Pervaiz was out at work, leaving me with no money and only the bare essentials at home, milk, bread, chapatti flour and lentils. I was too depressed to leave the house alone and I lived for Mummy's visits and trips to the shops with her, where she bought me and Junaid some treats. Her visits also meant she took over the care of Junaid.

Mummy worked in her friend Linda's designer baby clothes shop and no longer handed all her wages into the big house, keeping it to spend on her children and grandchildren, working part time meant she was able to visit as often as she did. I was struggling to cope and often thought of escaping. To where though? In the early 1990's, Glasgow was still blissfully ignorant to the problems faced by Asian children, forced marriages being the biggest problem. No one can help, is what I told myself. Days could go by and I didn't wash. I had a love hate relationship with food. Some days I starved myself and other days I binged, vomiting it up in the toilet afterwards. Binge eating days were usually when Pervaiz had done the weekly shop. There were no supermarket visits for us, instead the halal butcher shop is where the shopping was done. Along with the meat he bought biscuits, gulab jammins, sweet rusks and other calorie laden deserts for when visitors came. They rarely did so I ate it all and then vomited it all up again. I did the cooking of the breakfasts, lunches and dinners and was not very good at it. Pervaiz only drank tea for his breakfast, was never at home for lunch and preferred to eat his dinner when drunk so he never noticed the lack of taste in my cooking. Mummy preferred to concentrate on cooking without teaching me so she could get all the praise for a meal well cooked and I didn't mind not learning. Fights were a daily occurrence in the flat and some days were worse than others, especially after a night of rough and uncaring sex. These were the days in which I thought of killing myself to escape the misery.

When Junaid was eight months old I was rushed to hospital early one morning, bleeding. The nurses and doctors thought I was having a miscarriage. I was left on the trolley in the cubicle while other patients were dealt with, Pervaiz left to drop Junaid off to Mummy in Glasgow and to go to work. He had a corner shop which needed to be opened and that was more important than my unexplained bleeding. An hour or so passed when a nurse appeared and told me, 'Do you think you can manage to give us a urine sample? The doctor wants to check if you are pregnant.'

I nodded and she helped me up and onto a wheelchair and I was wheeled into the toilets. Feeling slightly woozy, I got up, entered the cubicle and shut the toilet door. Before I could sit down I passed several huge clots, I opened the door and the nurse told me to get back onto the wheelchair and rushed me to the ward.

'Have you had anything to eat? I was asked.

'We are going to prepare you for theatre and do a procedure called a D and C,' I was told, 'Find out what is causing the bleeding.'

I was embarrassed more than anything else so I said nothing. What would I tell my family? What would they say? Mummy and Zanera were called to be on standby, they shared my rhesus negative blood and the doctors were worried I might need a blood transfusion unaware of what was causing my bleeding, preparing for the worst. When I came round from my anaesthetic and D and C, Mummy was sitting in the chair next to the bed. The doctors have told her I had internal bleeding, a blood transfusion wasn't required, just some stitching to close the tears causing the bleeding, I have refused to tell them what has caused it and on my chart at the foot of the bed there is a question mark. Pervaiz had told them my stitches had burst, after the baby and Mummy asked if this was true, I went along with it not knowing what else to say. How else do I tell her what really happened? Not believing for one minute this to be the case Mummy never questioned further, scared to hear the truth although years later she told me everyone knew sex with Pervaiz had caused my bleeding. After her visit she had returned to the big house where the women all gossiped about what had happened. Eight months after a baby is born the stitches are healed with no danger of them ever bursting, still nobody cared enough to do anything, and the next day I left the hospital to go back and live with Pervaiz.

He began to say that he was going to marry again and make me live with wife number two, Abbas did it so why shouldn't he? It's what I was used to and grew up with, was his taunt for a while. He stopped saying this when I told him go ahead I couldn't care less, I said I would even give my permission. In my mind I thought if he got married again, then he would stop having sex with me.

During my pregnancy Amirah had returned from Kashmir and marrying her off was being discussed. Fatima had decided Amirah was to be given the same fate as me and was looking to marry her off to Abbas's nephew in Mirpur. Lucky for Amirah her time in Kashmir had been a godsend, mixing with the other English born children who had been banished for their 'troubles' she heard all about the agencies being set up in England to help. Scotland was way behind in dealing with the cultural differences compared to England. With the knowledge she gained from the other young people she met, she had secretly contacted the Social Work department and plans were being made to escort her from the house on her 18th birthday saving her from a forced marriage and what would probably be a life of misery. Abbas was powerless to stop her leaving, but he never disowned her for her defiance in the way he disowned me.

One day I upped and left Pervaiz. Amirah had been living in a hostel for the homeless with other young white teenagers and young people for several months and I had spoken to her a few times when she visited the big house, if I happened to be there visiting also. It was easier for her because she had Social Work involved. I envied her confidence and freedom. The night before Pervaiz had had friends visiting from England and whenever I took in cups of tea for them, Pervaiz spoke to me like I was a piece of shit. One friend off his in particular told him off, asking him to speak kindly to me as after all I was his wife and the mother of his child. Pervaiz laughed and refused to treat me with any respect. The next morning I left with Junaid and my gold from the wedding and went to The Hamish Allan Centre. We were provided with emergency accommodation until somewhere suitable to place us was found. I pawned the gold, which provided us with money so we would be financially secure. I got £3000. Amirah had stayed there for a few nights until she had been moved to a suitable hostel for the young so it seemed help was finally available. The fears and worries of young Asian women seemed at last to be taken seriously. The first night on my own was terrifying especially when one of the reception staff came to tell me Abbas had rung to ask if I was there. My absence had been noticed and with Abbas' contacts there was no hiding place. I rang Pervaiz, he was Junaid's father and regardless of how he treated me, I wanted him to know his son was safe. Pervaiz begged me to come home or at the very least meet him somewhere. He didn't shout or get angry instead spoke nicely, he sounded strange. Alone in a homeless centre and terrified of going to the big house, yet missing the security of my family, I agreed to meet Pervaiz a few days later and we met in McDonalds. We talked over coffee and he put no pressure on me to return, instead asking that I stay in contact with him and allow him access to Junaid, and I agreed.

Over the next few weeks I went from hostel to hostel, never settling in any of them, being surrounded by people and a culture I had no understanding of. The hostels were filled with white women fleeing abusive marriages or partners. They didn't understand me or my culture, I had nobody to talk to about my fears and worries, nobody to understand my dilemma. The abuse and the drinking they understood but not being able to go back to my parent's home they couldn't understand, or my fear of another forced marriage if I returned.

Throughout this time I stayed in touch with Pervaiz, allowing him access to his son, he became my 'friend' and encouraged me to socialise with the new friends I was slowly beginning to make, offering to watch Juniad, eventually having him more often than I was. We divorced Islamically in front of witnesses during this time, his cousin and a friend, thus making it official. Pervaiz said it three times.

168

'I divorce you, I divorce you, I divorce you.' And under Islamic law we were divorced. He also wrote it down in English and signed the piece of paper and gave it to me. I was happy to be divorced even though Islamically our marriage was never legal – Islam is against forced marriages. Legally, under the British laws, we wouldn't be divorced for another two years.

Having avoided any contact with the big house I bumped into Abbas and Mummy one afternoon purely by chance. Mummy was happy to see me and Abbas was pleasant and I was talked into visiting with Junaid the following day. I arrived in my trousers and polo neck, my hair cut short to a bob, which with my unruly hair resembled a bush unlike Amirah's sleek smooth version. Everyone was being nice to me even Fatima. No one made any remarks about the changes in me, nobody shouted and screamed and as always, I was fooled by their falseness.

'Ju come home, no stay hostel no look good. Vat vill people think?' Abbas started. 'Vee get Junaid back from his father, ju go college study jor Social Work and then vee find ju a new husband. End of the year ju getting married again.' I listened as he went on, Fatima smiling. Mummy was in the kitchen making cups of tea, keeping out the way of the discussions even though they involved one of her children, as always, no change there. For most of the afternoon I listened to him as he talked at me, agreeing to everything but the husband, with Abbas insisting there will be a husband. Taking a break I went to visit Amina in the house next door, we hugged as I entered.

'I'm thinking of coming back, I miss everybody and don't like being alone, I'm not happy,' I told her outlining Abbas's plans for my return. 'I don't want to get married again though and have told them.'

'Did they tell you Waquas is coming next month with his wife and the kids to stay for six months?' she asked.

'No! Oh my god, they haven't mentioned it. Mummy hasn't said anything either,' I replied.

'Don't say I told you,' she begged, fearful of the drama it would cause for her.

I reassured Amina I wouldn't tell, I knew what misery they would cause if they thought she had shared a family secret, and I decided then what I was going to do.

When I returned to the big house, Abbas demanded I tell him what my thoughts were and I asked him.

'Can I think about it? Can you take me back to the hostel and I will call you in the morning?' I knew my answer was no but I was too scared to stand up for myself face to face with him, hoping away from his glare I would find the courage.

Reluctantly he agreed knowing the law was on my side and he couldn't stop me. I knew it too and with a smile on my face I gathered Junaid's things, said my goodbyes and left. I was unaware then that it would be last time I would ever visit the big house.

The thought of living in the same house as Waquas even if only for six months was enough to change my mind and all night I wondered how I would tell Abbas, and at the same time thought how clever they were at manipulation. I had got caught up in their fake niceness, I had believed their lies. Possibly Junaid would have been returned to me, he was now spending most of his time with Pervaiz and his family and there were discussions of me signing custody over to them. I was struggling to cope with Junaid and giving him up to his father seemed like the only option available to me. There would have been no college and there would most certainly have been another husband. I would have been married off in months not the year they had promised. The next morning, at 11 o'clock when I could put it off no longer, I rang the big house. Abbas picked up right away. I pictured him, on the couch in the family room, sprawled out across it, Fatima and Mummy sitting on the couch opposite, waiting to hear what I would say.

'I've thought about it and when I get married again I want to pick my husband,' I blurted out, not even saying hello.

'Vat ju say?' Laughing he continued, 'Who bluddee vana marry ju? Ju bludee stupid, a joke!'

'If you are going to marry me off again, then I don't think I want to come back, I want to live on my own,' I told him with confidence even though my heart was thumping at standing up to Abbas. I mentioned nothing about Waquas because Abbas had not told me he was coming and it would have got Amina into trouble. I had told about Waquas's abuse and in the end nothing was done about it, but he knew I'd told. The thought of facing him terrified me. I would not have gone back to live in the big house even if Waquas was not coming to stay, I was sick and tired of always being made to feel worthless and unloved. Abbas didn't even try to sweet talk me with false promises of no marriage.

'Ju are bludee dead to me then, I have no daughter called Aisha, she is dead,' he spat through the phone.

I hung up, dead daughters don't talk.

Chapter 10   Being disowned and waiting to be owned

After that phone call my life changed forever. Junaid was spending all his time with his father while I was out experimenting with my new found freedom. I didn't leave Glasgow when Abbas told me I was dead. I didn't run away from my home like so many other Pakistani girls were doing up and down the UK, to escape the misery of a forced marriage or a miserable life. I stayed in Glasgow but I still spent the next two decades running. Running from myself. I stood out like a sore thumb everywhere I went, so different in appearance and life experiences from the new people I was meeting. In one of the hostels I had met Gaynor, a few years older than me, she too had left an abusive relationship.

Gaynor had four young children and at the weekends her mum would watch them and Gaynor took me out a few times with her. I had never been out at night, never been to nightclubs, never wore 'Western clothes', never hung around with guys as freely and openly as I was now doing, I had never had a life. All the things I had been protected from in the past, now at the age of 21 were available to me. Money wasn't a problem as Pervaiz had been giving me a few pounds here and there to allow me my nights out, anything to keep me from being a mother to Junaid and I gladly took the money. Pervaiz decided to take Junaid to Pakistan and I allowed it. I was too busy socialising and without Mummy's help I was unable to be a mum. When Abbas had told me I was dead, Mummy too behaved like I had died and I lost all contact with her. I began smoking marijuana and taking speed with my new friends and trying my hardest not to fall apart.

Some days I wanted to scream loudly, just scream and let it all out. My family didn't want me and I was losing my son. Even though I had made the choice to let him ago it still felt like I was losing him. The only option I saw as available to me, apart from continuing the life I had, was returning to the big house and there were so many times I almost picked up the phone and asked to come home, begging, in my head, to be allowed to come back from the dead. Anything would have been better than the loneliness of having no family. I thought really seriously about going back but then I thought again. Junaid would have been raised as I was, always put down and belittled for being my son and Mummy would have been made to feel guilty if she showed him love and attention. Abbas would have made sure Junaid was returned to me if I went back to the big house and did as I was told, Pervaiz would not have been allowed to keep Junaid from me. If I was married again, as I'm sure I would have been, my son would gain a step dad and who knew what misery that would cause him. I visualised the life we would have thanks to Fatima and Abbas's next choice of husband.

'We will find her a husband who hates kids and white women. She has no shame ruining our family honour in the way she has. Who does she think she is?' is what I imagined them saying.

Happiness would not be allowed for the gori's children. The best place for my son, I believed, was with his father's family, going to live with his grandparents like I had done all those years ago. It was the time in my childhood I was happiest and I hoped it would be the same for him. The only problem was he would not be returning for a long time. Even though deep down I knew I was doing the right thing for the wellbeing of my son, it broke my heart. Two weeks after they had gone, I wrote a letter to Pervaiz begging him to bring Junaid back. There was never any chance of that, they had been planning this for months. That was why he had been encouraging me to go out, exploiting my insecurities, making me feel inadequate, watching me fall apart. He saw his chance to take Junaid from me and acted on it and if I'm honest I did nothing to stop it. I was too caught up in my misery and self-loathing. The drugs helped, there was nothing else in my life. Every hostel worker and every women's refuge worker I spoke to had no idea what to say to help me. The cultural issues were too difficult for them to understand, so I smoked more marijuana and took more speed. The amphetamines (speed) gave me energy and my brain buzzed. I was constantly on the go, hiding my fears and worries. In the evening I smoked marijuana, relaxing with my new found friends and blocked out the pain.

A letter arrived from Pakistan written by Pervaiz's older brother. In it he pointed out all my wrong doings and how they didn't feel living with me was the best thing for Junaid, I lived a Western lifestyle now and not a very respectable one, from what they had heard. He also told me Junaid was happy and settled, and finished it off by stating that I could have more children if I missed Junaid. All I wanted was Junaid and another child was not something I had considered. I continued taking drugs and struggled to cope in a culture in which I did not belong, I still felt Pakistani. If a psychologist was to predict what I would do at this stage, they would say the chances were I would become promiscuous, and I didn't disappoint them but fulfilled their predictions. The baygerat (without shame) became a baygerat. Looking for love and finding what appeared to be love in so many wrong places. I slept with men if they showed me a little kindness, mistaking the sex for love and when they lost interest soon after I slept with them, I hated myself a little more. During my entire life I had been brainwashed into believing I was trash, worthless and so I expected to be treated in that way, behaving in ways which fulfilled Abbas and Fatima's hopes and aspirations for me. I was given a two-bedroom flat in a tower block in Thornliebank. Finally I had somewhere to call home.

The big house had fewer people in it. Amirah had escaped to Manchester, having had enough of the constant lectures from Abbas to return home. She had enrolled at college and was studying for her 'O' Grades she had been forced to abandon when she was taken out of school and sent to Pakistan. Abbas allowed Amirah to visit the big house, he took her out for lunch and met her for coffees and supported her financially. He was still her father and the fact she had chosen to leave home never affected their relationship. At this point in our life we had little to say to each other, both Amirah and I were caught up in our struggles to survive. I was dead to Abbas but Amirah was very much alive, more proof of the difference in the treatment of me.

Abbas had wanted me aborted because Fatima was coming over from Kashmir, a pregnant white mistress would have been difficult to explain and Abbas would make sure I never received any love or forgiveness from him. Although Amirah was pregnant soon after moving to Manchester and unmarried, she had not been banished from the family for her sins. I understood that Abbas must love her in a way he didn't love me to forgive the shame she was bringing onto the family. Living far away, her 'shame' was hidden even though it is no secret amongst the gossiping faction of the community.

Yacoub had been living in the big house, he was working and bringing a wage in, handing very little into the housekeeping and so causing frictions. There had been a huge fight one Friday night when he handed over £20 out of his weekly wage. He had been doing this for weeks but this time Abbas slapped him hard across the face furious that his son had spent the money Abbas wanted for whoring. Yacoub packed his bags and moved out. He had prepared in advance for this moment, knowing it was coming and knowing he wouldn't back down to the bullying Abbas. He was no longer a boy and almost as tall as Abbas. He was no longer scared. We tried to maintain contact which was weird. We had never been allowed to bond with each other and we were finding it difficult to do, now we were able to do so. I met Yacoub a few times after he moved out of the big house and even though he was my baby brother I was really nervous around him, wanting him to like me and at the same time fussing around him and treating him like a prince, like all Pakistani boys are treated. Yacoub had always been different to the other boys and had always preferred to do his own tasks, never bossing his sisters around and my behaviour made him uneasy. The very life he had escaped from, I tried to recreate each time we saw each other. Still Yacoub was never disowned either but soon after, he moved to Manchester and chose to sever all contact with the big house. He has never contacted anybody from the family since, preferring to live his life quietly away from their poisonous reach; the backstabbing, the gossiping and the hypocrisy. Over the last few years thanks to Facebook we have slowly been trying to build a relationship.

Zanera wasn't allowed to talk to me, forbidden by Abbas and her husband, Rasoul. Everybody else in the big house, aunts, uncles and cousins, were also told to sever contact. Apart from Yacoub, there was only Amirah. I could have talked to her but she lived in Manchester and there was unspoken envy and resentment from me because she was forgiven and I was not. Also our childhood had been spent avoiding each other thanks to Fatima and her cries of 'Apoo ik doosray nal khedo (You all just play together)'. Her cries ensured we would never play together. It wasn't what Fatima said but the way she said it, we knew by the sarcastic tone in her voice that if we played together it was a bad thing. We were all strangers to each other.

I had nobody and so I decided I wanted a baby. I had been given a two bedroom flat because the council thought I was

178

pregnant. A savvy friend I met from school days told me to take her urine sample, she was pregnant, to the doctors and get a letter. If you take that to the council you get a house, easy as that, she said and here I was in a two bed room flat and not even pregnant. It worked. By now I was mixing mostly with white people. At first I tried so hard to stay within the Pakistani community but I didn't quite succeed. I ended up making friends with Pakistani girls who were happy to socialise in the Western culture with me rather than their own culture, and Pakistani boys who were only interested in bedding me with no chance of a relationship never mind marriage. If I returned to the big house there would be any number of eager men willing to make me a wife and give me babies, such was the desire for a red passport.

Every night I would be in tears, lying in bed wide awake well into the small hours. There are no words to describe the pain and loneliness and the utter desperation I was feeling. There was not a single person in the world to whom I could turn to for help and support, I had nobody whose name I could write in the 'next of kin' sections of any forms I had to fill out. 'Keep smiling and keep going otherwise they have won,' was what I told myself over and over again. A smile on the outside to hide the pain inside. I had grown up in the big house so was an expert at hiding my feelings, I could do it.

I started dating a white man, Jack, and three months later I had stopped smoking marijuana and stopped taking speed, and I was pregnant. All I had done for the last three months was cry, cry for hours and hours at how my life had turned and for

Junaid. I was full of self-pity and self-loathing. Night after night without fail I cried but now I cried in his company instead of alone in the dark. Anything could trigger me off. I decided I wanted a baby and he agreed, telling me he wanted a baby too. The youngest in his family, he was the only one without a child and he didn't for a minute consider my fragile state and the wider implications of what we were planning, but instead focused on my tears and how he could stop them. I conceived the week we stopped using contraceptives. The ache in my heart eased a little. I was happy I had been given the chance to be a mother again. Welcomed into his family, I instantly bonded with them and they were delighted with the news after the initial shock. Mum, Gran Kate, Dad, brothers, sisters and grandchildren all living happily with normal relationships. I looked forward to visiting their house in East Kilbride, Sundays were the best for visiting because the entire family arrived for Sunday dinner and the house was full and it reminded me of the big house but without the unhappiness. Here there was laughter, good banter and acceptance. It was just the number of people that reminded me of the big house. Twenty or thirty people in the big house was normal. In total there were 11 who lived there but then there was Tabassum and her husband and children who visited, Abbas's brother Haroon and his family and other first cousins of Abbas and Fatima. In a Pakistani household that can amount to a fairly large number. In Gran Kate's house on a Sunday there were usually 15 people there for dinner.

As my pregnancy progressed I began spending more time over there. Being pregnant meant I lost contact with Gaynor and the other friends I had made while living in the hostels. We had been friends or so I thought, but that was when we were all taking drugs and now I had stopped we had nothing in common. With no family of my own, my unborn child's family became my family and they welcomed me with open arms.

I was almost six months pregnant when Mummy defied Abbas and came to visit. News of my pregnancy had travelled to the big house and so she arrived to lecture me on how I should have waited and got married. Mummy's ways and thinking were whatever Fatima and Abbas told her.

'You've got a cheek to say anything, you have four children to him and you never married him. And you never married Zanera's dad either, so please spare me the lecture.'

The truth hurt and my family's way of dealing with it was to avoid it. They would never discuss the hypocrisy in their stupid arguments and rants. Away from the big house it was easy to question the flaws in our upbringing. Oblivious or choosing not to see the life her children had been forced to live, Mummy didn't like hearing what we were able to now tell her. For a time she refused to believe how cruel Fatima had been and even now finds it hard to understand the problems her children faced as they grew up. My relationship with Mummy has always been a minefield, happily chatting one minute and boom, an explosion the next. Most of the time I never see it coming but I would say something and off she would storm, red in the face, cursing and swearing at her misfortune to have such ungrateful bastard children. Fatima who had looked after all the children had told Mummy on a regular basis that we were 'ungrateful' and so she believed her, brainwashed into thinking the worst. Her chance of a normal relationship with us was damaged beyond repair.

For the next three months Mummy visited on a regular basis and we tried to create a mother-daughter relationship, both of us smiling on the outside but screaming at each other on the inside. We were walking on egg shells, scared to say the wrong thing, the thing that would trigger an argument. When I gave birth to my second son she was there and fussed and clucked like any proud grandmother. Babies she is good with, anything older not so good. Later she told me that when she returned to the big house she was met with taunts from Imtiaz and Jamal.

'Does he have blue eyes and blond hair?' asked Jamal.

'Bet she's calling him John,' Imtiaz laughed at her.

My son had brown eyes and jet black hair and holding him in my arms I was overcome with emotion. His skin was olive and I was reminded of Junaid. This was a bittersweet moment in my life. The joy of being a mother again and the sadness of not having Junaid. The birth of my second son, Nathaniel, helped stop the tears and I soon busied myself with the role of being a mum. This time round I had positive support from his dad's family. There were still times when I cried for Junaid but I was told by those around me that time would ease the pain.   When Nathaniel was a few months old, Mummy brought a video with her on one of her weekly visits.

'It's Junaid's 3rd birthday party, I've watched it already,' she said excitedly.

I made us tea while she pottered around checking on Nathaniel in his Moses basket. A few weeks had passed since Junaid turned 3, Mummy was sending a parcel in the post and had enclosed some gifts and a card from me. Settling down to watch the video with her I felt my heart sink and tried not to cry, I was seeing him all grown up and laughing and I could see he was adored by his father's family. Standing on a chair, in front of a table laden with food and the birthday cake, the wall behind decorated with balloons and banners and birthday cards, he was talking to the camera about the gifts he has received and pointing to the cards behind him. Unable to stop the tears I got up after a few minutes and switched it off. The first ten minutes had shown me all I need to see and know. Mummy didn't understand why I was crying and kept asking, 'What's wrong hen?' We are not a huggy family so she kept her distance and didn't try to comfort me. The times we have tried to hug have been too awkward. My tears meant I was unable to answer her for a while and also my anger towards her stopped me, I was scared of what I might say. She had watched the video and thought I would enjoy it as much as she had. Once I calmed down, I explained to her 'I sent clothes and a card. On the wall behind him they have every bastarding birthday card sent to him, apart from the one I sent. I saw them getting him to point to your card asking who sent that and he replies nanny, who sent this khala (aunty), who sent this, his bloody little friend across the street. Where the hell was my card? They were showing off the presents you and other people gave him and ignoring me completely.'

I allowed my son to go live with his grandparents, the least they could have done was acknowledge me, but Junaid was not told of my existence, the boy without a mother. I finally heard through Mummy that they had told him I had died in the hope that he would never try and contact me as he got older. They thought that this was in his best interests. I busied myself with being a mother to the son I had, promising him I would not be the type of parent I had grown up with. I would do my hardest to be nothing like the three of them. I was trying to create a home for us, but I really had no idea how to.

The circumcision of Nathaniel at eleven weeks old destroyed my relationship with his father. A Protestant, he saw no need for his son to undergo unnecessary suffering nor could he understand why I thought it necessary. My thinking was very much Muslim and baby boys need to suffer, and even though I was not a very good Muslim I tried my level best and somewhere I did it to please Abbas. All male Muslims are circumcised, it's what makes them Muslim. There was never any question in my mind of whether it was being done or not. Refusing to budge on my decision, I took him to Dr Maddock's surgery one Saturday morning along with Mummy. She was paying the £50 that was charged to do it privately rather than putting up with a year long wait on the NHS. She had phoned to book the appointment weeks before. When Junaid was circumcised he cried for two days, inconsolable, sleeping for little half hours and then painfully wailing for hours on end. Dr Maddock asked if Nathaniel felt pain.

'He's a baby,' I told him, gently taking him from his arms after the snip. 'All babies feel pain.'

'He is a very brave baby he only flinched, no screams. Maybe he will not need painkillers,' he smiled at me. Remembering Junaid and his screams, I smiled back and told him I would take the painkillers he was offering for him. Returning to my flat with him and Mummy, I waited for the screaming. He stirred and I put him on my breast where he fed contently before falling asleep. At tea time he woke up for another feed and Mummy changed his nappy. A task I was unable to face because of the blood, yet I still sneaked a look at the blood filled nappy. Once he was changed it was back on the breast for another feed and sleep. At eleven thirty Mummy was yawning and I told her I would phone a taxi for her and send her home, insisting I would be fine. Locking the door I went to bed with my boy who still did not scream. The next morning he woke for a feed and he was gurgling and cooing full of delight as I fussed over him. Being a mum second time around away from the evil of the big house and the misery of the marriage I had, was completely different. I was happy. When my relationship with Nathaniel's father ended it was because of the constant arguing. We had argued over the circumcision, and when it had been done we continued to argue. I didn't want any more arguments in my life. I had a failed marriage and now I had a failed relationship. In my heart I knew I was doing the right thing. Mummy nagged constantly saying that I should try again. 'You've made your bed you need to lie in it, hen,' she said.

'I don't like the way it's made and I want to make it again,' was my simple reply. I walked from a miserable forced marriage and lost my son in the process, so for me to stay in a miserable relationship was never going to happen. I had sacrificed too much to be unhappy with a man, any man. I continued to see Nathaniel's grandparents, still visited them regularly. They didn't judge and tried hard not to take sides with their son. They were glad to still have their grandson in their life.

My relationship with Mummy was breaking down again. I was fed up of pretending everything was okay. I had unresolved emotional issues and I asked too many questions. 'Why did you stay with Abbas and Fatima? Why did you not leave? We could have been happy,' I told her. Mummy was still living in the big house and had her own issues to deal with and preferred to distance herself from me, maybe it was easier to stay away than listen to the constant questions I asked.

Nathaniel had celebrated his 1st birthday and weeks had passed since I had spoken to her. Once again unable to keep that smile plastered on the outside, she had given in to her demons and was bed bound, wrapped up in the safety of Prozac and strong painkillers. For over a year she had been listening to 'Your daughter is a slut', 'Wearing short miniskirts, the whore,' 'Posing for dirty magazines AND being in blue movies is what I heard too', 'Living with a white man and their baby not even married, no shame.' Even lying in her bed there was no escape

186

and they came into her room and described the shame Amirah and I brought on the family and the community. They do not care that she was on the verge of a massive breakdown. She was wailing and moaning and clearly needing help, instead they made her demons worse. They ignored or forgot that Abbas had four children to her and was still living in sin with her. As is the way in most Pakistani homes, the sins of the men were never discussed.

When Mummy stopped visiting I just saw it as another rejection. She lived fifteen minutes away and I saw her once a year and Amirah and Yacoub, living in Manchester, she visited five maybe six times a year. Visiting me and going out and about with me meant she had to listen to the lectures from Abbas and the others in the big house on how she was seen walking down the street with me and my bastard child and how the community was talking about us and how we had no shame. It was easier for Mummy to stay away from me to please the big house. When things got really difficult for me to deal with, I started smoking marijuana again although I stayed away from the other drugs the people I socialised with were trying. When I was living in the hostels I had tried speed as well as marijuana but had said no to the Ecstasy tablets, cocaine and even heroin when some of the other women were using. Heroin always terrified me and I never felt life was so low that I had to inject. I enrolled at college, keen not to be a single parent sponging off the Government and I studied for the next year and a half. Social Work was still my passion especially working with children but I chose to do an NC in Computing, not choosing to follow my dream because despite everything I still wanted to please Abbas. A Social Worker in his eyes was not a good profession so I chose something completely different, something he would approve of. I made lots of friends which I was finding easy to do but holding onto friendships I was not so good at. My lack of family meant I became very full on and intense with the friends I was making in a very short space of time. I had no family and tried to recreate it with my friends, suffocating them with my neediness. There were always new friends to be found. I got another white boyfriend but we were totally unsuitable for each other, both of us carrying truckloads of baggage. Thomas was meeting a friend at my college one afternoon and asked me out on a date. I had never met him before and didn't know his friends but we arranged to go for dinner the following Thursday night at Mother India in the city centre. Thomas was from Dublin and he told me over dinner that he was working as a builder and saving money to return home. I told him my entire life story which is what I always did in any new relationship. Sharing everything so there were no secrets. It always felt important for me to do this, I had to tell about my family set up, my forced marriage and about Junaid, I was different to the white people I was mixing with. By the end of the night Thomas had asked me to be his girlfriend and I said yes. For now ignoring that he said he wanted to return to Dublin. All that mattered was that he wanted me that was enough. Thomas was like all the men I have dated, kind and caring. Thomas made me feel special and loved but the voices of Abbas and Fatima were stronger and I soon began having doubts. I'm sure we brought out the worst in each other and when he moved in a few weeks after we started dating, Nathaniel's dad, understandably, went ballistic.

Three months after Thomas had moved in I agreed to move to Dublin with him. Thomas was in touch with his father back home and was getting excited about the Celtic Tiger. Dublin was in the grips of an economic growth and Thomas wanted to be a part of it. His father shared the news and stories of cousins and friends all doing really well and would beg his only son to return. Thomas tried to persuade me to move over with him and make a new life. At first I refused. On the plus side, I was at college, having passed the NC Computing course I had enrolled and was half way through my HNC in Business Studies. On the minus side, my relationship with Nathaniel's father was full of arguments and he had begun to discourage me from visiting his parent's home. I had been close to his sister, Rachel, but she too was withdrawing from me the more I was arguing with Jack. Jack wanted me back, he said he wanted us to be a family and my refusal to go back meant he began treating me in the way Abbas and Fatima had. Mocking me and arguing over silly things and finally stopping Nathaniel from visiting, knowing how important his family were to me and my son. I still tried to keep in contact with them until the day I turned up at Gran Kate's door with Nathaniel and Rachel refused to let me in, taking her brother's side over mine.

The lack of contact I had with my own family and now this rejection meant I didn't stop to think about what I was about to do but instead I packed up my life, put it into storage and flew out to Dublin to make a new home with a man I barely knew. This was becoming a pattern in my life, running away.

Chapter 11　Dublin is my new home

Dublin was the best thing I ever did even though at first it was terrifying. Knowing only a handful of people, I was even lonelier than when I lived in Glasgow. Being so far from the drama of life with my family was liberating. I was no longer worrying that I would bump into someone who would report back that I was wearing a mini skirt, was talking to men, going to pubs and living like a gori. What else did they expect me to do? If you live amongst white people like I was, having no other option, well apart from returning home to be forced into a marriage, then it's difficult to live like a Pakistani. At last I was free from all the backstabbing and nasty rumours that I had to put up with in Glasgow and the people of Dublin welcomed me with open arms. Being Scottish was enough; the Irish have a great love for the Scots. The fact that I looked different was never questioned and I soon made friends.

At this time my relationship with Thomas ended, unable to withstand the different people we were both becoming. Thomas was back home, surrounded by friends and family and managed to find work the first week after we had arrived. We were living with his parents at first and then moved into the flat we were going to be renting, he was out all day while I was struggling to find work. I had applied to endless shops to work as a Sales Assistant. I also was dealing with the fact that I had taken Nathaniel away from his dad and extended family. Even though Nathaniel had not seen them for almost two months, I had let

Jack know I was moving and he realised too late that he wanted his son in his life. I still stressed over it. Not seeing his dad for so long had made it easier for Nathaniel to not miss him, two months is a long time for an almost four year old boy and he had stopped asking to visit while we had still been in Glasgow. Thomas had a good relationship with Nathaniel and accepted him and when we broke up I continued to stay in the flat and we tried to stay friends for Nathaniel's sake. I was changing in Dublin, I was no longer as needy and clingy.

I had run away and it felt good, it felt good knowing that the big house were completely ignorant as to how I was living my life. Two months after I had moved, Mummy came to visit and stayed for a week. As she was leaving she told me she would never be back to visit, the fear of flying was too much for her to make the journey again. I suggested that she could get the ferry and Nathaniel and I could meet her at Belfast and then travel to Dublin but she said the ferry made her sick. Mummy was just looking for an excuse not to come back, no more criticism from the big house if she severed contact with the dead daughter. I never wanted to return to Glasgow which meant there was a possibility I would never see her again. My relationship with Mummy was built on criticism and resentment. When she was pregnant with me Abbas had demanded she abort, over and over they argued. Then Fatima had arrived and she had to share her man with his wife. There is a part of Mummy that resents me for having had the strength to walk away from the big house, while she stayed and I thought if I never saw her again then that was life and I would get on with it. Having another relationship break down and losing contact with Thomas's family, although I still saw him it seemed silly going to visit his parents who I didn't really know anyway, made me think of Gran Kate and what Nathaniel was missing out on.

'I'm going home,' I tearfully told Majella, my neighbour and friend. 'I don't really know anyone and it was a stupid idea. My relationship was over and what's the point of staying, I need to be near Nathaniel's family. And no matter how fucked up they are, my own family.'

'Give it six months, sure you've only been here a few months. If you still feel the same then go home, at least you can say you tried,' Majella replied.

There was nothing really for me to go back to, no home, no family and no real friends. At least here in Dublin I had a roof over my head and a friend who seemed to care. Majella was my neighbour and married with two young children. She was tiny, so tiny she could get away with wearing clothes for a thirteen year old girl. She wore her dark hair in a sleek bob and even with two young children always managed to look good. She dressed to please herself and not what the latest fashion dictated and whenever I was out with her, it was guaranteed that somebody would comment on her bag or coat or boots or something. When Thomas and I had moved in she introduced herself and told us if we needed anything to just knock at her door. During the day when Thomas was at work, I would spend time with Majella, taking the children to the park if it was nice, staying at home or going to Bewley's coffee shop in Grafton Street. When my relationship ended she would sit with me in the evenings while I cried over my failure to maintain a relationship. She had been with her husband, Sean, since they were both 12 year olds, and years later they were still happy. A lot of my friends took drugs and Majella was no different. In the evening when she had put the children to bed she rolled a spliff or two to relax. I spent many evenings with her, getting high and talking about our lives.

I ended up staying in Dublin for just over three years. Unable to find a job I had applied for a government funded course aimed at encouraging women to get back to work, Majella had told me about it. I was accepted along with eight other women, mostly older, some with children my age. For the first week we get to know each other over endless cups of tea and coffee and discussed what our business idea would be. The course we were on was setting up a business and learning all the different aspects to it. I was not bothered about what we did, I was just glad to be doing something with my time. Instead I listened mostly to the ideas they were all coming up with and watched them, all laughing and joking. Every group setting always has someone who is the leader and in our group it was Carmel. She was in her 50's and I learned over the week that she was a widow with two grown up children. Her idea was a florists, she spent most of her time gardening and so to her it made sense. Ann, was also in her 50's, married with two teenage sons. Ann's idea was to set up our own beauty salon, offering all the usual beauty treatments along with tarot card readings.

194

Niamh was a few years older than me and was the course co-ordinator, she sat in with us some of the time and listened and took notes, looking to us all as if she was taking our ideas seriously. Another idea suggested by Karen, a married woman in her 40's, was a dog walking agency, advertising and getting clients and walking their dogs while they were out at work. The five days passed by in a blur of brainstorming with no idea being the one we could all agree on. I was excited and happy to be getting to know all of the women. Fiona was the same age as me and had a seven year old daughter. She too was a single parent, the only other one on the course. We hung out together, chatting and getting to know each other. The women were fascinated by my life story and as always I was asked lots of questions. The following week we had a visitor. Pearse O'Rahilly was introduced to the group and we were told he was going to help us in deciding what our business idea would be. Pearse was an editor and I thought it had already been decided that we would set up a free, monthly, community newspaper with local news, an entertainment guide and a section for children, along with the usual classifieds and advertisements. An Irish version of The Glaswegian is what I thought of it as. Most of the women on the course were against the idea, telling Pearse their writing skills were woeful and that they hadn't written anything since their school days. He reassured everyone that with his help we would be able to write a piece ready for publishing. Pearse was then hired to be the editor and came in three times a week for meetings and one to one discussions with us on editorial content for the newspaper. He also helped in getting advertising and taught us how to set up interviews for the articles we would be writing, how to source information and most importantly how to write a good article. We would need to learn all these skills before we were ready to print our first edition.

Nathaniel was at school from 8.45am to 1.30pm which fitted in with my course hours, his school was a ten minute walk from where I studied, allowing me to drop him off and collect him without having to pay for and rely on childcare. Majella had asked me one day why Nathaniel was not enrolled at school and when I told her he was only four years old she had laughed and said in Dublin children attended school at four and she arranged an interview for the local primary school for me and Nathaniel started the following Monday.

Pearse thought I had a talent for writing and nurtured it, and with his help and praise I began writing every night. My thoughts and ramblings, straight from my head onto paper, no censoring of anything. I would write pages and pages about the state of the world and even tried poetry. Just as when I was a child and books were my best friend, now pen and paper became my best friend. I never wrote about the big house, I was nowhere near ready, emotionally I was still a mess. Ann was a huge support to me on the course. I think she saw the lost little girl trying hard at being strong. We became friends instantly and during the years I spent there, I would refer to her as my Irish mammy and her husband Martin, my daddy. I spent Christmas with them, birthdays and any other special occasions. Weekends and evening were pretty much spent with them also.

Fiona and I were designated to be the nightclub reviewers for the newspaper, both being the youngest there was no need to vote, it had already been decided by the older participants on the course. Up until this point I hadn't been clubbing in Dublin. I had been happy to stay in and write my journals or spend my weekends round at my Irish family's home. Before our first review I rang the chosen nightclub and explained who I was, where I was calling from like Pearse had coached me. The woman I spoke to was extremely helpful and delighted that we had chosen their club. She asked for both our names and told me we were on the guest list. Fiona was more excited than I was by this news telling me we could review The Kitchen, The Red Box and the Temple Theatre and that getting on the guest lists for those clubs would be amazing, no more queuing and no more paying. Ann and Martin were babysitting and off I went for my first Dublin nightclub experience. The doormen were not as nice as the woman on the phone and mocked my name, accent and told me neither names were on the guest list. When Fiona tried to explain they refused to allow us entry. The review was still written based on the doorman's manners, or lack of and it was published in the first edition of The Dublin News.

My article on 'Dublin's Shame' about child prostitution visible on the streets but with nothing being done about it, was also published and was chosen to go on the front page of the newspaper. I celebrated with Ann and her family. As for my own family, back home, it was if they didn't exist. There was no one to share the news with. I could have called Mummy but it had been months since I had last spoken to her and my resentment towards her for not calling me to see if I was ok, meant I didn't call her. Good moments like these were always tinged with sadness, reminders that you were alone. At the age of 28 I had never moved on from smoking marijuana even though I could have had access to Ecstasy and cocaine. Most of the people I was mixing with were taking them, I was never tempted, happy getting high with marijuana. Dublin changed that and in Dublin I was tempted. I was far away from home and nobody would know I had taken Class A drugs. Fiona was out most weekends, queuing to get in to all the trendy nightclubs, taking illegal drugs as is the norm for many young people. Every week she would ask me to come out with her and every week I made my excuses and stayed in, until the next edition of the paper was being prepared and she chose the Temple Theatre for the next nightclub to be reviewed. Once again Ann offered to babysit. This time we were ushered in politely as is the norm when you are on the guest list. Treated like VIP's we were given free drinks and we mingled amongst the clubbers asking questions which would help write the review. Fiona was the photographer for the evening. The collecting of the information I need having been got out the way, I took my first ever Ecstasy, just a half to ease me in. Slowly I sensed the change, my skin began to tingle, my senses sharpened and my heart was certainly beating faster. I started to dance and spend the next few hours lost in a trance on the dance floor, leaving only to get a drink and have a cigarette or go to the bathroom. Eyes closed hearing the music. 'Silence' by Delerium, a song that will forever remind me of Dublin and of the years I spent living there. At the end of the night I was still high and I went to a party with Fiona and her friends, taking the other half of my pill when I got there but refusing the lines of coke, happy to be on my E buzz. I didn't care that the hard-core ravers found it amusing.

My hair had been cut short before I had left Glasgow and now away from the prying eyes I took it up a level. Entering the local barbers one afternoon, after spending days walking past waiting for it to be empty of customers, I coughed and the owner looked up and informed me, 'I'm a barbers, I cut men's' hair.'

'I want it shaved off,' I told her.

'What? The lot of it. Are you sure?'

I told her I had never been surer of anything. She shaved my head down to a number two and over time became a friend as well as my barber. My hair grew pretty fast so visits were regular. I bleached it blonde and then dyed it whatever colour suited my mood, shades of reds, blues and purples. It was when it was electric blue I got the most comments. Along with the constant hair dying, I was also getting tattoos and piercings, three tattoos and a tongue, lip and belly button piercing, my nose was pierced already thanks to my fake wedding. I wore a hoop through my bottom lip and a smaller hoop through my nose.

Pearse had great faith in my writing talent and encouraged me to write my memoirs. We would meet some

199

Saturday mornings in a little coffee shop near St Stephen's Green Shopping Centre, frequented by writers and journalists. To me Pearse was a father figure and I adored our time away from the course, relaxing over coffee and discussing life. I shared some of the big house stories with him, trusting him with my emotions, knowing he would not exploit them. He was never sleazy or touchy-feely with me and I instinctively trusted him. I was not ready to write my memoirs. It was still too raw and it was too painful to examine the past under a microscope, which is what writing them would have entailed. Being constantly told I would amount to nothing, it was hard to believe anything else, even when there were good, kind people telling me different. Soon I was tempted to try Ecstasy again and this time I was hooked, the come downs bad though they were, were worth it. Ecstasy was first used in the 1960's to treat married couples in therapy, the effect of the tablet allowing them to open up and explore their feelings honestly and that was what I did. Everyone around me was happy and accepting, nobody gave a damn that I was of Pakistani origin. Abbas had talked me into believing I would never be accepted by white people but only by Pakistani people. Here in Dublin, lost in the music, on the dance floor surrounded by friends, well apart from Fiona, the rest of the friends I was dancing with were clubbing friends, friends I met only on the dance floor, still I knew it was just another lie. White people were accepting me, it was the Pakistani side who had let me go. Really believing that it was all lies would take a while. Of the two races that make up my mix, white, in my experience, is more accepting and forgiving, less judgemental and less controlling.

Living in Dublin I became a very spiritual person, spending most of my time with Ann and Martin it was inevitable. Ann more than Martin was into spirituality and she would talk to me for hours, helping me discover who I was, helping to stop the pain from the past affecting the person I was today. It worked a little, but I was still constantly changing my hair, getting piercings, more tattoos, smoking marijuana, crying out for help and at the same time insisting I needed no help. Ann and Martin knew I smoked dope and allowed me to smoke in their company, never making me feel like I was a failure, never judging and telling me off. Instead they allowed to make my own choices and mistakes. I kept smiling determined not to end up like Mummy, bed bound, dozed up on Prozac and wailing.

Ann played a game with me one afternoon, getting me to close my eyes and talking to me, getting me to imagine I am walking through the woods into a house and having me describe certain things along the way. It was a test to see how I see myself, at the end she was amazed and laughed at me a little, not unkindly.

'You see yourself as white with blond hair. And look at you, you're brown, my dear,' she smiled.

The voices in my head told me I was a gori, it's all I had ever heard. The mirror showed one image and in my head it was the complete opposite. Even though I knew I was mixed race with brown skin I saw myself as white. I had moved to Dublin so

I could escape the ways in which Abbas and Fatima still controlled Mummy, discouraging her from having a relationship with me and escaping from my need to be loved by Abbas. However I began to realise I carried the big house madness with me, inside my head. I had brought it along and allowed it to affect my everyday life. Escape wouldn't be a possibility for many years to come.

I discovered Reiki - a Japanese technique for stress reduction and relaxation that also promotes healing. I was writing an article on the topic for the newspaper as it was becoming the 'in thing to do'. As part of the interview the Reiki Practitioner offered me a free session, three really. Reiki is always done over three hour long sessions, preferably within seven days for maximum results, she told me. Healing was the part that attracted me, lying down on the practitioner's table with a blanket over me, the lights were dimmed and scented candles were burning, while background music of the ocean and other soft and gentle sounds of nature were playing. Eyes closed with the healing hands travelling over the twelve chakras was heaven for me. I loved it and after the first session booked the next one before I left. A few months later I had saved up the money and enrolled on a weekend course to learn Reiki.

Having becoming friendly with a Reiki Master, I was intrigued by the whole process of changing yourself and your attitudes, and the results that come from learning this technique. I arrived at the Temple Bar Healing Centre one cold wet February morning. It was Valentine's Day and this was a gift to myself. There were six of us and the Reiki Master, we sat and listened to his talks and he performed different relaxation and meditating sessions. We discussed our hopes and fears for most of the morning and were then initiated and our ability to heal was unlocked. At the end of the session I was told by my Master to stay away from drugs, until I have completed the course at least. I had met with him a few times before the weekend and had been honest with him about my drug taking. I smoked that night and returned the next day to complete the course. I began a slow process of change rather than the quicker way it could have been had I listened to my Master. For me smoking marijuana was the only thing that stopped me from cracking up completely, when I have been in my darkest hours, alone in the world with not a single person to call, it has been the drug that had saved me, getting high to make everything alright in my world.

Before my Reiki initiation I felt sorry for myself and would cry for my lost childhood. My childhood was gone and no amount of tears would bring it back or change it. I became aware of the children who were suffering much worse than I ever did. I recognised I was an adult, I was free, children all over the world are suffering, and every minute of every day and in comparison to many my childhood was nowhere near as bad. After that weekend, the self-pity started fading and I was able to talk about my childhood without any tears. It would take many more years before I would learn to like myself though.

Half way into the second year of the business course I left. Friction between myself and the woman in charge was enough reason for me to walk out. Niamh had not really said or done anything to cause me to walk out, it was my problems and issues with authority that had created the friction. I would give her attitude whenever she spoke to me, I was looking for ways in which to sabotage something I was good at and that I enjoyed. Meetings with Pearse and the others on the course did not persuade me to go back, really I needed an excuse to give it up and she was it. My head told me I wasn't good enough to be there, even though my writing was being praised. I felt like a fake who would soon be caught out. I couldn't believe I deserved the title 'Journalist,' so I did what I always did and would continue to do for years, not knowing how to stop my self-destruction, I walked away. I sabotaged chances available to me, never believing I was worthy of it. Happiness had been denied to me in my childhood and as an adult I didn't know how to accept it.

I stayed in touch with Pearse after I left and we would meet for chats and feedback on the writing I continued doing with his encouragement. It was not for the newspaper. I stayed in touch with Ann and Fiona and continued to visit Ann as always. Fiona I saw every other weekend for a night of partying. I also found a part time job in a clothes shop near the Ha'ppeny Bridge. I worked four days a week from 9am till 2pm. I now relied on Ann for childcare and she happily took Nathaniel to school after I had dropped him at hers in the morning and collected him when he finished school at 1.30pm. After I finished work I would go to Ann's and she would have something ready for me to eat, most evenings we stayed for dinner. Sitting round sharing stories and watching Nathaniel perform his plays. He was five coming up for six and loved singing and dancing. Nathaniel was happy and loved and I had put to the back of my mind his family back home. At the weekends Nathaniel and I would go to the cinema, shopping, trips to the park and on rainy days art galleries and museums. Every other month we went to Belfast and would spend the day shopping and having lunch and then strolling through the city before we returned home to Dublin. One of our favourite times was St Patrick's Day when the River Liffey was turned green to celebrate; it was the colour of the river we liked rather than the actual day. Too many people getting drunk and fighting meant we never stayed around to watch the celebrations. Phoenix Park was another favourite and we would spend days exploring it. Majella had moved out of the flat and into a house, she had wanted something bigger and with a garden. We still stayed in touch. Life was good. Working part time I earned enough to get by. I was never one for saving my pennies instead spending them on creating happy memories.

Nearly two years had passed and I knew it was time for Nathaniel to visit his dad and grandparents for Christmas. This was the first time they had seen him since we left, although we kept in touch with letters and phone calls. I could never understand why Jack and his family would not visit us in Dublin even when I told them they could stay at our flat if they visited. Jack said he would never set foot in Dublin, too many Catholics for his Protestant mentality. When I said there were many Protestants living in Dublin too, he said he didn't care. Jack flew out to Dublin the day after Nathaniel finished school for the Christmas holidays and waited in the airport for an hour until it was time for his flight back to Glasgow. I didn't understand but then I wasn't a Protestant. Coming back three weeks later Nathaniel was heartbroken, missing them every day. The love from Ann and Martin unable to compensate for the love from his grandparents, aunts, uncles and dad. I would have stayed in Dublin forever, happily settled and loving life, but I promised Nathaniel we would go back.

Four months later we flew back to Glasgow, leaving behind our belongings in Ann and Martin's attic. I planned on shipping them over once we had settled in our new flat. For months I had been organising our return with the help of his dad. Our relationship had for so long been arguments and accusations. Jack never let me forget that I had left Glasgow and taken his son and never forgave me for moving Thomas in either, so it was nice to be able to talk about positive things and plan our return. He told me had found a place for us, a friend of his was renting out a two bedroom flat in Shawlands, and not long after that phone call I booked our tickets and we said our sad farewells, promising to stay in touch and visit. Once again I returned to Glasgow.

There was no two bedroom flat. Jack had just wanted his son back in Glasgow and told me what I needed to hear. He had tricked me into returning to nothing, arriving at Glasgow Airport laden down with luggage. Jack suggested that I go into a homeless unit and he would take Nathaniel to his mum's house.

He had seen no other way of getting his son back. Instead I rang Mummy at the big house.

'Hello, may I speak with Margaret please?' I said in my poshest voice, which by then had an Irish twang. My voice was not recognised and Mummy was called to the phone. If the big house knew it was me calling Mummy, I would be sworn at for daring to call and the phone hung up by Fatima or Abbas or one of their children. The only way to speak to Mummy was to lie, to pretend to be a friend and not her child. Knowing there was nothing she could really do to help, I wanted to tell her my problems anyway. I just wanted to have somebody to call even though I know it is pointless, I was secretly hoping she can help. After her only visit to see me in Dublin, phone calls to the big house and to speak to Mummy were sporadic, although I had called to let her know I was returning to Glasgow.

'Oh hen, you know you cannae come here,' she started, panicking already.

'I'm not stupid,' I told her, 'I've got nowhere to go, is there not anybody that can help? One of your friend's maybe? I really don't want to go to a hostel.'

She told me to call back in five minutes, which I did.

'Aunty Wilma says you can go to hers. Have you got a pen?'

'Hurry up and write it down.' she said, desperate to get me off the phone, not wanting to have to explain who she was talking to, the dead daughter.

I arrived at Aunty Wilma's. The last time I saw her I was fifteen years old. A huge fallout between her and Mummy had caused a rift, and a chance meeting had re-established their friendship while I was living in Dublin. There was no awkwardness and I was told to stay as long as I needed while she fussed over me. I thanked her over and over again.

'There is nothing to thank me for, couldn't have you sleeping on the streets,' she replied.

We stayed up late into the night, catching up on all the years and she was the same kind Aunty Wilma from my troubled childhood. The next day Mummy arrived and the awkwardness began. She criticised my hair cut and the colour - it was peroxide blonde and shaved down to a number two; tut tutted at my piercings, thankfully the tattoos were covered up or she might have gone crazy. The differences between Mummy and Aunty Wilma were huge, especially in their treatment of me.

'Why does she not like me? Why can't she be nice?' I asked poor Aunty Wilma.

Aunty Wilma never had an answer for me, instead she listened and soothed without any judging, allowing me to cry my eyes out. Mummy found my relationship with Aunty Wilma difficult to witness, envious of the closeness even after I hadn't seen her for so many years, forgetting her own bond with her step granddaughter, Mirrium.

Nathaniel had to be enrolled at school and it was decided by Gran Kate that he went to the one near her house. His two older cousins went there too so it would not be as daunting being the new kid mid-way through term. A week after returning, he started school and moved in with his gran. My relationship with Kate was improving because my son was living with her now. It was the best thing to do, my son needed stability and I was unable to provide it. My head was all over the place from the alternative treatments I was trying, and taking Ecstasy wasn't helping either. I had no idea who I was anymore, the smile was starting to crack and after much discussions with Mummy and especially with Aunty Wilma, I decided that I would go back to Dublin, alone. Nathaniel seemed happy living with Gran Kate and I didn't believe I was a good enough mother to raise my son. The plan was I would come back to Glasgow in six months after having worked and saved the deposit for a flat and most importantly sorted my head out. Instead I became even more lost, spending the money I earned on drugs and partying, returning home twice a month to visit my son and buying toys and clothes to ease the guilt I felt at leaving him behind. I was sleeping on friend's floors and couches, going from job to job, never lasting more than a few weeks anywhere. Drifting from one short-lived fling to another, never being faithful, looking for someone to love me when really I needed to love myself. I knew I had to rid myself of the voices from the big house; I just didn't know how to, or if it was even possible. I avoided visiting Ann and Martin and although I still rang them, I made excuses whenever they asked me round for tea or a chat. I was too busy trying to silence the voices of Abbas and Fatima.

The Reiki wasn't working for me anymore and so I tried a technique called Re-birthing. I had a chance meeting in a coffee shop one afternoon with an older man, I was reading one of his leaflets and he began a conversation with me. Re-birthing along with many other alternative therapies was his forte. Over coffee he explained the re-birthing process and once again I was fascinated by something that promised to heal and booked an appointment for the following week. Stephen assured me it would take no longer than an hour. At £35 per hour I was worried about the cost especially as I was flying to Glasgow the next day to visit Nathaniel for the week, staying at Aunty Wilma's as there was nowhere else I could go. We started by discussing my life, and Stephen took notes, we talked about my childhood and life as it was now. After the discussion I laid down on the table, similar to one used by beauticians and a blanket was placed over me. Stephen got me to meditate and I entered a trance-like state, aware of his voice yet floating, I was taken to my earliest memory and then gently moved through the years until I reached the present. The session lasted four hours and I cried for most of it, he told me all my life I had been held down and was craving love and had many issues that I needed to address. I had been unprepared for my re-birthing; he had assured me on that chance visit the week before that most sessions never went over the hour, some lasted maybe two. Stephen told me he allowed the session to go on as he felt that I had to deal with all the emotional baggage I carried. He also said it was one of the most difficult re-birthings he had witnessed – difficult for me because I had so many negative beliefs about myself. He allowed me to pay what I owed in dribs and drabs over the next few months and advised me strongly to stay away from all drugs. I had been honest with him about my drug use, as I was with most people, but once again I didn't listen to advice.

I flew out to Glasgow early the next morning and spent the day with Nathaniel. Smiling and laughing and trying to pretend to him everything was ok when in reality I had abandoned him, left him with his grandparents and dad. After a few hours Nathaniel would want to go back to his grandparents. I ignored the feelings of hurt we were both experiencing. That night I went to see some old friends and unable to get Ecstasy tablets, we made do with acid. A stupid thing to do when I knew I was emotional and had been told not to. In my defence, I had been told I was stupid since I was eight years old, so I behaved stupidly. Spending an afternoon trying to rid myself of these thoughts and beliefs wasn't enough. Looking back on this part of my life, I am amazed I survived to tell the story. I had a pretty bad trip, I arrived at Aunty Wilma's still tripping, looking and behaving like a complete wreck, at 8 o'clock the next morning. My nails had been bitten down and I was picking at the skin, refusing her offer of a cigarette, telling her I had given them up, muttering to myself, unable to sit at peace.

'Since when?' she asked confused. Yesterday I was sitting in the very same seat puffing away. I just kept telling her I needed to be locked up in a psychiatric ward. Aunty Wilma got up to make another round of teas and coffees and then she quietly rang Mummy. I really gave her a fright she would later tell me, and as she was totally unaware of my drug taking, she was convinced I was having a break down. Aunty Wilma demanded Mummy come over immediately and when she arrived they rang the out of hours NHS service and I was taken to some medical practice where I was seen by a doctor. Mummy wanted to come in and sit with me, worried about my mental state but I insisted on going alone. Once in the office I blurted out, 'Get her away from or I will kill her.' The doctor asked who and I told him the whole sad story and that I was tripping on acid. 'Please lock me up or I will kill her,' I cried tears streaming down my face. He agreed to send me to the Southern General Hospital's psychiatric ward, a place Mummy had been to many times. Transport was arranged and I told the doctor to tell Mummy to go home, that I wanted to go on my own. Arriving on the ward the doctor spoke to me for a minute, then I was left to sit in the corridor outside his office while the hustle and bustle carried on around me. My smile had finally slipped and I had cracked up, begging to be admitted. Hearing the moans and cries of the ill people round about did not scare me, and I looked forward to joining them. I had wanted to scream for so long, let it all out but instead I had just kept smiling. Time passed and I got up and knocked on the door, reality was kicking in and the drugs were wearing off.

'Come in,' shouted the doctor.

'I want to go home,' I told him entering the room. Telling me to sit down he listened to me, listened when I told him the acid trip was wearing off and that I did not belong in there.

212

'Why did you threaten to kill your mother? Where is that coming from?'

I told him about my upbringing and the rebirthing and the acid taking which had caused all my emotions to become messed up.

'I never had any intentions of killing my mother,' I reassured him, worried I would be locked up against my will, a danger to Mummy. 'It was just anger at the unfairness of our life in the big house and I suppose at my mum for allowing it all to happen.'

Passing a small bundle of A4 paper towards me he asked me to write about my childhood. Looking at him I laughed that he thought my childhood could be written on a few pages.

'You are going to need more paper than that.'

He rang Aunty Wilma and told her he was sending me to her in a taxi and advised she sent me back to Dublin the next day, and to keep me away from Mummy and the big house. He told me to seek counselling and limit my drug use. Aunty Wilma organised my plane ticket for the next afternoon and her son Joseph, who I had met again a few times since my return to Glasgow, drove me to Prestwick Airport once I had said goodbye to Nathaniel. I was disappointed at letting him down and I promised him I would soon be back for good.

Returning to Dublin and my ever changing clubbing friends meant days spent writing, sitting in coffee shops, coming down from the drugs of the night before, trying and failing to deal with my past, writing down my rambling thoughts and not much else. Pearse was telling me all the time 'write about your childhood, you have a fantastic story to tell', and I began writing little bits but not much as it was still too painful.

I spent Christmas Day alone and in the evening I made my decision to return to Glasgow for good and face my responsibilities and my demons. Two weeks later I arrived at Glasgow Airport and this time Joseph was there to collect me. I stayed at Aunty Wilma's until I found somewhere to live. Joseph along with his wife Zarah were regular visitors and it didn't take long for a friendship to develop between us. Mummy came to visit too but the tension and the unsaid words as always ruined it. It was rare that we spent a few hours together without any fallout. I spent my days flat hunting and when Nathaniel finished school I collected him and spent some time at Gran Kate's helping with homework, staying for some dinner and story before bedtime.

My evenings I spent sitting talking with Aunty Wilma, talking about the big house. She was always on my side and saw the unfair treatment where Mummy was blind. With her I could imagine what a mother daughter relationship would be like, never judging and always accepting, full of love and kindness, all the things Mummy was not allowed to be. When Mummy did try and be kind and loving to me, I always found it was forced and it didn't come naturally to her, almost like she did it because she was my mother and that's what mothers do. There had been no love and affection when I was growing up, and now that I was grown up I found it difficult to accept her love.

A few weeks later I found a flat and moved out, Nathaniel was happy staying with his grandparents and I felt I had no right to force him to leave. Instead I decided to wait until he was ready to come to live with me again. I had let him down by leaving him behind for six months while I went to sort myself out. I saw Aunty Wilma on a daily basis until I found a job, working full time at the House of Frasers, a department store. Even then I visited at the weekend. It was round this time that I applied to volunteer at Child Line. I felt a need to give something back and wanted to make a difference in children's lives. It was on this course I would meet Marie who was studying for her Diploma in Counselling; she had applied for a placement as part of her course. It was to be a three month training course, the training took place every Saturday morning. Marie would tell me later that when I introduced myself to the group the first morning we met she thought I was some rich little Arab girl from Newton Mearns who had decided to do something other than spend Daddy's money. Marie seemed really sure of herself and full of confidence, I never imagined we would become such good friends. When she introduced herself, I looked at her and saw a tall, blonde, slim and trendy woman. She wore her hair in curls, loose and down to her shoulders and was very articulate. During the course of the three months, Marie and I worked together on a one to one basis and she realised pretty quickly she had got me wrong. Slowly we went from meeting with the group on a Saturday to meeting at the Sub Club on a Saturday night. Marie loved the club as much as I did, although she never took Class A drugs, happy with a vodka and red bull. I loved being in her company because she accepted me as mixed race, saw me as white and Pakistani too. She had a daughter, Dharma, three years older than Nathaniel, and Sonny, her boy, was the same age as Nathaniel. She would invite us both over on Sunday afternoons when all her family would be visiting, and allow us to be part of a loving family life.

Seeing Mummy so down trodden and miserable, full of bitterness and negativity was becoming too much, especially with my training course. I was changing and making choices that would benefit me, I was putting myself first and so one day I didn't call her as I had always done, I avoided visiting Aunty Wilma on the days I knew she went, and it was relatively easy to avoiding seeing her.

'You should phone her,' Aunty Wilma would often say.

'There is nothing to stop her picking up the phone to me and she never has,' I always replied stubbornly. 'She has my number and never calls me.'

For the next four years we would have no contact at all. Hearing bits from Aunty Wilma, I at times was aware of what was going on in Mummy's life, and that was how I learnt of her being forced out of the big house at the age of 60, but I was too busy living my life and falling in love for the first time.

Chapter 12 Ben and Ruby

I had made up with Mummy after bumping into her one
afternoon and she invited me to visit her in her new home. She
had chosen to stay on in Mosspark when she had been thrown out
of the big house, she had lived in the area for nearly thirty years
after all. Visiting her later that week I couldn't get over how
happy Mummy seemed, I didn't think I had ever seen her this
happy. Nathaniel and I visited often and at weekends we stayed
over. At this point in her life Mummy still had a relationship
with Zanera and one day I came to see Mummy and she was
there with her youngest daughter, Amber. At first it was awkward
with Zanera, years of no communication and with completely
different lifestyles, we had little to say to each other. I was eager
to please her and babbled away while she sniggered at some of
the things I was saying. I was very much a 'gori' in her eyes and
I ignored the way I felt whenever she sniggered or mocked.
Ignored the fact that it took me back to my childhood. With my
son, my mum and sister in my life I was beginning to allow
myself to be happy, allowing myself to feel good about myself. I
was starting to believe that maybe Mummy and her children did
deserve to be happy as a family, even though I was not on
speaking terms with all my siblings, it was a start.

Soon after meeting Mummy, I moved back to Mosspark
to be nearer her and rented a two bedroom flat not far from where
I had grown up. I was starting to make friends that were lasting
instead of the usual few months here and then a few months there

in ever changing circles of acquaintances. Aunty Wilma was still a huge part of my life, as was Joseph and his wife Zarah and their three children. I was a regular at the Sub Club and could be found there most weekends with my best friends Marie and John Paul, meeting up with Joseph and Zarah was a given also. The Sub Club was my home from home and I loved the way I felt whenever I was there. Accepted by almost everyone on the dance floor it was where I danced and lost myself in the music.

It was in the Sub Club that I met Ben, he was out with a group of people Joseph knew and introductions were made and we ended up chatting and dancing for most of the night and at the end of it we exchanged numbers. We chatted on the phone over the next few weeks, getting to know each other and eventually we arranged a date. I had never experienced old fashioned courting and it was as strange as it was refreshing. We began dating and he introduced me to his family, I felt bad that I wouldn't be able to introduce him to all of my family. I had told him about my upbringing and my forced marriage, my son Junaid and that I had been disowned for refusing another marriage. It would take my return to the Pakistani community and the way I was treated there for Ben to realise there was no point in me trying to contact Abbas. He was forever telling me, 'You only have one dad, make up with him, Aisha.' Ben could not understand that my father did not want me, that there would never be any chance of me coming back from the dead. Within months of dating Ben asked me to marry him, telling me he wanted to spend the rest of his life with me and to have a family.

I heard Abbas's voice 'Who bludee vant to marry ju? Idiot.' I told Ben one day we would get married and that I didn't want to rush into anything.

Nathaniel got on great with Ben too and we went on a holiday to Tenerife the first summer we were dating. A few weeks after we returned, I sensed I was pregnant but buried it away in the back of my mind, knowing I would have to deal with it sooner rather than later. My period was also late and by the second week Ben knew too. We both prayed that when I peed on the pregnancy test it would show I wasn't pregnant. Even though Ben had said he wanted children, we both felt it was too soon. We had been trying to convince ourselves that my period was just late, even though my cycle was regular. At the age of 35 I was pregnant, again. I had had no desire to have any more children. I had my two boys and even though Junaid was not part of my life he was still one of my boys, he was my first born son. Nathaniel had known about Junaid, had grown up hearing stories. I felt it was easier this way rather than try to explain to him when he was older that he had a brother in Pakistan, less of a shock, I thought. Nathaniel had wanted a little brother or sister for such a long time and now at the age of thirteen he was finally going to be a big brother.

I called Yacoub and shared my news with him and he was delighted.

'Congratulations, sis, I'm happy for you. Man, I'm gonna be an uncle again.'

I worried about what the rest of my family would think and say, even though I would never hear their opinion or comments, I still worried. 'Three children to three different fathers, see we said she was a slut.' I voiced my fears to Yacoub and he replied, 'Oh for God's sake woman. Who cares what they think, they are hardly ones to judge. It's not like you have been having babies every other year with random men. You had Junaid after you had been forced into a marriage, you had Nathaniel to be a mum again after Junaid went to live in Pakistan and it's been what 12, 13 years since you have been pregnant. Stop stressing over them, they are nobodies. Keep telling yourself that and you will be fine.'

I always felt much better after I had spoken to Yacoub and decided I would tell Nathaniel that day. I had taken a few days off work from my job in House of Fraser and went to meet him after he had finished school. Ben was at work but this was something I needed to do alone with Nathaniel. I took him into town and let him pick a new pair of Adidas, his latest fashion obsession, and then we went to The Social, on Royal Exchange Square for something to eat. We sat down, Nathan ordered a cheese and tomato pizza with fries and I asked for a coffee. We were chatting about school and his friends when, at the table across from us, a woman happened to lift her weeks old baby out of the pram, Nathaniel looked over and commented on how tiny the baby was. I thanked the gods for the timing and told him.

'You are going to be a big brother.'

'Oh my god, Mum, you're pregnant? Are you keeping it?'

'Of course I am, I'm not going to tell you I am pregnant and then have an abortion. I spoke to Uncle Yacoub and he is happy for me. I just need to tell Nanni now.'

Nathaniel after his initial shock was happy and told me he wished it was a girl. He finished his pizza and fries and we left and went to see Mummy. I hadn't planned on telling her on that visit but Nathaniel unable to contain his excitement, shared the good news.

'Nanni, I am going to be a big brother.'

Mummy was devastated at first asking, with a look of horror on her face, 'Is it true?'

For a second I felt shameful and dirty, knowing that Mummy is thinking only of what Abbas and Fatima would say when the news travelled to their door, as it no doubt would. When I told Zanera, she at first thought I was playing a prank on her and when she realised I was serious she said, 'Oh...well you have done it before so I'm sure you will manage this time too, and Ben is really nice.'

Ben had no other children and as he was an only child his parents were ecstatic by the news that they were finally going to be grandparents. His parents, Ella and Fraser, were both in their 60's and had given up hoping that they would one day hold their grandchild, instead they comforted themselves with three holidays a year and weekends away to all over the UK. At my eighteen week scan I asked what the sex of the baby was and I was lucky to be told; some hospitals don't reveal the sex. Too many Asian families are disappointed if it is a baby girl. Not me, I was overjoyed when I was told I was having a baby girl, as was Nathaniel. Ben, being a man, would have preferred his first born to be a boy to carry on the family name. He soon got over it because really there was nothing he could do to change the situation and he was excited about becoming a father. I was spending a lot of time with Ben and his parents and this was triggering my longing for Abbas and the Pakistani side of me, which I had managed to suppress for so long.

Ben's family was very small in comparison to mine. There was him and his parents, his maternal aunt Janet who was a widow without any children, and his maternal grandparents, Gran Lily and Papa Albert both of them were 85 and in good health. His family made me long for my family, my family that did not want me, and being pregnant was making me deal with issues and emotions I had hidden away. Issues and emotion I had never properly dealt with. Throughout my pregnancy and my crazy mood swings Ben was my rock. He never yelled, he never shouted, he just calmly talked to me and held me if I let him. My relationship with Mummy was going through a rocky patch and we didn't speak for a few months, only making up towards the end of my pregnancy. It seemed like that's the way my relationship with her had been my whole life. This time we had fallen out over my decision to spend Christmas Day with Ben and his family. Mummy had spent every Christmas since I had been disowned, in Manchester with Yacoub and Amirah, never really

222

caring whether I had anybody to spend the day with. Christmas was never celebrated in the big house so it didn't bother me if I had to spend it alone. Mummy told me I thought more of Ella than I did of her and it was obvious she resented the closeness I had with Ella. Mummy was unable to see that she had a closeness with Naeem and Amina and especially Mirrium, that she didn't have with me but I never gave her grief over it. That's just the way it was. Zanera had also been distancing herself from me as my pregnancy progressed instead of getting closer it seemed like we were pretending to be a family when we didn't know how to be a family. Zanera used the excuse of Rasoul, her husband, finding out she had been visiting and that he had been angry and told her to stay away, and for a peaceful life she did as he told her to.

Ruby was born in the first week of January and was my spitting image, although Ella was convinced she was Ben's double. Looking at her and seeing me as a baby I promised her that she would be the most loved girl in the world. Looking at her and seeing the way Ben was with her, made me think of Abbas and how he had not even came to visit me on the day I was born. How could parents not love and protect their babies? Why did they go about trying to destroy emotionally, the very thing they had created? I threw myself into being a mother. This time round I needed little help and joined breast feeding groups and went to mother and toddlers' mornings held in the local church.

At the weekends, when Ben was off work, we would do things that families do. Saturday mornings he would get up and I would get a lie in, he took Ruby swimming and sometimes Nathaniel would go too. After their swimming session they would return and we would go to Gran Ella and Grandpa Fraser's for lunch and if the weather was dry a trip to the park, and if not maybe the Gallery of Modern Art or the Kelvingrove Museum, Ruby's favourite two places to visit as she got older. On the surface everything was perfect, underneath I was still in turmoil. I had a happy family and a happy life so why couldn't I be content? Abbas had told me only people like him would accept me, and white people would always view me as a trash. And Fatima had ensured that 'the gori's children' would never know happiness.

Ben had asked me to marry him on numerous occasions and I laughed it off each time using my forced marriage as an excuse to never get married again, claiming it had put me off. It's only a bit of paper, what difference does it make? The truth was I didn't think I was good enough to be his wife. Hadn't Abbas told me the last time I ever spoke to him that nobody would want me? Even though white people accepted me and never thought of me as trash for having a Pakistani father, the voice of my father would not allow me to believe it. I felt I needed to return to the Pakistani community to finally believe that I was lovable and deserved happiness.

Just after Ruby's first birthday I left Ben and moved into a main door flat on the south side to be closer to my

Pakistani side. Understandably Ben took the split badly and it was only after months of long chats late into the night that I convinced him that there would be no next man moving in. That was his biggest fear, that and the thought of his daughter forgetting him. I promised I would call him every morning so he could say 'good morning' to Ruby and call him every night so he could say 'good night', and that he would come for dinner every Tuesday night and spend the night before her birthday and Christmas overnight at our new home. We also agreed to go on holidays together with Ruby. I told him I wanted my daughter to be her father's princess and even though I was taking her away from him by moving out, I would do my best to keep it amicable between us.

Moving to the south side was exciting, I was once again surrounded by Asian people, after having lived in Hamilton, where I had moved to just before Ruby's birth. Hamilton was Ben's place of birth and where his family still lived as did he, and there the number of Asians was few and far between. I began taking Ruby to the local mother and toddler's group and was surprised to see so many Pakistani and Indian mothers. In Hamilton there had been no Asian mums at the groups I had gone to. The group was on every morning, and every morning Ruby and I would be there, me happy to be mixing with Asian mums and Ruby happy to be running around and playing with the other toddlers. Some afternoons Mummy would visit and on one visit almost a year after I have moved into the flat she said that Zanera had asked if she could come and visit. I had not spoken to Zanera since her husband had told her to stay away, bumping into her rarely and even then she hurried off without talking, scared she would be seen and the crime of talking to her sister reported back. Oh, the shame.

I agreed to her visiting even though Nathaniel was against it. 'Why do you even bother with them, Mum? They don't care about us really, coming in and out of our lives whenever they want to. If you want to see them go ahead, but don't expect me to get excited, I mean Ruby is two year old, and now they want to come and meet her.'

It was strange seeing her again and again it was a little awkward also. She was wonderful with Ruby and told me she was happy to have a niece. Amirah had four boys, I had two as did Jamal and Yacoub had one boy. I remembered Fatima's curse and asked Zanera if she remembered it. Zanera laughed nervously, the big house was an emotional topic for her. I reminded her of the day not long after she had been married and Fatima had shouted at me and Amirah over something trivial like not ironing the clothes or making the beds quickly enough. Fatima shouted that she hoped and prayed we would never be blessed with boys, only girls, and then we would know how hard it was for her. She continued to shout that she hoped our future daughters would shame us like we were shaming our parents. I was 12 years old when Zanera got married, yet I can hear Fatima's voice as clear as if it was said yesterday.

Zanera, like Mummy, found it hard to discuss the big house, instead they both chose to bottle everything up inside and

226

forget it ever existed or pretend it was all happy times. Zanera spent most of her time playing with Ruby, besotted as was everybody who met her. Ben and I had worked hard on raising a happy girl who knows she is loved unconditionally. My relationship with Zanera was a strange one, I allowed Zanera to pass remarks and look down her nose at me, I allowed her to make me feel inferior and dirty. I was so happy to be in her life again and for Ruby to have an aunty that I could deal with the way I felt around her, for the time being.

When I told Yacoub I had met with her and Amber and they wanted to meet him too if he ever came to Glasgow for a visit, he told me to tell them no thanks. He didn't want to be a secret in anyone's life. I told him it would be different for him; he would be allowed to go to Zanera's home, be welcomed and he wouldn't be a secret, he was a male after all and all his sins would not even be questioned. Again Yacoub told me, tell them no thanks, if my sister is not allowed then I am not visiting either. Personally, it didn't bother me at all that he was welcome and I wasn't; I was a girl, he was a boy. Some girls are punished for their sins and most boys are forgiven. It was the culture and traditions I had been dragged up in and I never questioned it, I just went along with it.

By now I had also begun to get friendly with a few of the Asian mums at toddlers group and we would sometimes go for lunch after toddler group was over, or miss the toddler morning and I would invite them to mine for a coffee morning instead. One woman, Farah, was from Sheffield and had married a Glasgow boy, a love marriage, and had moved up to Glasgow to live with her new husband and her in-laws. Farah had been married for four years and had two daughters, Iman and Laila. The best thing about our friendship was she knew nothing about my background or family set up, like so many of the other Asians I was meeting.

'Oh, so you are Abbas's daughter. How is your father? I haven't seen him for ages.'

These people were well aware of the fact that I had been disowned yet thought nothing of asking a question to which they knew the answer. I always replied honestly that I had not spoken to him since I was 21 years old and as far as I was aware he still lived in Pollokshields. Farah's in-laws lived on Glenap Street just off Albert Drive in a large four bedroom tenement and had lived there since they had first arrived in the UK. One morning Farah's mother-in-law turned up to the toddlers group, her curiosity about the gori's daughter getting the better of her. Farah was a little embarrassed and told me so when I arrived and saw her. Don't worry about it, I told her, she just wants a little gossip that's all. I got Ruby settled with a toy, got myself a coffee and made my over to say 'Salam a lekum (hello).' Mrs Khan was a pleasant old woman and asked how Mummy was doing and then tried to place which daughter I was, getting me confused with Amirah. When I told her I had been married to Pervaiz she said to me, 'Hai hai, tuu Aisha eh, hai meh pachanai vee nee. Kee aal eh? Twaara murra teek taak eh? (Oh my, it's you, Aisha, I didn't even recognise you. How are you? How is your son?)'

I told her I hadn't seen him since he was a baby and she spoke a little about how she had felt sorry for Mummy and her children. I listened and answered her questions for another few minutes then made an excuse that I was going to check on Ruby and made my way to the other side of the hall. After that morning I never saw her again; having satisfied her curiosity she saw no need to return to a hall full of screaming children.

My relationship with Zanera was purely on her terms and she called and visited whenever it suited her or Amber. I had not met her two older children, my nephews who I had last seen when they were toddlers. Being boys and being quite into their religion and brainwashed by their father they chose to stay away. I made myself available whenever she visited even if it meant cancelling plans with other friends. Amber and Ruby had a special bond and Ruby lived for her visits. No matter what was planned I cancelled so they could spend time together. Zanera was very critical of me and often laughed at me or ridiculed me, it was almost as if she was Fatima and Abbas rolled into one. She would laugh at my hair when I had it professionally straightened to look more Pakistani. She would laugh at the clothes I wore, maybe because they weren't like her shalwar kameez or the sari's she wore, although Amber rarely wore traditional clothes. Nathaniel tolerated Zanera because I seemed so happy, but often told me to stop running after them. If he had been younger when we had made up then maybe he would have been happier, he was 12 and wise when he had met his aunt for the first time. Nathaniel said he saw through the fake act they were putting on and he hated the fact that we were not allowed to visit them at their home.

Sometime I felt that although only 14, Amber was more westernised than I was. She was unable to speak Mirpuri, although she understood some of it, she rarely wore Asian clothes and often told me she would be marrying a white man because they treated women way better than the Pakistani boys she knew. When I told her that the family would never allow it, she laughed and said, 'As soon as I am eighteen I am walking out that door, not running away, walking with my suitcase and they will not be able to stop me. If they think my fate lies married to a horrible, fat, old man and living in Pakistan then they are mistaken. This is Britain, not back home and I have rights.'

I admired her courage and knowledge, thankfully the laws were changing and forced marriage was being spoken about in mainstream media ensuring that when the time came for Amber to leave home, it would be an easy choice for her to make. Knowing the law is on your side and will not return you to your parents because you have chosen to take control of your own life is something I did not have when I was growing up.

At the beginning Zanera visited often during the week for an hour or two before she collected Amber from school, and at the weekend she would bring Amber with her. Ben met them again too and for a while I played at happy families. Ben although aware of my upbringing was still unable to understand

230

what it had really been like, having known only love and kindness from his own family. I would take Zanera and Amber to Ben's parents' home and they met the extended family too. That's what families do, isn't it? Six months passed and Zanera severed all contact, sending a text to say Rasoul had found out again, someone saw us walking along Kilmarnock Road and this time he was livid. She said in the text that he had screamed at her that I was a bitch who would lead Amber astray. Explaining to Ruby why Zanera and Amber no longer visited or called would have been heart breaking, and I said she had gone to Pakistan for a holiday.

Amber had introduced me to the latest Bollywood music. I was stuck in the music of my childhood and the new singers were pretty rubbish I told her. I had never listened to the new stuff preferring my golden oldies. Amber insisted I at least listen to Imran Khan, a singer from Holland, who sang in both English and Punjabi. I humoured her and listened and told her it was rubbish.

'It will grow on you, aunty, believe me,' she laughed. Amber was correct and the music all of a sudden grew on me one afternoon, like thousands of other Asians I played his album, 'Unforgettable' on repeat. He was playing a concert in Glasgow and I told Amber I would get tickets and we would go. Lucky for me the concert was being held in the local church where I went to for the toddler's group and I managed to get us free tickets. Zanera wasn't interested, telling me it would be full of young people and that there would inevitably be fights. Still, just before she sent that final text she allowed me to take Amber. A few of the Asian mums from toddlers were going too and it looked like it was going to be a good night. When concerts by Asian singers are organised they are usually 'ladies only' events, otherwise most ladies stay away because there will be males there. Unless it's a pricey event held in the Glasgow Concert Hall attended by the elders in the community, then it is mixed. For this event tickets cost £5 and it was mixed, and on the night Ben took Ruby to his house while I got ready to go to my first ever Asian concert. Zanera picked me up at 6.30 pm and dropped Amber and I off at the church. We had a brilliant time and I was probably one of the oldest in the crowd, there were about 150 people there, mostly males, young and in their late teens. There was a bhangra dance act, some hip hop dancers and then a lot of running around by the promoter of the night, a young boy in his late teens. Eventually at 9pm Imran Khan came on the stage and the crowd went wild when he started singing 'Amplifier' and then 'Bounce Billo.'

'He's not even singing live, that's rubbish,' said Amber, disappointed that her pop idol was lip synching. Imran Khan sang a few other songs, thanked Glasgow in his heavy accent, he is Dutch after all, and exited the stage. Making our way outside, we were approached by a woman with several girls. I didn't recognise her.

'Hi Amber, how are you? Where is your mum and who is this?' she said, looking and smiling at me.

'Hi Aunty Ghazala, this is my aunty, my mum's sister,' Amber replied, forcing her smile.

'Ah, which sister are you?' Ghazala asked me.

'Aisha,' I told her. I didn't know then that as my relationship with Zanera and Amber ended, a new relationship with this woman in front of me would begin.

Chapter 13 Pollokshields

Returning to the Pakistani community was like coming home, at first. For the first time since I had been disowned, I was Pakistani. I went to Pollokshields, the heart of the Pakistani community. An area I had avoided because I wasn't welcome anymore. I wore shalwar kameez (Asian clothes) again and celebrated Eid – a Muslim celebration after the month of Ramadan, I spoke the language and socialised with mostly Pakistani people. Up until the age of 21 I had lived life as a Pakistani girl/woman. Even though certain people in the big house viewed me as a 'gori', my upbringing had still been Pakistani, it was all I had known and I missed that part of me. I struggled for so many years with my identity. Being disowned meant I was no longer allowed to be Pakistani and as I was not sure how to be white, there was a constant internal battle.

Having tried Reiki and re-birthing, I began another immersion, this time into the Pakistani community. I was desperate to raise my daughter in the culture and traditions I remembered from my childhood in Mirpur. Even though the people in the big house were unkind, I knew there were good decent Pakistani people. I had spent the happiest years of my childhood in Kashmir, being raised by my Pakistani grandparents and aunt. I was accepted as a Pakistani child, never made to feel shame for being the gori's daughter, I was allowed to be me.

I returned to the community wholeheartedly, and some friendships with my white friends ended as they couldn't understand how I could switch so easily into the role of a Pakistani. They couldn't understand that this was part of me and I had to embrace it. I understood how they felt. They had only known me as a white girl with an Asian name and now I had changed to someone they didn't recognise. They would only accept me in their life and as a friend if I continued living like a white person, as a Pakistani woman I was something they did not want in their life. Apart from my few true friends, who have stuck by me no matter who I am.

My relationship with Zanera and her family should have prepared me for the way I would be treated in the wider Pakistani community, but I was blinded by a strong need for acceptance. Through Zanera I met Ghazala, who accepted me more than my own sister Zanera and her children ever did. Ghazala was married with six children, ranging in age from 24 to 4 years old. It was her second marriage. From the start she became a huge part of my life, although I rarely visited her at home. Ghazala lived with her parents, unlike many other married Pakistani girls do when they are married. They were old and they had no other children living in Scotland with whom they could live. She told me from the start not to be offended because I would not be allowed to go to her home.

'My parents are old, innit yaar (friend), don't mind them and their ways. It's just, you know, you ran away and had kids without marrying their fathers so it looks bad, right. They know your dad too, so it would be disrespectful to him to have you sitting in our house. I think you are cool though, and who knows in time they might come round when they see the changes you are making and that.'

It's just the way it was and having been raised in a Pakistani home I knew not to question it and told her I understood. I didn't visit Zanera at her home because her husband had said I was not allowed to, so I didn't expect strangers to be welcoming.

Pollokshields is the hub of the Pakistani community. Many families have moved out to surrounding areas, mostly staying in the South Side of Glasgow where the houses were cheaper than the west end. All families returned to Pollokshields weekly if not more often, for shopping and for visiting family and friends, for the feeling of being 'back home' with the streets full of Asian butcher shops, sweet shops, material and gold shops and of course the gossiping, which is rife in the community.

In Pollokshields you have Asian dentists, doctors, opticians, shop keepers and if you chose to go about your daily business in the 'ghetto', then you can do so without speaking to any white person. So many of the older generation are unable to speak English, choosing not to learn it. Fatima is one of the many elders who speak little or no English even after having lived here for over 40 years.

Ghazala was a bubbly outgoing person and liked by everyone. She was also the biggest backstabber I had ever met, happily discussing everyone's business with me. Safe in the knowledge that I would never repeat it because most of the people she bitched about I had never met and probably would never meet. Once she told me about her friend's nineteen year old daughter who had gone on a week's holiday to Spain. While there she slept with six men and by the time she had returned from her holiday, a so called friend had blabbed and the gossip spread.

'Silly bitch, honestly what on earth was she thinking?' Ghazala said after telling the story.

'Silly bitch? What would you say if she had been mixed race instead of Pakistani, or white?' I asked.

'I would think she was a slag,' she replied.

We argued over the unfairness of her judgement.

'I can't help the way I think. Half caste girls have a reputation for being easy, same as white women.'

Sometimes it was easier to keep quiet than continue discussing certain topics with her. Realising she would never change her opinions and beliefs handed down from her parent's generation. Knowing she would never use the term mixed race preferring to say 'half caste', no matter how often I told her it was an insult. Towards the end of our friendship she showed her irritation whenever I used the word paki. Telling me 'I don't really like it when you say Paki. Say Pakistani.' Arguing that she used the word all the time was met with 'It's different for me.' I knew why it was different for her and that would be the main reason our friendship lasted for such a short time.   It was different because she was 'pure' and I only had a Pakistani father. Arguing that having a Pakistani father allowed to me say 'paki' if I wanted to was pointless.

Ghazala smoked marijuana and drank alcohol, undercover. Most things which are forbidden or 'haram' in their religion are carried out undercover. Yet really everyone knows everyone else's business so there is no secrecy. People just don't ask you to your face, preferring to gossip about you behind your back. Her husband, Khalid, was aware of her getting drunk and getting high and was not too bothered, her parents were oblivious to it. Khalid was so happy to be living in the UK and escaping the poverty of his life in Mirpur, that he overlooked many of his wife's behaviours. Like so many other Pakistani people in the community, she sometimes prayed on Friday - Jumma prayer. If you pray on Fridays then the sins you have committed all week are forgiven by God.

'You should pray, at least try to pray on Fridays,' she often said to me. The only time she prayed on a regular basis was when her life was in turmoil. Then she remembered God. Believing bad stuff happened because she wasn't praying, for a few days maybe a week or so she would pray and read the Quran five times a day, the standard requirement for a Muslim. She would pray for her life to be transformed and for her problems to be solved, this didn't happen and the praying inevitably stopped. I put up with the never ending hypocrisy so I could be part of the community. What was I thinking? Right from the start it was clear I would never be accepted. In denial I refused to acknowledge it, ignoring the signs. Ghazala's was the one of the few homes I visited and even then it was on the occasions her parents were away to England visiting one of their other children or on a trip to Pakistan. Most of the Pakistani friends I was making were happy to be acquaintances and share their deepest darkest secrets. Happy to come into my home to drink and get high away from the prying eyes of their families. Happy to go clubbing and socialise with the opposite sex. Not so happy about inviting me into their homes. I allowed it. Being part of their double lives so I could fit in somewhere and finally belong. The Pakistani side of me had been looking for acceptance for so long that I ignored all the double standards and one sided friendships.

Most of the females I met had been through the standard forced or arranged marriage. Of those that stayed in the marriage some had affairs, those that divorced were soon married to another unsuitable cousin. So many forced or unsuitably arranged marriages causing untold misery and sadness, all for the sake of izaat (honour). One girl I knew was onto her third marriage and that was as miserable as the other two. A first cousin, her dad's nephew, from 'back home' who was openly gay and made no attempt to hide his sexuality. Still her parents married her off to him, allowing him to come and live in the UK to make money to send to his poverty stricken family back in Pakistan. Her dad only thought of his sister and how her life would improve if she had a son living in the UK; his daughter's needs and wants were irrelevant. I was told often by many different people that most married couples were having affairs. I wasn't surprised. With so many marriages arranged purely for the sake of the red passport or izzat (honour), it was inevitable. Ghazala once told me that it was easy to spot the women who were having affairs. She said that all of a sudden a married woman would start losing weight, start dressing in their fancier outfits, ones maybe saved for weddings or Eid, start getting their eyebrows and other facial and body hair waxed regularly. For this they would be seen visiting any one of the number of Asian hairdressers in Pollokshields and so the gossip would already have started. 'So and so is never out of the hairdressers on Maxwell Road, getting everything waxed and threaded, hair-cut and dyed, she must have a lover.' Many of the married women in Pollokshields have husbands who work in carry outs and takeaways. Long unsociable hours, leaving at lunchtime and not returning till after midnight gives the women they are married to plenty of time to conduct their illicit affairs. That's not to say all Pakistani women who are married to carry out workers are having affairs. I met a few families through Ghazala where the men worked in the carryout business and they had a happy marriage. According to Ghazala none of these couples were cheating, or not that she had heard of anyway. Gay Pakistani men and women have come up with new ways of outwitting their parents, finding husbands or wives on marriages of convenience websites. When I was first told this by Ghazala and some of the other friends I was making I refused to believe it. I searched on Google and yes it is true. I was amazed at the lengths Pakistani people go to so they can live a happy life. A gay man from Glasgow may 'marry' a lesbian woman from Manchester after finding each other on these websites and lying to their families that they have fallen in love and want to marry. This keeps the

240

family happy, as long as they are not the 'forced or arranged marriage type of family', and blissfully unaware of their child's sexuality. A baby may also be produced, again to keep the family happy. Sadly many gay men and women are forced into marriages with the opposite sex. Many of the men, like white men, live a double life. Mixing and socialising with other Pakistani gay men and satisfying their desires. I never met an openly gay Pakistani woman although I did meet many men and I was very surprised to learn from these men of the undercover gay community which exists within the Pakistani community. Another one of their many open secrets.

Child sex abuse is also rife in the community and I know from my own experiences that this exists. Many women and young girls confided in me that they had been sexually abused, as did some of the men I had got to know. It seemed like we all had a story to share when it involved sexual abuse.

'My uncle abused me for years, right up until I was married at 17. But I'm fine about it, I don't need counselling and would never report him. Ever!' said Najma, an older woman who I had spoken to at the ladies gym I went to. 'You're the first person I have ever told.'

There is no outcry when a child is sexually abused in the community. If the child or adult survivor of abuse, finds the courage to tell then there is disbelief at the telling not the horrific crime. Virginity is highly valued in the Pakistani community yet some men think nothing of raping their daughters, sisters and nieces. It's another one of the community's many open secrets and in my opinion one of their most horrific. Everybody knows, everybody keeps quiet to stop western society finding out. Shame on the community if white people find out that Pakistani paedophiles exist. Izaat (honour) will be ruined. So the abusers continue abusing knowing they will never be stopped because of this thing called 'honour' which really is more valuable than their children's' innocence. Pakistani parents put 'honour' before their children time and time again, and by coming back into the Pakistani community I was seeing the results of this on a daily basis. Many miserable and unhappy children and young people. Controlling every part of their lives and then forcing them into miserable marriages.

Borderline anorexia is also a problem for young girls, boys and some adults. For many, sadly, eating is the only thing they can control and when you see the big chubby elders of the community, their children, especially daughters, are like stick insects in comparison. For almost a year I listened to horror stories, listened to the exploits of the Pakistani people and became tangled up in their deceit and drama.

White people are not drama free but the Pakistani community being so small and interwoven makes it seem never ending. Everyone really does know everyone. Was this the way I wanted to raise my daughter? Again I asked myself, what I was thinking? The community I was disowned from all those years ago no longer existed, not outside Pakistan anyway. If it ever did. Instead it had become diseased and corrupted. All the things I wanted to protect my daughter from are happening in the

242

Pakistani community. The drinking and drug taking culture, the sleeping around culture, the being disrespectful to parents and elders culture.

Pakistani people think they are better than the 'white trash' they despise when in reality some of the people I met were far worse. I am not for a minute suggesting all Pakistani people are trash, some of the ones I met were good people. Writing my story made me analyse a lot of things. I had started to challenge the voices of Fatima and Abbas in my head, that for so long had been whispering 'white equals trash'; and wanted to escape from the Pakistani community. I had got away from the people who believed this yet behaved in ways which they proclaimed to despise. If they thought white people were trash then me being mixed race white would mean they believed I too was trash. And what of my children who were only quarter Pakistani? How could they ever be accepted? Regardless of what I had or hadn't done, regardless of the changes I was making to fit into the Pakistani community, many would always view me as trash.

Within a few weeks of writing my story I unfriended most of my Pakistani Facebook friends. I explained to those that contacted me and asked why, that I needed to be away from a community that viewed me as the gori's daughter, for a while, and we have never spoken since. I think they are envious of my ability to remove myself from a culture they too despise and are stuck with. They are offended by my need to remove myself from the double standards and sheer hypocrisy that they know exists, yet are unable to leave. Where would they go? All they know is the Pakistani community. I at least had my white community to return to. I had been living there for most of my adult life.

Ghazala was one of the few who I still spoke to. Excited by the book, excited when I told her my lecturer at university could see my story as a movie. Excited by the idea of fame and money. Asking if she could play a part in the film and asking if I would take her on holiday and buy her a Range Rover Vogue, in black please. Four months or so into the writing she called round. As usual I was at my dining table, typing away on my laptop.

'For fucks sake, yaar (friend), have you not finished that yet? To be honest I'm getting fed up listening to you go on about writing all the time,' she said as she sat down.

'Books aren't written overnight, some people take years to complete them,' I replied getting up to put the kettle on. Hiding my hurt at her unkind words. Something I was doing more and more in her company. My questioning the flaws that exist in Pakistani people and writing about it was causing our friendship to fall apart. My refusal to say white was trash and constantly telling her the Pakistani people I was meeting were worse in their attitudes and behaviours than my white friends, was causing us to argue instead of the easy banter we usually had. If white was trash then the Pakistani side was just as trash if not trashier, I argued, to no avail. Even faced with hard facts Ghazala refused to change her opinions.

It was round about this time I decided to move and not leave a forwarding address. Living in the south side was making me feel unsafe. Word was out that I was writing about Abbas and my upbringing, writing about Pakistani people, writing the truth. Many people had shared their deepest and darkest secrets, worried I would write about them and reveal their identity. I decided to move to a predominantly white area to escape the feeling of living in a goldfish bowl. Everything I did was scrutinised and discussed by the gossipers. I was living in fear, jumping every time I heard a noise, scared somebody would turn up, threatening me to stop writing and bringing shame on the community. I had heard the stories of what they had done to their own children so I felt my fears were justified.

I had tried so hard to fit in but I would never belong. Because I have a Mummy and not an Umee jee. Becoming somebody I wasn't, to please the Pakistani community that would never accept me anyway, was a waste of time. Having a Pakistani father wasn't enough, I needed the Pakistani mother to be accepted and to be forgiven for all my sins.

This time round I did the disowning and distanced myself from all things Pakistani. I ran away this time from the community I had been running to. Nobody knows where I live and it is liberating. Knowing I won't bump into anyone from the community has helped with my writing, allowing me to feel safe to continue and not worry about what people are saying. Even though I had heard from Mummy that people were saying I was writing a book about Islam and the prophet. I told her to let those people know that I have no desire to be a female Salman Rushdie. It's about Pakistani people not about Islam. I will leave it to the scholars to write about their religion. It's my life story, it's what happened to me when I was growing up and the effects that had on my life and choices I made and the person I was for such a long time. It's about the way I was treated by Abbas, Fatima and Mummy. It's about some Pakistani people believing they are better than everyone else, when really they are just like everybody else. There is good and bad in every kind of people but I am accepted by my white friends. They see past the Pakistani blood. I will always struggle to be accepted by my Pakistani side. They are unable to see beyond my white mother.

Chapter 14 Mummy

When I started writing, Mummy's biggest fear was that I wrote something bad about her; discussing the past and the big house was always extremely emotional for her. Tears and denials of any wrong doing to her children. Tales from her childhood and how she had suffered more than we possibly ever could. I remember the first time I told her about the ways in which we had been treated by Fatima. Told her what it had really been like for the gori's children. Mummy screamed and shouted that it was all lies and that I had made it up. The past was something we chose not to discuss to enable us to have a relationship, the guilt over making her unhappy meant I left some of the mean things she did out, scared to hurt her feelings and witness yet another breakdown. On one occasion when talking about the past she said, 'You'd be as well calling the book 'The Gori's Daughter's Revenge on her Mother!''

I reassured her it was nothing to do with revenge, on anyone. It's my life story and what happened to me, how I felt growing up. There was no way however to write it as a happy story no matter how hard I tried. Mummy chose to live with Fatima and Abbas, the consequences of that choice affected her children deeply. Growing up she was everyone's Mummy but ours. Everyone was encouraged, by Fatima, to call her Mummy and it became her nickname. Mummy was scared to show us love and kindness so she would stay in Fatima's favour, showering Fatima's children and grandchildren with praise while criticising her own, believing everything Fatima told her, never believing us when we told our version of events that was how she was with us. Even when she had been thrown out of the big house she refused to believe us, her children, when we told her stories from our childhood. All her children told the same story, so it wasn't make believe. She had allowed herself to be manipulated and turned against her children. I guess it hurt more thinking about Mummy because she was our real mum. It was easy to understand why Fatima hated us but I found it hard to understand why Mummy didn't show us any love, until I started writing and the big house was revisited. When I was disowned at the age of 21, my relationship with Mummy was a joke. I begged her to leave the big house so I could visit her in her new home and try to be a family.

'I want Nathaniel to stay overnight at his nanni's like he does with his dad's mum.' Mummy refused to listen, too brainwashed by Abbas and Fatima to even contemplate leaving the big house. All her children begged her to leave yet Mummy never listened, until the year she turned 60. By then our attempts at a mother/daughter relationship had broken down completely and we hadn't spoken for four years. I stopped calling the big house to speak to her and she never called me to ask why. It was easier for Mummy to cut me out of her life than have to listen to the constant stories about me from the big house. Two months before her 60th she moved into a pokey wee one-bedroom flat, her new home, just like the one back in Huddersfield almost 40 years ago. This time there was no halal butcher shop underneath.

248

She had been kicked out by Abbas and Fatima who had put the house up for sale and were returning to Mirpur, to live for a few years due to Fatima's ill health. Mummy didn't know this and naively thought she would be going with them, to all live happily ever after. There would be no happy ever after for Mummy, no getting to live out her old age in the home she had spent her life working to build. There would be no ticket purchased for Mummy, only Abbas and Fatima. Mummy was no longer needed. Aunty Wilma had been keeping me updated with the events, yet still I refused to call her.

'If they weren't kicking her out she would still be living with them, it's not like she made the choice to leave,' I argued when Aunty Wilma discussed the subject of Mummy. There was a part of me that was angry with her for not having left a long time ago, for all the times she chose the big house over her own children and grandchildren. When I finally met her again she had been in her flat for eight months. I was foolish to think that rekindling our relationship would be easy. Mummy was never allowed to be our mum and didn't know how to be our mum. Even though she was away from the clutches of the big house, she still struggled with the added stress of living on her own, for the first time in her entire life. She missed Fatima's grandchildren, Imtiaz's children, with whom she had a close relationship. They still lived in the big house with the extended family. For 40 odd years Mummy was part of that family, no matter how crazy, they were all she knew and the grandchildren adored her. When I visited Mummy in her flat for the first time, it hurt me that she had pictures on display of Imtiaz's children, but there wasn't any of me or Nathaniel. Yet Fatima's grandchildren smiled from the photo frames on Mummy's tables and walls in her sitting room.

Ten years living on her own has not been enough to rid herself of Fatima's voice, which lingers loud and clear in Mummy's head, along with her childhood issues she has never dealt with. Mummy is forever telling people who will listen, 'My children hate me.'

I can only speak for myself when I say I have no hatred towards my mum, but for the longest time there has been anger. Anger that she allowed her children to be left in the care of Fatima, anger that she stayed in the crazy house, anger that we are unable to have a healthy relationship and mostly the anger was at her refusal to go for counselling.

'I'm too old to change, I cannae help the way I am.'

The last time I spoke to Mummy we argued over how she came to leave the big house, adamant she made the choice for herself and told Abbas, 'I'm no coming with you, I'm getting my own flat.'

I was angry and I argued with Mummy that for the past ten years she had told me she was thrown out of the big house with just £8 to her name, and then I stopped arguing. I let her continue with her new version of events. Days later I rang Yacoub and asked him what he knew of the time she was forced to leave the big house and the family.

'All I remember is how heartbroken she was when she got thrown out. It's what she's always told me. Working for all those years and not a penny to show for it, how Abbas had never paid any N.I. contributions for her and just how depressed she was.'

There was a part of me that doesn't want to portray Mummy in a bad light to get one over on Fatima, to show her she failed in what she had set out to do, that Mummy and her children were all living happily ever after, thank you very much. That would be a lie though because Mummy's family does not exist, destroyed beyond repair from years living in the big house. Out of the three children she has living in Glasgow, me, Jamal and Zanera, nobody visits and Jamal never calls Mummy either. Fatima had taken Jamal from Mummy the day we arrived back from Mirpur, insisting he sleep in her bedroom because Imtiaz and Anwar were in the same room. Jamal chose to stay with the Pakistani side and sever all contact with Mummy and his real brother and sisters. Zanera finds it difficult to be around Mummy and appeases her guilt with the odd phone call. Zanera finds it difficult I think because she was the oldest and suffered the most, Mummy took most of her frustrations with her life out on Zanera.

Since I started writing, our relationship has been strained and now we longer talk. If I don't call, Mummy doesn't think to pick up the phone and call, so I stopped calling, again. Dealing with my own issues means I need to distance myself for a while. The other two children, Amirah and Yacoub, live in Manchester and call, with visits when work and holidays allow

251

them to. When looking at our relationship with each other out of the five children, Yacoub and I have the only relationship. I speak to none of my other siblings and neither does Yacoub. Jamal chose to speak to none of us. Amirah and Zanera sometimes meet if Amirah is visiting Mummy from Manchester, but have no relationship aside from that. We just don't know how to be a family, it was never allowed and as adults it's difficult to suddenly become a family, more so with the baggage we all bring.

Apart from Yacoub and me, the others are all in touch with the Pakistani side of the family, Mummy included. She visits Naeem and Amina weekly and is very much part of their family. Pretending everything is 'hunky dory' no longer works for me and is the reason I am unable to visit Mummy or even pick up the phone. I find it difficult to show or receive affection from Mummy, I find it difficult to act like 'normal' people. When she calls me 'darling' or tells me she 'loves me', I cringe and am unable to tell her that I love her too. The big house thrived on back stabbing, gossiping, arguments and fights especially against the white woman and her children. Mummy finds it difficult still to show her children love. She tries but the voice of Fatima always wins over us, it's almost like she is fearful of being truly loving towards us to praise us, fearful of Fatima hovering to chastise her.

'Twaray bachay bown chungay hain? Twaray harami bachay nal aur pyar hain? (You think your children are better than mine, don't you? You love your bastard children more.)'

252

Mummy would be quick to side with her, changing her attitude towards her children to keep Fatima happy, instead of standing up to her and shouting, 'Of course I bloody well love my children more than yours, you harami (bastard) idiot!'

Mummy doesn't know how to be our Mummy, too many years of anger, bitterness, pent up frustrations have not allowed her to. Instead of getting better our relationship seems to be getting worse, especially since the birth of my daughter. Mummy finds it difficult to be consistent with her praise, preferring to please the voice of Fatima. I had no choice but to bear the brunt of that upbringing and believe I was worthless, I had nobody to protect me from it. Watching and listening to the way Mummy spoke to my daughter hurt, knowing how kind and loving she can be towards other children. The ability to be loving is there. She is not a monster, years of not being a mother or really a grandmother, means even away from the big house she finds it difficult. If she is unable to be a mother to us, then she is even more unable to be a grandmother.

I suppose I shouldn't really be shocked that Mummy is not so keen on the book. For a while she was happy, telling me her stories and filling in the gaps on what happened when Fatima arrived and how they all came to live together and what life was like when I lived in Mirpur. Towards the end of the writing her attitude had changed and so had her stories, protecting Fatima and Abbas from any backlash. Not realising that by protecting Abbas and Fatima it would destroy what little relationship we had. How can I be around someone that praises the very people that destroyed any chance of a family life for us? Even if she is my mother I am unable to.

Chapter 15 Killing my father with his kind of love

Even though in my father's eyes I was dead; he had been very much alive in mine. Why did I keep him alive for so long when there was never a chance of reconciliation? If I'm honest, I still hoped for the father/daughter relationship I had dreamt of when I was younger. Amirah had a relationship with him; he forgave her the fact that she had children and hadn't married the father, so in my mind I thought one day he would forgive me too. Jamal also had children and had not married the mother and Abbas spoke to him. It's a different set of rules for the males in probably all Pakistani homes. They can have children to white women without the inconvenience of marriage. The girls in the family can be killed for it under the guise of 'honour'. This hadn't happened to Amirah or I though, so I thought there was still hope even if it was just a glimmer and only in my head. When I began thinking about the actions of the adults in the big house, the glimmer of hope was slowly extinguished and with it came, in my mind, the death of my father. My own personal honour killing.

My first memory of Abbas is when I was in Mirpur. Jamal was sitting on his knee, playing happily and I was crying, he was leaving us behind to return to Glasgow, where the rest of the family were. Jamal and I were to stay with his parents and extended family. The next memory I have of him is when we returned to Glasgow, five years later. Abbas had never visited us in the time we had spent there, only Mummy had made the trip,

255

twice, to see her children. The months that followed my return were spent crying and trying to adjust to my new family. All I remember is hoping and praying I would be sent back to my family in Pakistan, the only family I had known. Even at that young age I knew I wasn't liked very much by any of my three parents and their behaviour towards me was making it difficult to like anything in them, Abbas especially. Abbas was not a monster, he was a charming man and had after all managed to talk two women into living with him, together. He never practiced any of his charm on me. His children to Fatima he adored more than his children with Mummy. With my brothers and sisters he was sometimes loving as well, it was just me that he hated all the time.

I remember knowing from a young age, maybe ten, that Abbas had demanded Mummy have an abortion when she was pregnant with me. Hearing it from the older two girls or maybe when Mummy was having one of her meltdowns. How I came to know at such a young age isn't important I guess, I just knew and so did the other children. Maybe that's why he hated me, I used to think, because he didn't want me born in the first place. I was proof of Mummy's defiance staring him in the face. Maybe that's why the other children treated me differently too, they could sense I wasn't wanted. It didn't matter that he had no time for me, all I wanted to do was please him, to see him smile at me, speak kindly to me and praise me for doing well at school, like he did with the other children. He was affectionate towards the other children but the only time I got to hug my father was the day he forced me into a marriage, then it had to be done, surrounded by family and friends it would have looked shameful if he hadn't hugged his daughter. A Pakistani daughter leaving her father's house on the day of her wedding is a sad and tearful occasion. Some brides even wail hysterically and faint at the idea of being separated from their fathers. My wedding day was much less dramatic.

From a very young age we had chores to do and on a Saturday morning I would wake early and tidy the kitchen, cleaning out the cupboards, the fridge, pulling out the cooker to sweep and mop behind it. I always did this without being asked to, all so Abbas would give me a few pounds and tell me I had done a good job. The money would have been a bonus, it was the praise that I did it for, hoping for a hug or that he would ruffle my hair. That was something I saw him do, often, with all the other children, even Mummy's. Sadly moments like those between Abbas and I were rare. More often than not, on Saturday mornings, the gleaming kitchen went unnoticed. Still the next week I cleaned and kept on hoping.

Pakistani girls are taught to cook from a very young age. I was 10 when the responsibility of preparing the dough for chapattis was given to me. By 11 I was being taught how to make the chapattis and when I started secondary school I was learning to cook curries. Cooking was not a task I excelled in. Abbas was my teacher and that's the reason I failed. I have always been nervous and clumsy round Abbas, his constant put downs and sneering along with his volatile nature had me that way.   Abbas enjoyed cooking and in a culture where the vast majority of men do not cook it was my bad luck that he took it upon himself to teach me how to cook curries the summer before I started secondary.   A few weeks into the holidays and once again I was called in from the back garden where I was hanging out with the other children.

'Aisha, ju come inside.'

Never needing to be asked twice I made my way into the kitchen wondering what he wanted.

'Vat I tell ju last week? Ju too bloody big to be playing outside.   Come wash jor hands, ju make the curry today.   Hurry up.'

A few months before my 13th birthday I was hardly too big to be playing outside in the enclosed back garden but learning to cook at such a young age was to prepare me for my future wedding, enabling me to cook for my future husband and in laws so I could impress them with my culinary skills. I never really learned or impressed anyone with the skills he gave me. The worst time, and thankfully the last ever lesson, was when Abbas arrived home with 3lbs of the finest lamb, cut and prepared in the family butcher shop.   He was planning on making lamb and potato curry, or rather to have me be the chef that afternoon.   The kitchen sink looked out into the garden and I stood beside him as he barked orders at me.   My mind kept wandering to the others playing outside, so I had not been paying attention.   Leaving me to continue following his instructions, he went through to the living room where Fatima and Mummy were sitting.   I began to peel the onions and my tears mingled with the tears caused by the chopping of the onions, next the garlic and then tomatoes and green chillies. Mixing in the spices and salt I filled the pot to half way with water and put it on the gas turned up full to get it boiling, then turned down a bit to let it simmer, all the while thinking how unfair it was. I was not even a teenager and I was learning lessons in being a good wife. When Abbas finally returned to the kitchen, I had tidied up and was sitting reading a book at the table. World War Three went off in the kitchen, Abbas screaming and shouting at me like a man possessed.

'Oh ju bloody stupid fool, what ju done? Vat this pucking bakwass (rubbish)?'

Trembling with fear, I did not understand what I had done wrong and stared at him, not saying anything, too scared to say anything, his anger and utter disgust at me had turned me mute.

'How much vater ju put in it? Ju no bludee listen when I tell ju put half glass in?'

How could I tell him I remembered half of something and thought he meant to fill it half way up? How was I meant to know that the juices from the 8 large onions and 6 tomatoes would add to the water I had poured in? The pot was full to the top with water and the finest of lambs was only just salvaged by Abbas. His rant continued while he scooped the meat out and boiled the water off, then returning the meat and cooking it slowly so as not to ruin the already delicate lamb. Over and over again he told me I was useless, stupid, thick, good for nothing and his favourite insult was telling me I was ugly – ironically I look like him. Still I loved him and wanted him to love me, even just a little. The main things I hated doing for him were making his omelettes or ironing his shirts because no matter how hard I tried they were never ironed properly or too much salt in his omelette or not enough chillies. If Mummy or Zanera were around when he asked me, I would beg them to do it for me. When Amirah got old enough to do the job I would beg her too. Knowing he wouldn't complain because according to Abbas, they could cook and iron better than me and if I managed to persuade them to do the task then I was free to go to my bedroom and my books and escape from Abbas and his blatant dislike of me and the fact that nothing I ever did would be good enough. He was never able to see how nervous he made me. I messed up even the simplest of tasks.

When I outgrew my clothes or shoes or needed something new I would tell Mummy, she would tell me, 'I've nae money, hen, go ask your faither.' The 80's were a very successful time in the big house, we had two homes in Glasgow and one was being built back in Kashmir, no expense spared. There were two cars and a van in the drive. All the bedrooms in the big house had televisions and video recorders and the children had the latest music players when they came out. When we went to secondary school we were given £5 each to spend on sweets over the course of the week. £5 a week was a lot of money when I was a teenager. Money was far from short in the big house and yet Mummy never had any to give. The only money she received was her child benefit and even that she turned over to the big house and there was never a wage packet with her name on it. I hated going to beg Abbas for money. It would take me a few hours to pluck up the courage, saying it over in my head before I went to see him and always I ended up stuttering and stammering and always he told me he had no money, I would have to wait for another day to buy whatever I needed. I quickly learnt to stop asking, if my shoes were worn out or my coat was too small or something needed replacing so be it. It was easier to accept that I could have nothing than to go begging to be always told no, not yet, maybe next week there might be money to spend on you.

Throughout my childhood and most of my adult life Mummy could be heard saying 'You're just like yir faither' and I would protest loudly that I was nothing like him. I was secretly pleased but outwardly denying I was anything like him. It was just another reason for him to dislike me, out of all the children I am the most similar to him, stubborn, determined and as an adult I would become unfaithful like him too. Now I can see he was threatened. He was threatened by my intelligence, my sense of justice, which had been instilled in me from his parents, and my honesty. He had been busy creating a house full of anger, violence, lies and misery. Anger caused by the two women having to share him and violence directed at Mummy for daring to stand up for herself under any circumstances and lies as to what he was getting up to away from the home he had created. All the while I was being raised by the very people who had raised him, of course we were going to be alike. My return from Kashmir and my strong character was not appreciated in the flat on Albert Drive, nobody was allowed to question what went on in there. Fatima ruled while Abbas partied away from the madness he had created, and Mummy was sent out to work. Any attempts I made to question their flaws was dealt with by giving me a stern telling off and if I persisted, which I did often, at first anyway, then I would be given a slap and that would stop me. I stopped the questioning and accepted everything they told me, I was eight years old what else was there to do? With nobody to stick up for me I quickly learned to hide, escaping into my books.

Two women at home and Abbas out all the time. When he was home his mood depended on how his outside life was doing. By the time I was a teenager I would learn that he had a gambling addiction and was also addicted to paying for women. When he had done well and won some money on whatever he gambled on, then he would hand out twenty pound notes to the younger children when he arrived home, myself included. He was always jolly and full of good cheer, laughing and smiling. He had two women at home but he still set up a home with another. This time he carried this out in the traditional style of the Pakistani men. This woman and children he kept in a separate home, over in the east end of the city. Aunty Marion, as we would call her, visited the big house a few times until their affair was made public. Her husband was a friend of Abbas and one afternoon he rang the big house. When Fatima answered and told him he was out, his friend demanded to know where and soon began crying, saying that his wife had been missing for three days and he had a feeling she was with Abbas. Abbas had been gone from the big house for three days. Coincidence? Mummy took the phone from Fatima and asked the friend if he had no shame, how dare he ring and accuse their husband of this rubbish, Fatima started cursing him too, encouraged by Mummy's rage. The phone call ended with Mummy screaming at him never to phone the house again and the children were all sent to our rooms while Mummy and Fatima had a crisis talk, even though we heard everything anyway. In a twisted way this was the beginning of their bond, united against their man's womanising ways. Aunty Marion and Abbas had run away together and she would be his other white woman for years, although she would no longer visit us again. Her oldest child, a girl, looked like Marion's husband, her father, and the two youngest looked like Abbas. We all discussed it amongst ourselves, the children that is. I'm sure the adults noticed it too, although we would never dare mention it to them as it would guarantee a tongue lashing and a slap. Her children looked like me and I looked like Abbas, from that we decided they were his, even though nobody ever spoke about it.

I wonder what he would think if he realised how his words and actions have affected me my whole life, how I believed I was unlovable because my own father didn't love me. I suppose I don't need to ask him, because the truth is he doesn't care. All little girls are born and dream of being their daddy's little princess. I was a little girl born with the same dream, I was no different to the other little girls in the big house, yet he never allowed me to be a princess. He wished me dead before I was born, and then got his chance to tell me I was dead years later.

Freeing myself of wanting my father's love has changed my life beyond anything I could have imagined. I had lived the dream for so long I saw no other future. I was destined to fail. I ended up jumping from one friendship to another and one relationship to another. I moved home and changed career frequently, always running. All these were ways in which I sabotaged my happiness, never believing I deserved any. I was always cheating in relationships, Abbas was my role model and hardly the faithful type, and in a sick sort of way I wanted to be like my father. I'm thankful I didn't aspire to be like Mummy, in a fucked up relationship with beatings on top of it. I won't lie, there were relationships that were abusive but I got myself out them quickly, the fear of ending up like Mummy stronger than any feelings I had towards the men in question. In the year it has taken me to write this story I have slowly been killing my father in my imagination and now he is dead in my eyes, like I was for him all those years ago. I no longer believe I am worthless, unlovable or destined to fail. I no longer believe in cheating in a relationship because I no longer want to be like him. For the first time in my life, I no longer dream of being accepted by my father.

There are many parts of me that remind me of him. My love of old Bollywood songs is in part thanks to him, my time in Kashmir had meant all I heard was Asian music and that's where my love for these songs was created. Back in Glasgow, Abbas would call all the children into the living room where he would be watching some old Bollywood movie and tell us to sit and watch with him and when a song would come on, and in Indian movies there can easily be twelve or fourteen songs, would boast.

'This is vat real music is, no tha rubbish ju all listen to.'

Sometimes we would laugh and snigger behind our hands and whisper to each other, mocking the actresses and actors of the bygone era.

'She looks like Madonna and look, he could be George Michael.'

Childish behaviour yes, we were children after all and being forced to watch movies from the 50's and 60's in a language we didn't speak fluently or understand fully was not something the children looked forward to. In my case, to be honest, I didn't mind because Abbas was always in a good mood when watching his beloved movies so there was little chance of him being angry, and the music reminded me of the happy and carefree times when I lived with his parents. Even though I would be in his company for three hours or more, typical length of Indian movies, he never acknowledged me. Even though I was there in his company with everyone else, for him I didn't exist. I have always been dead to him, I just refused to see it. Only looking back can I see how much of a puppy dog I was, eager to please my owner. This eagerness was what made me clumsy, scared of how he was going to react no matter what I did. I can recall no tender kind and loving moments between Abbas and I. I never laughed and joked with him, never relaxed around him, if he wasn't shouting, belittling, criticising or controlling then he was silent, and has been silent for 20 years. He has no interest in my life, not even the slightest, apart from to criticise.

In my head he was far from silent, in my head he was always shouting or mocking, in my head he was always there reminding me nobody would want me. If my own father did not want me then nobody else would, is what I always believed. Hating myself with such self-loathing, piercing and tattooing my body, shaving my head, long before Britney was even famous, mild meltdowns all because I lacked the attention of a father who did not care one iota whether I lived or died. A father who only heard of my escapades through the gossip grapevine and even then showed no interest for his out of control child. 'She's dead, do not mention her name in front of me.' The biggest thing for me is the happiness I have achieved almost instantly from taking the initiative and rejecting and, in my imagination, killing Abbas. All my problems, all the stresses of working, raising children, all the dramas surrounding family, all the everyday struggles we go through are still there. Still I feel so much happier. I would have killed him years ago if I had known how much it would have set me free.

Epilogue

Killing my father and disowning the community I had yearned to be part of was not as easy as it seemed. There were many times when I almost called someone just so I could speak and hear the language, and to find out what was going on in Pollokshields. I felt like there was something missing in my life without the Pakistani side. Ben became my rock during those moments and I would call him instead and we would discuss how I was feeling. Ben told me that he always felt like I had been given a little window from which I could look in on the Pakistani community and watch. He said the door had never been fully opened for me to walk through and be part of the community. It didn't take long for me to get over my trauma and replace it with happiness. Whether Abbas or the community accept me makes no difference, because I will always be half Pakistani. I own a tawa, a pan used for making chapattis, and in my bathroom there is a lota – jug used for washing yourself after using the toilet. All Pakistani homes will have these two items. I make curries, Nathaniel sometimes complains that I add 'curry' to the end of every dinner suggestion. I listen to my Bollywood songs from the 60's and I listen to Imran Khan, still on repeat. I no longer need to be part of the Pakistani community to feel Pakistani. I know how to be Pakistani because it is half of who I am.

Months after I had finished writing my story I enrolled at Glasgow University and have almost completed my degree in Social Work. I work part time at a children's charity and life is good and I am happy. I have my children, Ben and his family, Marie, John Paul, Joseph and Zarah in my life. Apart from Yacoub I have no contact with anybody from the big house and for the first time in my life I am content. Ben has been my best friend for years and neither of us had ever dated anyone since we spilt, preferring to focus on Ruby and her happiness.

We had taken Ruby and Nathaniel to Tenerife for their October holidays and when we came back after spending ten days together I missed him. I missed having him around every day and when we next spoke he asked if I would marry him. Could I do it? Could I say yes to spending the rest of my life with someone and being happy? I had to sleep on it, I didn't say yes to his proposal straightaway. I was scared and the self-doubts were trying to tell me I would never be good enough to be Ben's wife. I wish I could have said yes the moment he asked me, but years of feeling worthless don't evaporate overnight. Lucky for me Ben is very patient and understanding. Nathaniel was ecstatic when he heard, telling me I had to say yes and how great he thought Ben was. The next morning when I phoned Ben, I told him yes. We have set a date for the summer.

Also Available from Ringwood Publishing

Silent Thunder by **Archie Macpherson** is a refreshing return to the proud Scottish tradition of Adventure story telling; Archie Macpherson is a worthy heir to John Buchan and Robert Louis Stevenson."

Silent Thunder is well-written, fast paced, exciting, enjoyable and will prove to be a much appreciated throwback to the days of wholesome and engaging Adventure stories in the tradition of Thirty Nine Steps, the Gorbals Diehards, Treasure Island and Kidnapped.

We knew Archie Macpherson could vividly describe sporting events, now with SilentThunder, we know he can write exciting, high

quality fiction.

Set in Glasgow and Fife, **Silent Thunder** follows the progress of two young Glaswegian working class males as they refuse to be bullied by greater force, and stand up for what they know to be right, at considerable danger to themselves. They show the Glasgow spirit, do the right thing and have a go despite the painful consequences for themselves. They quickly find themselves thrust headlong into a fast moving and highly dangerous adventure involving a Scots radio broadcaster, East European gangsters, a computer genius, and secret service agencies from at least 3 major world powers. Starting out on Glasgow back streets the action quickly widens out and ends up in Fife, with an explosive climax on the iconic Isle of May.

Silent Thunder can be purchased in any of the following ways.

From the Ringwood website www.ringwoodpublishing.com for £9.99 excluding p&p, or ordered by post or e-mail for the same price. All copies signed by the author.

From www.amazon.co.uk either from Ringwood(a signed copy) or from Amazon (unsigned copy).From any good bookstore or online bookseller

The e-book version is available for £7.20 from the Kindle Book Store or Amazon.co.uk

A Subtle Sadness by **Sandy Jamieson** is a rigorous exploration of Scottish Identity and the impact on it of the key Scottish obsessions of politics, football, religion, sex and alcohol. It deserves to be read by everyone seeking to understand the Scottish character.

A Subtle Sadness focuses on the family and personal history of Frank Hunter, a sad Scotsman with a self-destruct streak enormous even by normal West of Scotland male standards. Frank Hunter is a product of Scotland's unique contribution to mixed marriage, with a Protestant father and Catholic mother. A man of considerable talents, in both football and politics, he brings a peculiarly Scottish approach to the application of those talents.

A Subtle Sadness is the story of a 100 year fight for Scottish Home Rule, from 1890 to 1990,

A Subtle Sadness is also the story of the emotional and political impact of Scotland's quest for the World Cup, with 5 consecutive qualifications in the crucial years from 1973 to 1989 covered by the book.

A Subtle Sadness covers a century of Scottish social, political and football highlights, with disasters and triumphs aplenty, culminating in Glasgow's emergence in 1990 as European City of Culture.

A Subtle Sadness is also a reflection on sadness, depression and mental health as affected by that Scottish identity and those key obsessions. And a searing scrutiny of the Scottish male capacity for self-destruction. Illustrating that capacity to the full, Frank Hunter's story is a memorable and haunting one.

A Subtle Sadness can be purchased in any of the following ways.

From the Ringwood website www.ringwoodpublishing.com for £9.99 excluding p&p, or ordered by post or e-mail for the same price. All copies signed by the author.

From www.amazon.co.uk either from Ringwood(a signed copy) or from Amazon (unsigned copy).From any good bookstore or online bookseller

The e-book version is available for £7.20 from the Kindle Book Store or Amazon.co.uk

Calling Cards by **Gordon Johnston** is a fresh and exciting addition to the ranks of Tartan Noir. It is a novel exploration of the impact of stress and trauma on individuals, encompassing their resort to addiction, recovery, and denial. It highlights the influence of the equally corrupting desires for success or revenge. Linking the small Scottish worlds of journalism and politics, it has been favourably compared to State of Play in its creation of an intricate network of linked strands, as it builds to a compelling climax that leaves many people changed forever.

"An anonymous email leads West End Journalist Frank Gallen on a quest to unravel the links between a campaign against a housing development proposal in Kelvingrove Park; personal and political corruption at the highest level in Glasgow City Council; and the increasingly frenzied activities of a Glasgow serial killer. Gallen and DI Adam Ralston engage in a desperate chase to identify the serial killer from the clues he is sending them, in time to stop him from implementing the climax of his campaign of killing."

"Calling Cards is a fascinating examination of people under stress. Extremely well-written in a fluid style very easy to read, it is both the story of an increasingly desperate hunt for a Glasgow serial killer, and an examination of how people cope under intense pressure. It marks the arrival of a new and very welcome addition, Gordon Johnston, to the ranks of distinguished Scottish crime writers."

"Calling Cards is a psychological thriller worthy of a place in the top rank. It is well-written, and easy to read with a fast flowing style."

Calling Cards can be purchased in any of the following ways.

From the Ringwood website www.ringwoodpublishing.com for £9.99 excluding p&p, or ordered by post or e-mail for the same price. All copies signed by the author.

From www.amazon.co.uk either from Ringwood(a signed copy) or from Amazon (unsigned copy).From any good bookstore or online bookseller.

The e-book version is available for £7.20 from the Kindle Book Store or Amazon.co.uk

School Daze by **Elaine McGeachy** is a hugely enjoyable romp through the social, sexual and professional dilemmas facing three recently qualified young teachers as they try to cope with the increased stresses in the modern day education world."

Caitlyn, Jamie and Jennifer all share an infectious enthusiasm for and deep love of their chosen profession. Qualifying on the same course, then based in the same Glasgow Secondary School, they work hard at becoming good teachers. Facing temptations including a highly attractive male pupil, a charismatic Head Teacher and a tall, dark and handsome mysterious stranger, they try to steer an acceptable course between their professional responsibilities and their desire for a fulfilling social life.

With great sensitivity and a refreshing absence of sensationalism, **School Daze** tackles the vexed issue of why smart, attractive young teachers risk reputation and career by romantic involvement with pupils.

"The dazzling tale that is **School Daze** will be loved by all young teachers, and by all those ever taught by a young teacher who wondered what passions might lie behind the prim face properly presented in the classroom. It is ideal school holiday reading material for both groups, highly recommended."

School Daze can be purchased in any of the following ways.

From the Ringwood website www.ringwoodpublishing.com for £9.99 excluding p&p, or ordered by post or e-mail for the same price. All copies signed by the author.

From www.amazon.co.uk either from Ringwood (a signed copy) or from Amazon (unsigned copy).From any good bookstore or online bookseller

The e-book version is available for £7.20 from the Kindle Book Store or Amazon.co.uk